PRAISE FOR

The Anomaly

"A volatile and compelling thriller that has you hurtling toward the mystery at the heart of the novel from page one...a gripping and moving blend of Blake Crouch's *Dark Matter*, the television show *Lost*, with a bit of *The Philadelphia Experiment* thrown in for good measure. I couldn't put it down."

—Terry Miles, author of *Rabbits*

"Brilliant...an immensely fun novel, an immersive experience that leaves the reader analyzing everything anew."

—Cherise Wolas, author of *The Resurrection of Joan Ashby*

"An extraordinary, fast-paced, disturbing novel, perfect for these extraordinary, fast-paced, disturbing times. Think Steven Spielberg meets Umberto Eco with a side order of black humor, generously sprinkled with genuine emotion."

—Sam Taylor, author of *The Island at the End of the World*

"Exhilarating, thought-provoking, funny, and devastating. *The Anomaly* is unlike anything else I've read this year."

—Laure Van Rensburg, author of *Nobody But Us*

"Fantastic...combines the best of American TV series with an impeccable mastery of the French psychological novel."

—*Elle* (France)

"Excellent...at once zeitgeisty, intelligent, and entertaining."

—*Charlie Hebdo*

ALSO BY HERVÉ LE TELLIER

All Happy Families

Atlas Inutilis

Eléctrico W

Enough About Love

The Intervention of a Good Man

The Sextine Chapel

A Thousand Pearls (for a Thousand Pennies)

The Anomaly

HERVÉ LE TELLIER

TRANSLATED FROM THE FRENCH
BY ADRIANA HUNTER

OTHER PRESS
NEW YORK

Originally published in French as *L'Anomalie* in 2020
by Éditions Gallimard, Paris

Production editor: Yvonne E. Cárdenas
Text designer: Jennifer Daddio / Bookmark Design & Media Inc.
This book was set in Horley Old Style by
Alpha Design & Composition of Pittsfield, NH

3 5 7 9 10 8 6 4

 Printed in the United States of America on acid-free paper. For information write to Other Press LLC, 267 Fifth Avenue, 6th Floor, New York, NY 10016.
Or visit our Web site: www.otherpress.com

Library of Congress Cataloging-in-Publication Data
Names: Le Tellier, Hervé, 1957- author. | Hunter, Adriana, translator.
Title: The anomaly / Hervé Le Tellier ; translated from the French by Adriana Hunter.
Other titles: Anomalie. English
Description: New York : Other Press, [2021]
Identifiers: LCCN 2021018164 (print) | LCCN 2021018165 (ebook) |
ISBN 9781635421699 (paperback) | ISBN 9781635421767 (ebook)
Subjects: LCSH: Doppelgängers—Fiction.
Classification: LCC PQ2672.E11455 A8613 2021 (print) | LCC PQ2672.E11455 (ebook) |
DDC 843/.914—dc23
LC record available at https://lccn.loc.gov/2021018164
LC ebook record available at https://lccn.loc.gov/2021018165

Publisher's Note
This is a work of fiction. Names, characters, places, and incidents either are the product of the author's imagination or are used fictitiously, and any resemblance to actual persons, living or dead, events, or locales is entirely coincidental.

And when I say you are dreaming,
I am dreaming, too.

—ZHUANGZI

A true pessimist knows that it is
already too late to be one.

—*The anomaly*, VICTØR MIESEL

. I .

As Black as the Sky

(MARCH–JUNE 2021)

There is something admirable that always surpasses knowledge, intelligence, and even genius, and that is incomprehension.

—*The anomaly,* Victør Miesel

BLAKE

It's not the killing, that's not the thing. Gotta watch, monitor, think, a lot, and—come the time—carve into the void. That's it. Carve into the void. Find a way to make the universe shrink, to make it shrink till it's condensed into the barrel of the gun or the point of the knife. That's all. Don't ask any questions, don't be driven by anger, choose the protocol, and proceed methodically. Blake can do all that, and he's been doing it so long he can't remember when he started. Once you have it, the rest just falls into place.

Blake builds his life on other people's deaths. No moralizing, please. If anyone wants to talk ethics, he's happy to reply with statistics. Because—and Blake apologizes—when a health minister makes cuts in the budget, culling a scanner here, a doctor there, and an ICU bed somewhere else, that minister knows that he or she's appreciably shortening the lives of thousands of strangers. Responsible but not answerable, we've all heard that tune. With Blake it's the other way around. And anyway, he doesn't need to justify himself, he couldn't give a damn.

Killing isn't a vocation, it's a leaning. A state of mind, if that makes more sense. Blake is eleven years old, and his name isn't Blake. He's in the Peugeot with his mother on a minor route near Bordeaux. They're not traveling especially fast, a dog crosses the road, the impact barely alters their course, his mother screams, brakes, too hard, the car zigzags, and the engine stalls. Stay in the car, honey, my God, you be sure to stay in the car. Blake doesn't do as he's told, he follows his mother. It's a gray collie, the collision has crushed its chest, blood is oozing onto the tufts of grass by the roadside, but the dog isn't dead, it whimpers, sounding like a mewling baby. Blake's mother runs in every direction, panicking, she covers Blake's eyes with her hand, stammers incoherently, she wants to call an ambulance, But, Mom, it's a mutt, it's just a mutt. The collie sputters on the fissured asphalt, its broken, twisted body contorts at a strange angle, wracked with gradually diminishing twitches, dying right in front of Blake's eyes, and Blake watches inquisitively as the life drains out of the animal. It's over. The boy puts on a cursory show of sadness, well, what he imagines sadness is, to avoid disconcerting his mother, but he feels nothing. His mother stays by the little body, frozen to the spot, Blake's had enough, he pulls at her sleeve, Come on, Mom, there's no point staying here, he's dead, let's go, I'm gonna be late for the game.

Killing is also about skill. Blake finds that he has all the requirements the day his uncle Charles takes him hunting. Three shots, three hares, a kind of gift. He aims swiftly and accurately, he can adapt to the crummiest old rifles, the most misaligned shotguns. Girls drag him to fairgrounds, Hey, please, I want the giraffe, the elephant, the Game Boy, yes, go on, again! And Blake hands out soft toys and games consoles, he becomes the dread of shooting galleries, before opting for a little more discretion. Blake also enjoys the things Uncle Charles teaches him, gutting deer and jointing rabbits. Let's be clear on this: he derives no pleasure from killing, from finishing off an injured animal. He's not depraved. No, what he likes is the specialized action, the fail-safe routine that gels with frequent repetition.

Blake is twenty, and using his oh-so French name—Lipowski, Farsati, or Martin—he's enrolled at a hospitality school in a small town in the Alps. Don't go thinking there were no other options, he could have done anything, he was keen on electronics too, programming, he was a gifted linguist, take English, for example, all it took was a three-month course at Lang's in London and he could speak it almost without an accent. But what Blake likes more than anything else is cooking, because of those idle moments spent writing a recipe, the time that trickles slowly by, even in the feverish activity of a kitchen, and the long, unhurried seconds spent watching butter melt in the pan, white onions reduce, a soufflé rise. He likes the smells and the spices, enjoys arranging combinations of colors and flavors on a plate. He could have been the most brilliant student at hotel school, but Seriously, fuck, Lipowski (or Farsati or Martin), if only you could show some courtesy to the clientele, it wouldn't do any harm. This is a service industry, service, do you understand, Lipowski (or Farsati or Martin)?

One evening in a bar, a—very drunk—man tells him he wants to have someone killed. The guy probably has a good reason, a work thing, a woman thing, but that doesn't matter to Blake.

"Would you do it, would you, for money?"

"You're nuts," Blake replies. "Completely nuts."

"I'd pay you, a lot."

The figure he offers has three zeros. Blake laughs.

"No. Are you kidding?"

Blake sips his drink, slowly, takes his time. The man's collapsed onto the bar. Blake shakes him.

"Listen, I know someone who'll do it. For twice that. I never met him. Tomorrow I'll tell you how to contact him, but after that, you never mention him to me again, okay?" And that night Blake invents Blake. For William

Blake, whom he read after having seen the film *Red Dragon* with Anthony Hopkins, and because he likes one of the poems: "Into the dangerous world I leapt: / Helpless, naked, piping loud; / Like a fiend hid in a cloud." And the word "Blake" itself, lake but with a hint of black, yeah, it was on the right track.

The next day a North American service provider registers the email address of one blake.mick.22, set up in an internet café in Geneva. Blake pays cash to a stranger for a secondhand laptop, buys an old Nokia and a prepaid card, a camera, and a telephoto lens. Once he has his equipment, the apprentice chef gives the guy from the bar the contact details for this Blake, "but there's no guarantee the address is still valid," and he waits. Three days later the man sends Blake a convoluted message that makes it clear he's being cautious. Questioning. Looking for the chink in the armor. Sometimes leaving a couple of days between messages. Blake refers to the target, to logistics and delivery times, and his precautions succeed in reassuring the man. They reach an agreement, and Blake asks for half the fee in advance: that alone is four zeros. When the man explains that he wants it to look like "natural causes," Blake doubles the sum and insists on having a month. Now convinced that he's dealing with a professional, the man accepts all the conditions.

It's the first time, and Blake is making this up. He's already extremely meticulous, cautious, and imaginative.

He's watched so many films—no one realizes how much hit men owe to Hollywood scriptwriters. From the start of his career, he arranges to receive the fee and contract information in a plastic bag left in a place chosen by him, a bus, a fast-food outlet, a building site, a garbage can, a park. He'll avoid anywhere too remote, where he'd be the only person visible, and anywhere too public, where he wouldn't be able to identify anyone. He'll be there hours ahead of time, scanning the area. He'll wear gloves, a hood, a hat, and glasses; he'll dye his hair, learn to fit a wig, to hollow his cheeks, or puff them out; he'll have license plates by the dozen, from every country. With time, Blake will take up knife throwing, half spins and full spins depending on the distance; he'll take up bomb making, and extracting undetectable poison from jellyfish; he'll know how to dismantle and reassemble a Browning 9 mm and a Glock 43 in a few seconds; he'll be paid and will buy his weapons in bitcoin, a cryptocurrency whose movements can't be traced. He'll set up his site on the dark web, which will come to feel like a game to him. Because there are tutorials for absolutely everything on the internet. Just have to search.

So, his target is a man of about fifty. Blake has his photo and his name but decides to call him Ken. Yes, like Barbie's husband. A good choice: "Ken" doesn't grant him a full existence.

Ken lives alone, and that's a good start, Blake thinks to himself, because he can't see how he'd find the opportunity with a married man with three children. The problem remains that at Ken's sort of age, a natural death doesn't leave many options: car crash, gas leak, heart attack, accidental fall. Period. Blake doesn't yet have the skill set for sabotaging brakes or tampering with steering, any more than he knows how to get hold of potassium chloride to trigger a heart attack; as for gas asphyxiation, that doesn't smell right either. Let's go with a fall. Ten thousand deaths a year. Particularly the elderly, but he'll work with it. And even though Ken's no athlete, a fight is out of the question.

Ken lives in a two-bedroom apartment on the first floor of a detached house near Annemasse. For three whole weeks Blake just watches and puts together his plan. With the advance, he's bought himself an old Renault panel truck, fitted it out with rudimentary trappings—a seat, a mattress, extra batteries for lighting—and he's chosen a spot in a deserted parking lot that overlooks the house. He has a bird's-eye view into the apartment. Ken leaves home at about 8:30 every day, crosses the Swiss border, and then returns from work around seven o'clock. On the weekend he's sometimes joined by a woman, a French teacher from Bonneville, ten kilometers away. Tuesday is his most predictable day, with the strictest routine: he comes home earlier, goes straight back out to head to the gym, returns two hours later, spends about twenty minutes in the bathroom, then eats in front of the TV, dawdles on his computer for a while, and goes to bed. Let's go for Tuesday evening. Blake sends his client a message, using their code: "Monday, 8 pm?" One day earlier, two hours earlier. The client will have an alibi for Tuesday at 10 pm.

A week before the appointed day, Blake arranges for a pizza to be delivered to Ken's apartment. The delivery man rings the bell, Ken opens the door without a moment's hesitation and looks baffled as he talks to the pizza man, who leaves again, still holding his box. Blake doesn't need to see any more.

The following Tuesday, he personally pitches up carrying a pizza box. He studies the empty street for a moment, puts on anti-skid overshoes, checks his gloves and then waits awhile so that he can ring the bell just as Ken's coming out of the shower. Ken opens the door, wearing his robe, and sighs when he sees the pizza box in the delivery guy's hands. But before he has time to say anything the empty box falls to the ground and Blake jams the ends of two stun batons into his chest. The shock knocks Ken to his knees, Blake drops down with him and keeps up the pressure for ten seconds, until Ken stops moving. The manufacturers promised eight million volts: Blake tried out just one baton on himself and nearly passed out.

He drags a dribbling, moaning Ken to the bathroom, gives him another zap for good measure, then in one horrifyingly violent move—that he's practiced ten times on coconuts—he grasps Ken's head between his hands, holding it by the temples and raising it up, then hurls it back with all his might: Ken's skull shatters against the side of the tub, and a diamond-shaped floor tile cracks from the force of the impact. Blood immediately starts to spread, viscous and scarlet as nail varnish, complete with its pleasant smell of hot rust. Ken's mouth stays open, inanely, his eyes wide, staring at the ceiling. Blake half opens his robe: the electric shocks have left no trace. He arranges the body as best he can to fit the hypothetical trajectory that gravity would have dictated following a tragic slip.

And just then, as he stands up and admires his work, he has a sudden, overwhelming urge to pee. It would never have occurred to him. Let's face it, assassins in films don't pee. It's so urgent that he even contemplates relieving himself in the toilet, at the expense of having to clean the whole thing thoroughly afterward. But if the cops take it into their heads to be just a teeny bit intelligent, or simply thorough, methodically following procedure, they'd find some DNA. Bound to. At least that's what Blake assumes. So, despite his pleading bladder, he continues with his plan, grimacing in agony. He picks up the soap, rubs it firmly against Ken's heel, crushes a trail of it onto the floor and throws it in line with the assumed slide: the soap ricochets and gets stuck behind the toilet. Perfect. Finding it will make the investigator's day, thrilled to have solved the enigma. Blake sets the shower to its highest temperature, turns it on, and—avoiding all contact with the steaming water—swivels the showerhead toward Ken's face and chest, then he leaves the bathroom.

He runs to the window, closes the curtains, and checks over the room one last time. There's nothing to suggest that a body was dragged for several meters, and pinkish water has started flooding over the floorboards. The computer is on, and images of English lawns and bloom-filled flower beds glide across the screen. Ken had a green thumb. Blake leaves the building, removes his gloves, and strolls over to his scooter, which is parked two hundred meters away. He starts it up, covers a good kilometer and then, finally, stops to pee. Shit, he's still wearing his black cotton overshoes.

Two days later an anxious colleague will contact the police, who will discover the accidental death of Samuel Tadler. Blake receives the outstanding balance the very same day.

All this happened a long, long time ago, and since then Blake has devised two lives for himself. In one he is invisible, has twenty surnames and as many first names, with corresponding passports of every nationality, but with genuine biometrics, yes, it's easier than you'd think. In the other he goes by the name Joe, and from a fair distance, runs a delightful Paris-based company that does home deliveries of vegetarian meals, with subsidiaries in Bordeaux, Lyon, and now Berlin and New York. His business partner, Flora, who is also his wife, and his two children complain that he travels too much and is sometimes away too long. Which is true.

MARCH 21, 2021

QUOGUE, NEW YORK

IT'S MARCH 21, and Blake's away from home. He runs through fine rain on damp sand. Long blond hair, bandana, sunglasses, yellow-and-blue tracksuit, every jogger's brightly colored invisibility. He arrived in New York ten days earlier, with an Australian passport. His transatlantic flight was so terrifying that he really thought his time was up, and the heavens were going to claim their revenge for all his contracts. In a bottomless air pocket, his blond wig nearly even parted company with his head. And now, for the last nine days, he's been doing his three kilometers under gray skies along the beach at Quogue, passing houses worth ten million dollars, at least. Dunes have been landscaped along what, for simplicity's sake, has been called Dune Road, and pines and reeds have been planted so none of the houses can be seen by their neighbors, which helps all the owners feel confident that the whole ocean belongs to them alone. Blake takes small, unrushed strides and then, as he has at the same time every day, he comes to a sudden stop opposite a magnificent single-story house clad with wide planks of cedar; it has huge floor-to-ceiling windows and a terrace with a staircase leading down toward the ocean. He pretends to be out of breath, bends double under the effects of an imaginary stitch, and also like every other day, looks up and waves to a man in the distance, a slightly chubby fiftysomething who's leaning on the balustrade, drinking a coffee under the awning. A tall, younger man with short, dark hair keeps him company. He stands a discreet distance away, with his back to the wooden cladding, anxiously scanning the beach. An invisible holster under his jacket swells the fabric on his left-hand side. Right-handed, then. Today, for the second time this week, Blake comes over to them smiling. He walks along the sandy path between broom shrubs and low grasses.

Moving steadily, Blake stretches and yawns, takes a towel from his backpack, wipes his face, then takes out a flask and has a long drink of cold tea. He waits for the older man to speak to him.

"Hello, Dan. How are you?"

"Hi, Frank," Dan–Blake says, still panting and grimacing because of a feigned cramp.

"Horrible weather for running," says the man, who's allowed his gray beard and moustache to grow since they first met a week ago.

"Horrible day, even," Blake replies, stopping five meters from them.

"I thought of you this morning when I saw the price of Oracle shares."

"Don't talk to me about it! But do you know what I can predict for the next few days, Frank?"

"No?"

Blake neatly folds his towel, stows it in his backpack, then carefully slips the flask in beside it before whipping out a pistol. He immediately fires three times at the younger man, who's propelled backward by the impact and collapses onto a bench, then three times at a dumbstruck Frank, who barely twitches, falls to his knees, and stays slumped against the balustrade. In both cases, two bullets to the chest and one in the middle of the forehead. Six shots in the space of a second, using a P226 with a silencer, although the waves smothered the sound anyway. Just another contract, no heroics. An easy hundred thousand dollars.

Blake puts the Sig Sauer back in his bag, picks up the six cartridge cases from the sand, and sighs as he studies the felled bodyguard. Yet another company hiring parking attendants, training them for two months, then spitting these amateurs out into the real world. If this sap had done his job, he'd have communicated the name Dan back to his bosses, along with a photo taken from a safe distance, and the company name Oracle that Dan had mentioned fleetingly, and they would have been able to reassure him, having identified one Dan Mitchell, deputy director of logistics at Oracle New Jersey, a man with long blond hair and more than a passing likeness to Blake, who actually trawled through dozens of organization charts to find a plausible lookalike among those thousands of faces.

Then Blake starts running again. The rain, which is falling more heavily now, blurs his footprints. The Toyota rental is two hundred meters away; its license plates match those of an identical car, spotted the week before on the streets of Brooklyn. Five hours later, he'll be on a flight to London, then the Eurostar to Paris, under a new identity. If his return flight is less turbulent than the Paris–New York trip ten days ago, everything will be perfect.

Blake is professional now, he never needs to pee on the job these days.

17

SUNDAY, JUNE 27, 2021, 11:43 AM

LATIN QUARTER, PARIS

JUST ASK BLAKE, you get the best coffee in Saint-Germain in this bar on the corner of the rue de Seine. A good coffee, and Blake means a really good one, is a miracle born of the intimate collaboration between excellent beans (these are freshly roasted Nicaraguan), finely ground, with filtered, softened water, and an espresso machine, in this instance a Cimbali that's cleaned every day.

Since Blake opened his first vegetarian restaurant on the rue de Buci, not far from the Odéon Theatre, he's been a regular here. If you're going to despair about life, the universe, and everything, you might as well do it on a Parisian café terrace. In this neighborhood, then, he's Joe, for Jonathan, or Joseph, or Joshua. Even his employees call him Joe, and his surname doesn't feature anywhere, except probably in the entry for the organization's holding company recorded on the trade register. Blake has always been obsessive about secrecy, or shall we say discretion, and he has daily proof that this is a good instinct.

Here, though, he lowers his guard. He does some shopping, goes to pick up his two children from school, and, since they've taken on a manager for each of the four restaurants, he and Flora even go to the theater and the movies. An everyday life, in which you can also be injured, but only because when you took Mathilde for her pony ride you accidentally knocked your forehead against the door to the box stall.

His two lives are completely sealed off from each other, perfectly watertight. Joe and Flora are paying off the mortgage on a lovely apartment, steps away from the Luxembourg Gardens, while twelve years ago Blake paid cash for a one-bedder near the Gare du Nord station. It's in a handsome building on the rue La Fayette, and the doors and windows are as bulletproof as the walls of a safe. The rent is paid by an official tenant whose name changes every year, a process made all the easier by the fact that he doesn't exist. You can't be too careful.

So Blake's drinking his coffee, with no sugar and no concerns. He's reading the book Flora recommended, but hasn't admitted to her that he spotted the author on his Paris–New York flight back in March. It's lunchtime, and Flora has taken Quentin and Mathilde to her parents'. He skips lunch because only this morning he arranged a meeting for three o'clock this afternoon: a contract that came in yesterday evening. A simple, well-paid job, and the client seems to be in a big hurry. He just needs to stop off at rue La Fayette to change, as he always does. Thirty meters from him a man wearing a hood and an unreadable expression is watching him.

VICTOR MIESEL

VICTOR MIESEL isn't short on charm. His face, which was angular for a long time, has softened over the years, and his thick hair, Roman nose, and olive skin could be reminiscent of Kafka, a healthy Kafka who made it past forty. He's big and tall but still slim, although the sedentary life inherent to his work has padded him out a little.

Because Victor writes. Sadly, regardless of favorable critical responses to two novels, *The Mountains Will Come to Find Us* and *Failures That Missed the Mark*, despite a very Parisian literary prize (albeit the sort that doesn't cause a stampede when it's trumpeted with a sticker on the book), his sales have never gone beyond a few thousand copies. He's convinced himself that there's nothing less tragic, that disillusion is the opposite of failure.

At forty-three, having spent fifteen years writing, he views the small literary community as a farcical train where crooks without tickets ostentatiously take first-class seats with the complicity of incompetent conductors, while modest geniuses are left on the platform—and the latter are an endangered species to which Miesel does not claim to belong. Still, he's not embittered; with time he's learned not to fret about it, accepting that he has to sit through book fairs, signing only four copies in as many hours; and when a comparable lack of success leaves whoever's sitting at the table next to him with time on his or her hands, they chat pleasantly. Miesel can come across as distant and aloof, yet in spite of everything, he has a reputation for his sense of humor. But surely any man worthy of being called amusing is always given this label "in spite of everything"?

Miesel makes a living through translation. From English, Russian, and Polish, the language his grandmother spoke to him when he was a child. He's translated Vladimir Odoyevsky and Nikolai Leskov, nineteenth-century authors whom no one much reads anymore. He's also ended up with some extraordinary commissions, such as—at the request of a festival—translating *Waiting for Godot* into Klingon, the language of Star Trek's cruel extraterrestrials. To put on a good front for his bank manager, Victor also translates entertaining English-language bestsellers that reduce literature to the status of a minor art for minors. This work has opened doors to reputable if not powerful publishers, not that this has helped his own manuscripts cross any of their thresholds.

Miesel has a pet superstition: in the pocket of his jeans he always carries a Lego brick, the most commonplace sort, two by four studs in bright red. It comes from the outside wall of a fortified castle that he and his father were building in his childhood bedroom. Then there was the accident at work, and the model stayed by his bed, unfinished. The child often sat silently studying the crenellations, the drawbridge, the little action figures, and the keep. Continuing the building process alone would have meant accepting death, just as dismantling the castle would have done. That was thirty-four years ago. Victor has lost the brick twice, and twice he's salvaged another identical one. Firstly, in a state of grief, then with no qualms. When his mother died last year, he slipped the brick into her coffin and immediately replaced it. This little red parallelepiped isn't his father, just a memory of a memory, a standard raised to his line of descent and to loyalty.

Miesel has no children. Romantically, he flits from one failed relationship to the next with his enthusiasm intact. He's too often distant, unconvincing, and has never found the woman with whom he'd like to share a good portion of his life. Or perhaps he chooses his partners in such a way that ensures he'll never achieve this.

That would be lying: he did come across *the* woman four years ago, at the Arles Translation Conference. She was in the first row during an in-conversation-with about "translating humor in Goncharov." He tried not to look at her the whole time. Then, because an editor buttonholed him—How about you translate Liubov Gurevich for us? What do you think? That would be great, wouldn't it?—he couldn't get away. But two hours later, in the patient line of people heading for their desserts, she was standing behind him, smiling. The truth, with love, is that the heart knows straightaway, and shouts it from the rooftops. Of course, you're not going to come straight out and tell the person you love them. They wouldn't understand. So, to disguise the fact that you're already hostage to them, you make conversation.

When they reached the final stage—chocolate fondants with whipped cream—Victor turned around and made his opening gambit. He asked her, stumblingly, how to translate *crème chantilly* into English. Yes, apologies for that, it's the best he could come up with. She laughed, politely, and replied "Ascot cream" in a husky voice that sounded enchanting to his ears, and she went back to join her friends at her table. It took him a while to realize that Ascot, like Chantilly, is a racecourse, but in England.

They'd exchanged glances that he liked to think were knowing, and he'd headed pointedly to the bar, in the hope that she would join him there, but she was caught up in a lively discussion. Thinking he was behaving like an idiotic teenager, he returned to his hotel. He couldn't find her among the photos of participants, but felt sure he'd see her again, and spent the next morning visiting all the workshops on a variety of pretexts. In vain. Neither was she at the closing night party. She'd evaporated. Over the last breakfast at his hotel, he described her to a friend involved in organizing the conference, but the words "small," "dark-haired," and "fascinating" have never gone far to describe anyone.

Victor came back to the conference for the next two years, and if he's going to be absolutely honest, it was to see her. Since then—and this is a serious professional error—he's slipped into his translations brief passages describing Ascot Racecourse or whipped cream. And it was in Gurevich's collected articles that he started these misdemeanors: in the opening text, "Почему нужно дать женщинам все права и свободу" ("Why women should be given freedom and all their rights"), he introduced the sentence "Freedom isn't merely whipped cream on a chocolate cake, it is a right." It was discreet, and who knows? After all, she was obviously interested in Goncharov. But no. If she read the book, she didn't notice the addition, and neither did the editor, or any of the readers, for that matter. Victor let life go on, and it's enough to break your heart.

AT THE START of the year, a Franco-American organization financed by the cultural department of the French Embassy in the U.S. gives him a translation prize for one of the thrillers that keep him fed and watered. In early March he flies to the States to receive it, and the flight hits appalling turbulence. The storm throws the plane in every direction for an eternity. The captain talks soothingly, but everyone in the cabin—and Miesel more than most—suspects that they're going to plunge into the sea, shattering on impact with the wall of water. For many long minutes he puts up resistance, clinging to his seat, straining his muscles to counter every jolt. He avoids the window that looks out into hail-filled darkness. And then, a few rows in front of him, he sees this woman. If he'd noticed her when they were embarking, he wouldn't have been able to take his eyes off her. Although not exactly like her, she is cruelly reminiscent of his vanished Arlésienne. Judging by her fragile quality, the delicacy of her features, the texture of her skin, and her slender body, she's little more than a girl, but tiny lines around her eyes suggest she's around thirty. The nose pads on her tortoiseshell glasses etch temporary fly wings on either side of her nose. From time to time she smiles at her neighbor, a man, older than she is, perhaps her father, and the plane's lurching seems to amuse them, unless they find it reassuring to pretend that they don't care.

But the plane plummets in yet another air pocket, and something in Victor suddenly snaps, he closes his eyes and lets himself be sloshed every which way, no longer trying to anchor himself. He's turned into one of those lab mice that's subjected to violent stresses and eventually stops fighting, resigned to dying.

At last, after what feels like forever, the plane escapes the storm's clutches. But Miesel is still prostrate, mired in a horrible impression of unreality. Life resumes around him, people laugh, or cry, but he observes it all through smoked glass. The captain announces that no one is to leave their seat until after landing, but Miesel is drained of all energy and wouldn't be capable of heaving himself from his in any case. As soon as the doors of the plane are open, the other passengers race out, impatient to get away from the contraption, but as the cabin empties, Victor stays where he is, in his seat by the window. A hostess taps his shoulder, and he agrees to get to his feet. At this point he remembers the young woman, with renewed intensity. He intuits that she alone can extricate him from this abyss of nonlife. He looks for her but she's out of sight, and neither can he find her in the line for passport control.

The head of the book office comes to pick him up at the airport, and shows concern for this disoriented, monosyllabic translator.

"Are you sure you'll be okay, Mr. Miesel?"

"Yes. I think we nearly died. But I'm fine."

His toneless voice worries the man from the consulate. They don't exchange another word all the way to the hotel. When he comes back to collect Miesel late the following afternoon, he gathers that the translator hasn't left his room all day, or even eaten. He has to insist that he take a shower and put some clothes on. The reception is being held at the Albertine bookshop on Fifth Avenue, overlooking Central Park. At the appropriate moment, on an insistent cue from the cultural attaché, Miesel takes from his pocket the thank-you speech that he wrote in Paris, and proceeds—in a droning voice—to say that the translator's role is to "liberate the pure language captured within a work by transposing it"; he professes limply all the fine things he doesn't think about the American author, a tall blond woman with terrible makeup who smiles to herself, and then he stops talking abruptly. Confronted with the growing discomfort in the room, the writer takes over the mic to give her heartfelt thanks and to announce that her fantasy saga is to have two further volumes. Then it's time for drinks and mingling; Miesel's expression is faraway.

"Jesus, when you think what this kind of party costs us, he could maybe make an effort," the cultural advisor mutters as an aside. The man from the book office half-heartedly defends Miesel, who has his return flight the next day.

Once back in Paris, he starts to write, as if following dictation, and the uncontrollable mechanism of this writing process itself plunges him into a state of profound anxiety. The book will be called *The anomaly*, and it will be his seventh.

"I have not made a single gesture in my life. I know that, from time immemorial, it is gestures that have made me, that not one movement has been made under my own control. My body has been happy to come alive, pulled by strings I did not attach. It is presumptuous to imply that we master the space around us, when we simply follow the curves of least resistance. The limitation of limitations. No takeoff will unfold our sky, ever."

Over just a few weeks, a graphomanic Victor Miesel fills hundreds of pages in this style, fluctuating between lyricism and metaphysics: "The oyster that feels the pearl knows that the only conscience is pain, in fact it is only the pleasure of pain. [. . .] The coolness of my pillow always reminds me of the pointless temperature of my blood. If I shiver with cold, it means my pelt of solitude is failing to warm the world."

In the last few days he hasn't left home at all. The final paragraph sent to his publishers shows just how close this derealization experience comes to being insurmountable: "I have never known how the world would differ had I not existed, nor toward what shores I would have driven it had I existed more intensely, and I cannot see how my passing will alter its movement. Here I am, walking along a trail whose absent pebbles lead me nowhere. I am becoming the point where life and death unite until they are indistinguishable, where the mask of the living man settles restfully in the face of the deceased. This morning, because the weather is clear, I can see all the way to me, and I am like everyone else. I am not putting an end to my existence but giving life to immortality. Ultimately, it is futile for me to write a final sentence that does not seek to change the moment."

Having set down these words and sent the file to his editor, Victor Miesel, overcome by a piercing anxiety that he cannot identify, steps over the balcony, and falls from it. Or throws himself from it. He leaves no letter, but the whole book leads him to this ultimate gesture.

"I am not putting an end to my existence but giving life to immortality."

It is April 22, 2021, at twelve noon.

LUCIE

MONDAY, JUNE 28, 2021

MÉNILMONTANT, PARIS

IN THE HALF LIGHT of dawn, a man with an angular face silently opens a bedroom door, his tired eyes trained on a barely visible bed where a woman lies sleeping. The shot lasts three seconds, but Lucie Bogaert doesn't like it. Too bright, too diffuse, too static. The director of photography must have been asleep. She makes a note that FX will need to work on the gamma and the contrast, and pixelate a painting in the background that's too obtrusive. She slightly alters the framing around Vincent Cassel's face, creates a subtle zoom toward him, and slows the shot down by a few frames to give it some rhythm. It takes her a minute. There, done. That's so much better. It's this attention to detail, this cinematographic instinct, that make her the favorite editor of so many directors.

It's early, five in the morning, and Louis's asleep. In a couple of hours she'll wake him—*to wake, woke, woken*—and make breakfast—*to eat, ate, eaten*—and yes, she'll help him go through the irregular English verbs in his seventh-grade curriculum. But for now Lucie hastily reedits the interior scene that she and the director Maïwenn will be looking at together later this morning. She stands up, her neck aching and her eyes dry. The large mirror above the fireplace reflects a small, slim woman with the ethereal figure of a girl; pale skin, fine features, and short-cropped dark hair. On her delicate Greek nose she wears large tortoiseshell glasses that make her look like a student. She walks over to the living room window. When she feels overwhelmed by the emptiness of it all, this cold glass is where she always comes to rest her forehead. Ménilmontant is asleep, but she feels the irresistible draw of the city. She wishes she could abandon her body and dissolve into everything outside.

A muted ding tells her she has an email. She sees André's name and sighs. She's angry, not so much because of his persistence as because he knows he shouldn't persist but can't help himself. How can he be so intelligent and so fragile at the same time? But love means not being able to stop your heart trampling all over your intelligence.

She met André three years ago, at a party thrown by filmmaker friends. She'd arrived late, and a man who was about to leave had stayed. People teased him, Oh, of course, the lovely Lucie shows up and suddenly André's not in such a hurry to go home... So this was the André Vannier of Vannier & Edelman, the architect who'd been mentioned to her. A tall, slim man who looked about fifty but who could well have been older. He had long hands and eyes that were both sad and cheerful, eyes that had managed to keep an enduring, youthful quality. She knew instantly that as soon as she said anything she captivated him, and she liked his being her captive.

They saw each other again soon afterward. He wooed her discreetly, and she realized that he was less afraid of ridicule than of making her feel uncomfortable. At first she rebuffed him, tactfully. But they still met regularly, and he always proved thoughtful, amusing, and attentive. She surmised that he wasn't proud of his bachelor life, a subject he avoided at every turn; she suspected a string of mistresses and precious little magic.

One spring evening he invited her to his apartment for a dinner. She was amazed by his eclectic group of friends: a very conceptual painter, an English surgeon just passing through, a woman who wrote for *Le Monde*, a librarian with quite a penchant for alcohol, and even one Armand Mélois, an exquisite, refined man who—she learned during the course of the meal—ran French counterespionage. Lucie also discovered André's vast Haussmann apartment, with its understated furniture, featuring a predominance of wood and industrial chic, cluttered with books, novels: a far cry from the cold, pared-back world associated with architects. And on one of the shelves a brightly colored plaster model of Mickey Mouse. She picked up the figurine and turned it over in her hands, astonished.

"It's hideous, isn't it?" André said, coming over.

Lucie smiled.

"I bought it so that something in my apartment defied acclimatization. You can't get used to ugliness. It's full of life. Ugly life, but life all the same."

All through the evening Lucie's eyes kept being drawn magnetically to that monstrous Mickey Mouse. And all at once, although she couldn't have said why, that Walt Disney mouse communicated something to her, it told her that happiness was possible with this man.

She introduced him to Louis. André wasn't calculating: he immediately liked the lively, funny child on the cusp of adolescence, and didn't try to make an ally of him. But he was no fool: in the battle for Lucie's heart, he had no need of an enemy.

One day when they were saying goodbye after lunch, she stepped out to cross the street and André snatched her arm and yanked her back. A truck thundered past her. Her shoulder hurt, but she really had almost died. All the color drained from André's face. They stood side by side for a moment and the sounds of the city seemed heightened around them. He was breathing fast, so was she, and with a gasp he hugged her to him.

"I hurt you, I'm sorry, I was scared, I thought... I love you so much."

And he stepped back, terrified by these words that had escaped him. He stammered another apology and left. She watched him walk away and noticed for the first time that he walked quickly and upright; he was still so young. She was very shaken, and it was two weeks before she contacted him; when they next saw each other he didn't mention it again.

But he'd said it. I love you. Lucie was wary of the words. It was too soon for her to hear them. She'd loved another man who used that mendacious verb too often and inappropriately, who humiliated her, abused her, and disappeared, only to come back and disappear again. She wanted to tell André that she was tired of all these men wanting her for her soft skin, her slim legs, her pale lips, what they called her beauty, its promise of happiness, and this was all they could see about her. Tired of the men who approached her like hunters, the ones who wanted to hang her on the wall like a trophy. She deserved more than impulsive desire, she didn't want to be toyed with anymore. She wanted to tell him that this was why she'd gradually gravitated toward him, it was why she was there. For the time he'd given her, for the gentleness she sensed in him, and for his respect too. She wished she could stop keeping him dangling in his role as the silent older admirer, wished she could make a decisive break, or surrender completely, let go. She settled for being ashamed that she was hard, sometimes cruel, by resisting her growing attraction to him.

Another winter went by, and then just over four months ago, after a dinner at Kim's, the little Korean restaurant in the Marais neighborhood where they'd become regulars, he said it again: "You know, Lucie, I care about you, and I know all the things that stand between us, against us. But if you ever want me as a partner, for however long you like, it's up to you to take the first step..." The way he looked at her then was ageless. A little disconcerted, she smiled at him; of course she knew she should give herself more time, but she was afraid he would tire of this pointless waiting. She thought of Caerus, the Greek god of the opportune moment, and decided to grab him by his characteristic tuft of red hair. Every part of her being drove her to sit down beside André on the banquette and kiss him tenderly. No British style rom-com would have dared a more wonderful opening scene. She had no regrets.

And from that rather miraculous moment she and André were together.

André was due to fly to New York to visit the Silver Ring construction site two weeks later, in early March;

she was just finishing editing the latest von Trotta and had nothing else planned before the Maïwenn more than a month later. He suggested they go together: they'd have plenty of time, they could pay their respects to the ducks in Central Park, drop in on the Klees at the Guggenheim, and even go to a musical on Broadway. She accepted without a moment's hesitation, on the condition that he also show her the Silver Ring site. It was her way of saying she wanted to "be a part of it." Back at her apartment she packed her bag breezily and well ahead of time, what books should I take, the Coetzee, why not, and also, there you go, a Pléiade collection of Romain Gary's work, it's not that heavy, and this black dress, yes, it really suits me, that skirt's too short, but I'll wear tights, it's very cold in March, and she was delighted to be feeling so frivolous again. Louis had agreed to stay with his grandmother for a while.

The flight was turbulent, terrifying even. While the plane was threatening to break in two and she was so frightened she was going to lose all self-control, André never stopped talking to her and smiling. She loved New York, a city she knew nothing like as well as he did. They were meant to stay a week, but it ended up being two. In a horribly overpriced salon in the East Village she had her long brown hair cut very short. "You know, I would never have had the nerve to do this before. I'm starting a new life." Of course, it was the worst cliché, but she was grateful to André for not pointing this out. She was aware how reassuring she found him, how much they could, yes, love each other.

And then they returned to Paris, and slowly everything started to sour. Faced with André's elation, with his arms wanting to hug her, and the kisses he inflicted on her the whole time, contemplating the friends he "absolutely must" introduce her to, like a spoil from some battle he'd won, she gradually withdrew. Why do cats that catch mice refuse to let them live? She wasn't designed for this sort of invasion; she would have liked fewer imperatives, a slower, more serene commitment. The avid longing of his man's hands frightened her, their oppressive lust gave her own desire no opportunity to bloom. He didn't want to understand, and the fragility that André had so adroitly disguised became palpable; and no, she didn't want to have to keep reassuring him, no, she wasn't duty bound to comply with his tyrannical appetite, she didn't need to appease his wounded narcissism, whether or not the wounds were inflicted by age, and she certainly didn't have to tolerate his puppy-dog eyes whimpering Choose me, take me. Why did he refuse to see that he was trapping her in his arms, and his bed? Why did she have to feel guilty for rejecting his advances when the very last thing she wanted was any sense of duty?

And then in early June there was that last dinner, the dinner where André wanted to win her back, when everything was already screwed, and he insisted that they go to Kim's, as if its already dated half-Zen–half-Gangnam décor could exercise some magic power over her. And he talked and talked over his cooling cream noodle *beosut*, listening only to himself, giving in to his excessive propensity for words, and each pretty pronouncement made their farewells all the uglier. She looked at him, he took her hand, which she surrendered to him, and all she wanted was to be somewhere else; a coolness stole over her heart, she smiled with no trace of anger at the charming gentleman who now looked old again, but why couldn't he see that she'd already left? Perhaps she didn't have enough energy, or just not enough love—God, but she hates that word. All the same, André had played his part as a salve, for the time it took her to scar, a sort of ointment with a smell that turned out to be fairly unpleasant and rancid, now that the wound had healed... But no, she was wrong, why revisit their lovely beginnings in the bitter light of their ending? She wasn't the one who'd used him, he and he alone hadn't lived up to their shared hopes.

She insisted on splitting the check, to signal in every possible way that there was now a him and a her, but no longer an us. And then he handed her a small book: *The anomaly*, by Victør Miesel. His name meant something to her.

"Here, you'll like it..."

She opened it at random onto this page: "Hope keeps us waiting in the corridor to happiness. If we secure what we hope for, we enter the anteroom of unhappiness." My God, metaphors, that's a bad start. A little further on: "Seduction has always been a commonplace craft; breaking up a major art." So she's an artist, then. Let's go with this major art.

She accepted the gift and left.

That was three weeks ago, long before André set off for Mumbai and the wretched Soyara or Suyara Tower, whose elegance he trumpeted to her even though she'd already lost interest in anything he built.

The email he sent yesterday is still up on her screen in bold blue letters.

In the end she opens it. Not a single sentence that doesn't sound gossipy, hollow, or ridiculous to her. Nothing she finds touching, but in all likelihood, there was nothing that could have reached her. "I would have liked the two of us to walk the longest possible path, together, and even the longest of possible paths." Trite nonsense. "I can never know whether you would have ended up liking the way I look at you, full of love and longing." She rolls her eyes. And finally this pathetic renunciation: "I don't expect a reply."

Lucie's not thinking of replying, anyway.

All of a sudden, her phone buzzes, a withheld number. How dare he, on a Monday morning, when it's still dark, with Louis asleep in his bedroom? Lucie picks up, furious, to stop the ringing. But it's a woman's voice.

"Lucie Bogaert?"

"Yes," she answers quietly.

"Captain Maupas. National police."

"But . . . there must be a mistake."

"Were you born in Montreuil on January 22, 1989?"

"Yes."

"Good. We're just outside your door. Could you let us in, please."

"But why? You'll wake my son."

"We'll explain. We have a warrant, I'm slipping it under the door right now. Open up, please."

DAVID

MAY 29, 2021

THIRD AVENUE, NEW YORK CITY

THE FICUS is thirsty. Its brown leaves are so dry they're curling up; some branches are already dead. Standing there in its plastic pot, it's the very incarnation of hopelessness, if indeed the word "incarnation" can be applied to a green plant. If someone doesn't water it soon, David thinks, it's going to die. In all logic, it must be possible to find a point of no return on the continuous thread of time, an irretrievable tipping point after which nothing and no one could save the ficus. At 5:35 on Thursday afternoon someone waters it and it survives; at 5:36 on Thursday afternoon anyone in the world could show up with a bottle of water and it would be No, babe, sweet of you, thirty seconds ago, I can't be sure, maybe, but now, what are you thinking, the only cell that could have set the whole thing going again, the final viable eukaryote that could have rallied its neighbors—Come on, guys, let's see some motivation, let's have a reaction, fill yourselves up with water, don't let yourselves go—well, the last of the last has just left us, so you're here too late, with your pathetic little bottle, ciao ciao. Yes, somewhere on the thread of time.

"David?"

A gentle man's voice stirs David from his existential, vegetal musings. He gets up and hugs a tall man of about fifty, only just older than he is but one whose hair is already white, a man who looks like him, as is only right for someone with whom he has a good deal of DNA in common.

"Hi, Paul."

"You okay, David? Is Jody not with you?"

"She'll join us as soon as she can. She's teaching her class at the Goethe-Institut, I didn't want her to postpone it."

"Okay."

David follows his brother into his office. A French Empire desk, oak bookcases, Art Nouveau crystal wall lights, carmine-colored drapes in thick velvet, and through the window a fine view over Lexington Avenue and, further over, on the corner of Third Avenue, the entrance to their Friday squash club. The room rather successfully disguises what it is—this office belongs to an oncologist, one of the best.

"Do you want coffee, David? Tea?"

"Coffee."

Paul slips a capsule into the coffee machine, puts a chic Italian cup under the funnel, and finds a way of avoiding eye contact with his brother for a few more seconds. He guesses that David, having heard him say his name too many times, already knows. In war films, when a soldier's spurting blood and the sergeant says, You'll be fine, Jim, you'll pull through this, Jim, it's never a good sign. The kindly rhetoric, the Italian espresso with its unctuous crema, this device of constantly delaying their conversation—it all indicates the worst.

"Here."

David nods, automatically takes the cup, and immediately puts it down on the desk.

"Go on. I'm ready."

"Right. You remember we did a biopsy during your scan yesterday . . . I have the results."

Paul pushes aside the cup, takes some photos from an envelope, and spreads them on the desk, facing his brother.

"It's what I was afraid of. The tumor in the tail of your pancreas, opposite the small intestine, here, is malignant. Cancerous. And it hasn't just spread into nearby blood vessels and lymph nodes, it's metastasized in your liver and your small intestine. Clinically, you're a stage 4."

"Stage 4. In other words?"

"It's too advanced for us to consider a distal pancreatectomy and splenectomy, that means removing the pancreas and the spleen."

David visibly reacts to the blow. His breathing is labored. Paul has a glass of water ready and hands it to him. His brother looks up into his eyes. It was because Paul noticed the characteristic unhealthy yellow in the whites of David's eyes that he insisted on running tests. David takes a deep breath.

"Prognosis?" he asks.

"It's too late to operate so we'll do radio and chemo to shrink the tumor."

"Prognosis, Paul," David says again.

"How can I put this? It's a bastard."

"Which means . . . ? What're my chances?"

"A twenty percent chance of surviving five years, that's it, that's what the statistics say. But probabilities don't mean a thing. We're going to try to do way better than that. I've set up an appointment for you with Saul to get a second opinion. He's the best. He's taking you on as an urgent case, he can see you tomorrow, and I already sent him your biopsy results and your MRI images."

"It's not worth it, Paul. I believe you. Let's do what you said. When can we start?"

"As soon as you can. As of now, you're off work for a good three months, at least. Let your people know right away. Do you have good medical insurance?"

"I think so. I never needed to check. But I guess so, yes."

David stands and takes a few steps. He's shaking with anger, but is it anger? His whole body refuses to be impervious to this. Oh Lord, why do we always go back over the last few weeks, why is it that we can't help wanting to gauge just how blind we've been? And all those days lived without a care, in the last bliss of ignorance, eating out, telling jokes, taking the kids to the movies, making love with Jody, playing squash with Paul, when maybe if he'd just had a scan, what, three months ago, the diagnosis would have been made and he could, perhaps, have been saved. David wonders whether some part of him had guessed, and whether that part of him didn't want to know.

"When did it start?"

"I don't know, David. There's no way of telling. The tumor could have been there for a year, or two months. No one can know. Every pancreatic cancer is different."

"Would it have been too late to do anything two months ago? After that hellish flight from Paris when hail trashed my plane, I was already kind of tired, remember? My pee was very dark too. And I didn't have time to get tests."

"I don't know. What I do know for sure is that we need to concentrate on what we can do now, and there's a lot we can still do."

"Are there new treatments? Drugs?"

"Yes, we'll try everything there is, plus, if you want, chemicals that are still experimental, revolutionary stuff that's not on the market yet, I swear it."

Paul's lying, because it's better than Well, no, David, there's nothing new, it's a bastard, like I said, we don't know how to deal with it, not a clue, we haven't found a miracle cure, we don't even know why patients say a particular protocol works better than another.

"It's a painful cancer, right?" David asks, sitting back down.

"I promise we'll do everything to minimize the pain throughout your treatment. Of course, there are undesirable side effects. Obviously. You get nothing for nothing."

Undesirable. Like hell. That's right, bro, yes, you'll puke up your guts, spewing from every orifice, you'll lose your hair, and your eyebrows, and forty-five pounds, and then what? All that to claw back what, maybe two, three extra months, a twenty percent chance of surviving five years, twenty percent, yes, but not from where you're starting, little brother, in your case it's a one in ten chance, not even that, shit, it's so unfair, it stinks... Paul draws up his chair and sits next to David, who's stopped moving, paralyzed, all his spark gone. Paul puts a hand on his already absent brother's arm, hoping this gesture will calm the icy panic sweeping over him, and he also hopes that just the touch of his hand can draw out and destroy the darkness, because it's insane but that's how it is, years of practice and hundreds of patients lost still haven't stopped magical thinking from surfacing every time, even in the depths of the most rational mind, and also right now—why now?—he suddenly remembers the bowling nights in Peoria when David bowled like an idiot and still got strikes, the fucking lucky jerk of an asshole, and the smell of pink marshmallows torched in the gas flames at Aunt Luna's place, and the sweet berry perfume that that blonde chick Deborah Spencer used to wear, the one they were both nuts about and who ended up sleeping with that meathead Tony the Dinosaur, wait, why did people call him that again? and David's speech at his first wedding, with Fiona, a totally half-assed marriage, by the way, it sure was half-assed, and that speech was so dumb and so funny and so wonderful because it was funny and dumb, and the birth of his, Paul's, son, also called David, and Baby David asleep in Uncle David's arms as he sobbed with emotion on the maternity ward, and everything that'll be lost, sayonara, and everything that cancer will drag down into its dark whirlpool, and then, out of nowhere, tears prick his eyes, it's brutally sudden, shit, an oncologist who goes and cries, what the hell is that? Paul turns aside, takes a Kleenex, and blows his nose loudly.

A ray of sunlight comes into the office. It's not great timing, but the fact that it comes in, the fact that it lends

David its golden light, makes it a beam of life, a fleeting miracle as the fickle sun heads west between the two skyscrapers on Third, at 5:21, a marvel that lasts exactly twelve minutes, spring, summer, and fall. At 5:33 it'll be over.

"Okay, David. I don't have another patient. Let's wait for Jody, I'll talk you through the protocol."

Paul explains, at length, and David listens without interrupting. But Paul will need to explain again the next day because he won't remember any of it. David will have been thinking of Jody, of the look of indescribable distress on her face, of the kids' eyes when he has to tell them that Daddy's very sick, Grace, Benjamin, my darlings, you both need to be very brave, you also need to help Mommy a lot and be very good, is that okay? He will have thought about his medical insurance, which is excellent, sure, but they'll make some inquiries and criticize him for hushing up his ten years as a smoker from the age of fifteen to twenty-five, he will have thought about the inescapable pain, the degradation of the final days, the cremation, even the music his friends will be made to listen to, something nice, don't you think, Paul, some rock, a bit of blues, but not God-knows-whose seriously depressing requiem, he will have thought, not for the first time, about the kids' school fees, about the mortgage on the apartment that he paid off early, what a moron, when—if you die—the life insurance pays off all the outstanding money owed, he will have thought about everything yet to happen and everything that will still happen, after. He will even have thought about strange things.

"By the way, Paul... in your waiting room..."

"Yes?"

"The ficus. You need to water it."

It's 5:33 and the sun slips away.

THURSDAY, JUNE 24, 2021, 10:28 PM

MOUNT SINAI HOSPITAL, NEW YORK CITY

THE FICUS in Paul's waiting room isn't dead. But David hasn't been back, and he won't see the sun glide between the two skyscrapers, or even the sun. Room 344 at Mount Sinai Hospital faces due north, and he will most likely vacate it in a few days. Death has taken up residence in his now-gaunt features.

In the battle against pain, they're complementing morphine with trials of a nanomedication being developed by the French, which means they don't have to keep raising the dosage. In the battle against cancer, the medical team have given up. Too aggressive, too invasive, too advanced.

Someone knocks at the door, but no one replies: next to an unconscious David, Jody is asleep in a chair, exhausted from so many nights spent by his side. The children have been at Paul's place for the last three days. The door opens, softly, lets in two men in black suits, wearing gold badges. The first man leans silently toward David, collects a sample of saliva from the corner of his mouth, stows the tiny spatula into a tube, and immediately leaves the room. The second man takes out a cellphone, photographs the intubated, dying patient, sends off the image, and sits down on a chair, unable to tear his eyes away from that emaciated face.

THE SPIN CYCLE

MARCH 10, 2021

EAST COAST OF THE U.S., INTERNATIONAL WATERS

N 42°8′50″, W 65°25′9″

ALL SMOOTH FLIGHTS are alike. Every turbulent flight is turbulent in its own way. It's 4:13 pm when Paris–New York flight AF006, to the south of Nova Scotia, sees the pillowy barrier of a vast cumulonimbus looming up ahead. The cloudy weather front is rising, and very quickly. It's still fifteen minutes away, but it stretches north and south in an arc that covers hundreds of kilometers, and it's already reached a height of nearly 45,000 feet. The Boeing 787, which is flying at 39,000 feet and was about to begin its descent toward New York, won't be able to avoid it, and there's a sudden flurry of activity in the cockpit. The copilot compares maps to the weather radar. This wide front wasn't forecast, and Gid Favereaux is more than just surprised, he's worried.

The impenetrable gray wall, its summit iridescent with dazzling sunlight, is homing in on them at breakneck speed, voraciously swallowing strata of clouds that feed and bolster it. Captain Markle switches to Boston's frequency and examines his instruments, including the weather radar, which is filling up with red 120 nautical miles ahead. He nods and puts down his coffee just as Boston broadcasts on its frequency.

"All flights on Boston Control. Due to exceptional weather conditions on the East Coast, all airports are closed except for KJFK. There have been no takeoffs on the Eastern Seaboard for thirty minutes. The situation has developed too quickly for us to warn flights any earlier. KJFK Canarsie remains open for all landings."

"Boston Control, hello, Air France 006, level three nine zero heading for Kennebunk. We have a monster up ahead. Request course three five zero for the next eighty nautical miles."

"Air France 006, Boston Control here. Maneuver at will. Contact Kennedy on 125.7. Bye-bye."

Markle grimaces and watches the horizon clog up inexorably from north to south. The sky's given him something to remember on his penultimate transatlantic flight. He connects to the airport.

"Kennedy Approach from Air France 006, we have enough fuel to skirt the front southward all the way to Washington."

A click, another woman's voice, but more serious.

"Sorry, 006. Negative. The conditions are the same well beyond Norfolk. It might even be worse in the south now. Come down to eight zero when you can and resume your course to Kennebunk. Keep within those parameters."

Markle shakes his head, snaps off the radio, and picks up the cabin mic to address his passengers in a reassuring voice, speaking first in English, then in not-bad French.

"This is your captain speaking, please return to your seats immediately, fasten your seat belts, and turn off all electronic devices. We're heading for a patch of very significant turbulence. Repeat: very significant turbulence. Please stow your bags and laptops under the seat in front of you. Cabin crew, please ensure passenger and cabin safety and then return to your seats. Repeat, after checking passenger safety please return to your seats immediately."

The cumulonimbus is getting closer, it's a supercell, but far from the standard type. There's not just one anvil-shaped mesocyclone spiraling high up into the atmosphere, but dozens of them, as if they were being lifted by an invisible hand, and all fusing together in the tropopause. Any vessels on the ocean must be in the grips of an apocalyptic depression. Markle's never seen anything like it in twenty years of long-haul flights. The storm of the year, at least. The stratospheric domes reach heights of sixteen kilometers. He could try to slip between two columns, but that would just mean flying straight into the one behind. The weather radar now shows a long diagonal band of red: a wall of water and ice.

"Did you see how quickly it's growing?" Gid asks anxiously. "We're gonna be dragged down like hell the minute we reach it. We'll never get through."

Gid is right to be worried, thinks Markle, even if he has only done one year of transatlantics and three of long-haul. He switches the mic back on to talk to the passengers in a jaunty tone, playing down the situation.

"Hello, folks, Captain Markle again. I'm asking you once again to remain seated, fasten your seat belts, and check that children have their seat belts fastened. Also, please switch off all electronic devices. We're very likely to experience an air pocket within the next minute. To all cabin staff, if passenger safety has been assured, please return to your seats straightaway... I'll wait for your confirmation."

"All in secure position, confirmed," comes the voice of the senior cabin crew officer.

"Okay, this is likely to be quite something, and I can guarantee you won't forget it, but I promise you it's safe so long as your seat belt is fastened. A roller coaster, for those who like their amusement par—" All at once, before even reaching the edge of the front, the Boeing has no air to support it, and it starts to plummet. Despite the soundproofing on the door to the cabin, Markle and Favereaux are sure they hear the passengers scream.

The plane spends ten interminable seconds in freefall before diving into the cumulonimbus in the worst possible place, to the southwest of the column, at an alarming slant, a thirty-degree angle adopted by the autopilot that has taken over from manual controls. The Boeing is instantly churned in spiraling currents of cloud, and just as instantly the cockpit lights up because it's dark as night, soot black, and there's a horrendous racket: hundreds of enormous hailstones pelt the windows, occasionally leaving impact marks on the reinforced glass. Those few seconds feel like an eternity, and then despite the tornado's gusts, the plane finds a warm, rising current and a semblance of support, producing that intense crushing trough-of-a-roller-coaster sensation.

Strapped into his seat, Markle pushes both General Electric throttles to the maximum, because damn, what *is* this bastard! I mean, you might expect doldrums like that on a Rio–Madrid, near the equator, but what the hell's it doing right up in the North Atlantic? Fuck, this is crazy, we have the most powerful engines around and fantastically supple wings, we can't just snap in two like some scale model, it's not possible. We got out of fixes dozens of times on the simulators, with engine failures, depressurizations, onboard computers dying on us . . . shit, we can't screw it up in real life. Markle doesn't think about his kids, or his wife, not yet, it may even be that pilots always die before they have time to watch their life flash before their eyes, and Markle is definitely not thinking of the passengers; right now, he's just trying to save this big, very heavy, and very clumsy Boeing, so he goes through procedures he's learned by heart and repeated over and over; he puts his faith in reflexes and his twenty years of experience. But it's still a hell of a thing.

Shaken, buffeted, and ashen, Markle and Favereaux concentrate on their instruments, battling it out with the storm, which, it will be established later, is the most violent and the most sudden in the last ten years. The warning light for the left-hand turbine indicates a fifteen percent loss of power, but the strong electric field is disrupting the aircraft's electronic circuits. All in all, the plane stands up to the tornado, stays more or less horizontal, eventually stabilizes, and, even though there's no letup in the hail and the surface of the windshield is pockmarked, there are no worrying cracks on the inner side.

As soon as the buffeting eases just a fraction, Markle talks to the cabin. He tries not to shout, despite the deafening noise in the aircraft.

"Sorry for this turbulence, folks. We're going to have to continue our course to New York through these clouds and stay in this spin cycle for at least..."

Blazing sunlight suddenly streams into the cockpit, the Boeing accelerates dramatically and silence returns; the disruption is instantly behind them.

Markle checks the controls in astonishment. The plane's flying perfectly well, with a steady thrumming sound, but all the instruments are malfunctioning. Despite their vertiginous drop and five minutes spent with no clear course, the altimeter is now stuck at 39,000 feet again, the weather radar refuses to display the least disturbance, and their course seems to be two six zero. He turns back to the mic that's connected to the cabin.

"Well, you saw for yourselves, we just emerged from the clouds without too much damage. Please stay in your seats until further instruction and leave all electronic devices switched off. Cabin crew, you are free to move, thank you. Please report to the cabin."

Markle cuts the mic and enters the emergency code 7700 into the transponder. He puts his headphones back on and calls Kennedy Approach.

"Mayday, Mayday, Mayday, Kennedy Approach, this is Air France 006. Following turbulence negotiating clouds and substantial hail, we have no injured parties but our instruments have failed, no altimeter or airspeed indicator, the radar's not working and the windshield is badly damaged."

The voice at Kennedy air traffic control is now a man's, and he's very surprised.

"Mayday received, Air France 006. Could you confirm the 7700 squawk code?"

"New York, Air France 006, I can confirm, squawk 7700."

The voice, with a clear note of complete bafflement, asks again, "Air France from Kennedy Approach, please confirm the transponder on 7700. You did say Air France 006, didn't you?"

"Affirmative, Air France 006, Mayday. I can confirm squawk 7700, we've come through a huge cloud of hail, the windshield is cracked and the radome is almost certainly dented."

The communication is interrupted for several long seconds. Markle turns to look at Favereaux, lost for words. He gave the transponder code three times, and Kennedy still can't identify them. Then the connection is suddenly back. This time it's a woman's voice, but not as lilting as the previous one. Not as friendly, either.

"Air France 006 Mayday from Kennedy Approach. This is air traffic control, what's the name of the captain on board, please?"

Markle's jaw drops open. Never in his entire career has an air traffic controller asked for a pilot's name.

"Air France 006 Mayday from Kennedy Approach. I repeat: who is the officer in charge, please?"

SOPHIA KLEFFMAN

FRIDAY, JUNE 25, 2021

HOWARD BEACH, QUEENS, NEW YORK CITY

BETTY THE FROG is found by Liam on a Saturday afternoon. She's in the kitchen, behind a radiator near the sink, completely dehydrated. She's light as a feather, translucent, a sheet of tracing paper someone crumpled and crushed into a paper approximation of a frog, its thighs and webbed feet clearly distinguishable. She sure is dead, Liam tells his little sister, your Betty sure is dead, he thinks it's really funny and starts dancing around with his arms in the air, Dead Betty, Dead Betty, and Sophia dissolves into tears.

Three weeks earlier Betty escaped from the terrarium, where she must have been bored out of her tiny mind, despite the pretty, damp mosses, the gleaming green plants, and the round, gray pebbles that Sophia chose for her, plus the half a coconut shell that acts as a swimming pool, but most of all the very-much-alive black flies Sophia fed her when she came home from school. Sophia had put the terrarium on a low table near her bed, and every evening she would get up, huddled in a blanket, and whisperingly describe her day to the frog, which sat motionless under the greenery. What Sophia wanted was for Betty to be safe, and happy too, but mostly safe, sheltered from predators, that's a word she learned, and she really likes it, maybe precisely because it sounds a little disturbing. But the frog escaped in spite of everything. She must have hopped around all over the place in search of warmth and moisture before ending up there, on the floor below, against the lukewarm metal of the convection heater. She'd been hungry and thirsty and her skin had cracked like the dirt in the yard when it hasn't rained for days, until—frozen in death—Betty had become an ectoplasm of a frog.

Sophia's scared to touch her, and Liam is too, even though he's showing off, squealing as he runs around the little corpse. Their mother says, Quiet, for goodness' sake, quiet down a bit, you'll wake Daddy, but their father's already coming downstairs in his T-shirt and yelling, What's this goddamn noise, April, can't you keep your kids quiet, just while I'm on leave, and weren't you supposed to go do the shopping? Lieutenant Clark Kleffman sees the really very dead Betty and his daughter, who's still crying, and laughs as he says, Well, Sophia, that frog of yours . . . you know what? She looks like an old Chinese dumpling!

Clark picks the frog up by one foot between two fingers and dumps it dispassionately in a bowl.

The Kleffmans are collectively resigned to burying Betty, and even though they know nothing about her religion, April decides that she's Baptist, like them; well, she didn't have a believer's proper, immersive baptism, but she spent most of her time in water. It simplifies things. The born-again frog will go to frog heaven. And in the end Clark will flush her down the toilet, that simplifies things too.

Betty was Sophia's sixth-birthday present. Thanks to her, Sophia learned a lot about frogs. Like, for example, they've been around for three hundred million years, they lived alongside the dinosaurs, there are thousands of different species, and an ingredient of insecticides, atrazine, is threatening their survival because their skin is permeable: ironic in light of the fact that they're "useful because they eat insects." And they're amphibians, like salamanders and toads. Besides, Betty is actually a toad, *Anaxyrus debilis*, Sophia carefully wrote out the name on a piece of card and stuck it to the terrarium, in fact, she may even be a male toad, the salesman wasn't too sure—You know, miss, Andy sighed, at least it said Andy on his badge, I'm sorry but this toad is barely an inch long, I can't make out the reproductive organs, maybe give it a name that works for both sexes like Morgan or Madison?—but Sophia called her Betty despite this advice. Betty always hid in her burrow or under her stone when Sophia came near the terrarium. She was terrified of the sound of the vacuum cleaner too. And the noise made by planes taking off from JFK airport and flying over Howard Beach. You could never see her because she was so scared of everything. She's a broad all right, Clark sniggered. Don't say stuff like that to Liam and Sophia, April sighed.

So, Clark Kleffman goes to take Betty from the soup bowl, and Sophia shrieks, "Betty moved, Mom. Betty moved!"

"What? Don't be silly, Sophia, Dad just tilted the bowl."

"But she moved. Look, it's 'cause of the water in there. It woke her up! Mommy, Mommy, put more water in, please!"

April shrugs, but still takes a glass, fills it with water from the faucet, and pours it over Betty. The amphibian moves one foot, then another, it's rising from the dead, absorbing all the water like a sponge, and now it's moving about in the bottom of the bowl and its skin is even gradually reverting to its normal greenish color.

"That's nuts," says Clark, stunned.

"She did what salamanders do in a drought, Mommy, you remember, we saw those salamanders, well, she did the same thing, she went dormant and waited for the rainy season."

"That's nuts," Clark says again. "I never saw anything like it, this dumb frog was one-hundred-percent dead from Deadsville, and now she's bouncing around like a whore in heat. It's nuts."

"Clark, please don't used words like that around the children," April says.

"Jesus, I'm in my own house, I'll talk how I like! What exactly am I to all of you, just a machine to pay the bills and go get itself killed in some country full of assholes, is that it? I fucking had it, April, I had it, do you get that?"

April looks at the floor, Sophia and Liam freeze. The air coagulates around Clark's anger.

Clark balls his fists, withdraws into himself, it's either that or he'll break everything. Fuck, he nearly died ten times in Afghanistan, and this is all the thanks he gets. Ten times, easy, that's right. Nobody ever gave a damn about them, they're almost not even good enough to die, they're not politicians' sons like those little assholes who hid in the National Guard way back in Vietnam days. Okay so last year they did replace those coffin-on-wheels Humvees, the regiment got a hold of some Oshkosh trucks, huge things, real bad boys, so ugly they're hot, and their armor's meant to stop a 13 mm. But, hell no, with armor-piercing bombs around they were just made of cardboard painted to match the sand.

Two weeks before Betty the Frog's resurrection, the Oshkosh was on the way to Kabul from the airbase in Bagram when it was hit by a barrage of Zastava fire, must have been, from the sound of it, they're the Syrians' entry-level semiautomatic. A bullet came through the window in the left rear door—indestructible glass, they'd been told—and it ended up in Thompson's chest, giving him an opportunity to gauge just how perfectly bullets were designed for bodies, and he screamed like crazy. Thompson was a mercenary with the paramilitary firm Academi, the poor sap was more dumb than messed up, and he'd lost his crummy job with a subsidiary of General Motors when the factory hauled its ass to a country where some other poor sap made the same spark plugs for thirty cents an hour. All Thompson wanted was a cabin in Montana, and to achieve this dream, he offered close protection to the engineers of Albermarle Corp.: four months they'd been prospecting for lithium, never daring to stray from the Kabul Serena Hotel, four months they'd been trying to get the exploitation rights contract signed ahead of the Chinese guys at Ganfeng Lithium. But—tough luck, Thompson—Academi's support vehicle had set out for Kabul without him and he'd had to hand over two hundred dollars for a ride on the Oshkosh, just for two hours of potholes, rubble, and corrugated iron in a godforsaken suburb ravaged by ten years of war.

While Sergeant Jack took care of Thompson, who was rolling the whites of his eyes and hiccuping up blood, Clark slipped into the rotating tower and started machine-gunning the area where he thought the shots were coming from, yelling every insult he'd ever known. His bullets, in their hundreds, winged their way to two dirt huts on a bare hillside, two pitiful homes that collapsed to dust in the onslaught.

The Oshkosh raced back to Bagram, where the operating theater was waiting for them. The infirmary was already crowded: the day before, one of the Afghan auxiliaries, a guy on the cleaning team, had blown himself up with a suicide belt when he was near the mess hall, screaming *Allahu akbar*—two dead, ten injured—because there was a rumor that some hooched-up soldiers had pissed out their Buds on copies of the Koran.

Maybe the story was true: slices of ham were definitely thrown into the cages at Guantanamo. The lowest trash always have the option of taking refuge in patriotism. They didn't need to find a bed for Thompson anyway, he was dead on arrival, and the inside of the truck was slick with blood. And one thing's for sure, they could always have tried pouring water over Thompson, but it wouldn't have brought him back to life. So, real sorry, but Clark doesn't give a damn, not a single damn, if he uses words like "broad" and "whore in heat" around the kids, sooner or later they need to learn what a shit world they live in.

"With all your bullshit, I'm exhausted," Clark says, "go do the fucking shopping, April, and take Liam. You, Liam, stop playing your goddamn video game and go help your mother carry the groceries. Come on, Sophia, let's put your frog back in her terrarium."

Sophia looks at her mother, who silently takes the car keys, and reaches for a grumbling Liam's hand; then she follows her father, who's climbing upstairs with the now completely revived Betty in the bowl.

There's a little Eiffel Tower stuck onto a stone in the terrarium, because the Kleffmans went to Paris for their wedding anniversary four months ago. They rented a one-bedroom apartment in Belleville, and the children slept on the convertible sofa in the living room. They visited Notre-Dame and the Arc de Triomphe, and explored Montmartre and the Champs-Elysées. And even with all that, Sophia insisted on going to see some amphibians. April gave in and took her to the zoo at the Jardin des Plantes, and that's where the child first saw a salamander, the extraordinary creature that can regenerate a damaged eye or even part of its brain.

Then Sophia, Liam, and their mother traveled home to New York on a scheduled flight so bumpy that the children didn't stop screaming for the last half hour. Clark did not return with them; he was given a new assignment that sent him from Paris to Warsaw, and then straight on from Warsaw to Baghdad, this time on board a C17, escorting two Abrams tanks and a bomb with a massive blast, the "mother of all bombs," eleven tons, ten meters, a monster. Clark stayed there nine weeks and eventually flew home to Howard Beach, with the hot metallic smell of Thompson's blood still on him.

Sophia's intelligence is April's pride, even though she's angry with herself for being jealous of her own daughter, of her spark and curiosity. At Sophia's age, April clung to her mother, coloring pictures of animals, mostly foals. When she and her sisters had to relocate their mother, who was losing her mind, she found hundreds of those pictures. It was absurd: scarlet foals and indigo foals, green foals and orange ones, every color of the rainbow got the treatment, but it was always, always, foals. She didn't remember this. In fact, she didn't remember anything from that time. She'd left her parents' home very young to marry a tall, skinny, fair-haired boy, such a tender, attentive kid, he wrote her a pretty poem on a piece of paper torn from a notebook, and handed it to her in silence, embarrassed by his own audacity:

Swing the bells
Play hide-and-seek,
I kissed April on the cheek

Yes, in those days Clark was thoughtful. He didn't have any qualifications, so he tried to become a realtor, then a driving instructor, but quickly lost his nerve with an indecisive client or a learner driver, and didn't manage to hold down any job. The army gave him a framework, it restored his pride. Aged twenty-two, this kid who looked no more than eighteen had his head shaved, was given a black beret, and, most important, a fifteen-thousand-dollar bonus. With this money and the guarantee of a regular salary, April managed to negotiate a loan, and right when real estate prices were at their lowest, to buy a discounted house in Howard Beach, its financially ruined owners having been evicted; in their rage they'd taken a hammer to everything they could when they left, breaking washbasins, the kitchen sink, the countertops, and even the wall to their bedroom. In a few years, when the Thwaites Glacier in Antarctica, a huge ice cube two kilometers thick and the size of Florida, has calved and started to melt, the house will be paddling in the ocean. But she and Clark couldn't really know this, and they straightened out the whole place, with April doing all the repainting by herself, despite her growing belly.

April tender, April shady,
O my sweet and cruel lady,
April blooming with pastel colors,

With the passing months Clark grew sure of himself, domineering even. She no longer recognized the sweet boy who wrote her poems. Military training had transformed him, muscled him up, hardened him. And when they made love, the reticent young man, so shy with his girlish young body, had become brutal and selfish. It was then that she started to be afraid of him. But when Clark finished his training and passed his final exam, Liam was already born, and Sophia was on the way.

April caught in the icy storm,
April soft, so sleepy warm,

And many years later, April tender, April shady happened to open a book lying around at her sister's place and she sat there with her mouth gaping like a carp washed up on the riverbank. His poem, his beautiful poem written just for her, was "Fall for April" by an obscure English poet, and that scrap of paper that Clark had given her on their first date, a treasure she still kept, like an idiot, folded in her wallet, was from something he'd studied in high school and painstakingly copied out. She went home with the kids and spent that night crying with anger and pain at this ultimate torpedoing of an image from the past, the now-spoiled memory of Clark, with all the awkwardness of a teenager, handing her a page torn from a school exercise book.

April, I fall for you

CLARK LIFTS the mesh from the terrarium and tilts the bowl, the frog slips out, bounces on the moss, and dives straight into her coconut-shell pool.

"We need to feed Betty, Daddy. She must be hungry."

"Let her rest, honey, and you're going to take a bath too, you can play in the tub like Betty."

Sophia doesn't say anything. She hears the door close downstairs, her mother's and Liam's receding footsteps, the car doors shutting, the engine starting up. Clark turns on the faucets, checks the water temperature, pours in some bubble bath and removes his shoes. Sophia hangs back. He frowns at her.

"Hurry up, Soph, in the water, quick, we don't have as much time as in Pari—"

The doorbell rings, interrupting the father. It rings again, Sophia hears thumping on the door. Clark rolls his eyes.

"Mr. Kleffman?" comes a woman's voice. "Mrs. Kleffman? Agent Chapman, FBI."

"Okay, Soph, I'm going down. You get in the tub, stay in the bubbles, and stop the water running when it's halfway full, you got that?"

Clark leaves the room, and Sophia can hear him downstairs raising his voice, then a man replies firmly, and then another. The argument is still going when someone knocks on the bathroom door.

"Can I come in, Sophia?" the woman's voice asks.

"Yes, ma'am," the child replies.

A lady comes in, she's smiling, she's black, her hair is smooth, it's cut short like Mom's, Sophia thinks, but she doesn't look as tired as Mom does. The FBI officer kneels down, strokes her cheek, gently, professionally: neuroscience has demonstrated that touch is a crucial means of reassuring children and making them feel safe.

Then the agent hands her a towel.

"Hello, Sophia, I'm Heather. Officer Heather Chapman. Dry yourself quickly, get dressed, and I'll wait for you outside, okay? Do you know where your mommy went?"

"She went to the store with Liam."

The woman leaves the bathroom and takes out a cellphone.

"I'm with Sophia Kleffman. Find out where April Kleffman is, probably the nearest supermarket, a black Chevrolet Trax, you have the license plate. She's with the boy, Liam."

The little girl is dressed, the woman hears her on the landing, and reaches out a hand to her. The shouting downstairs has stopped, her father has left.

"Come, Sophia, we're going to find Mommy and your brother Liam, and we'll go for a car ride together."

"Will we come back home after? Because we need to feed Betty."

"Betty?"

"She's my frog, ma'am. We thought she died, but she just dried out. Like a salamander."

The woman already has her cellphone out, she puts it away again.

"Don't worry about your frog. We'll take care of her too. Everything's gonna be fine. Call me Heather. Would you do that for me, Sophia?"

"Yes, ma'am."

JOANNA

FRIDAY, JUNE 25, 2021

PHILADELPHIA

"JOANNA," Sean Prior announces, "your brain is a Gothic cathedral."

Joanna Wasserman holds eye contact with Prior and disguises her consternation. Really? A cathedral? And Gothic? Flamboyant Gothic, at least, thinks the lawyer. Why not the Taj Mahal, the pyramids, or Caesar's Palace in Las Vegas? Although briefly thrown, she still manages to find a reply.

"Well, that's better than 'a man's brain.'"

"Excuse me?"

"Simone de Beauvoir. Her father always told her she had 'a man's brain.'"

Valdeo's CEO gives a knowing chuckle, as if he were best buddies with Simone, her father, and their dog.

Joanna laughs to herself. At best, Prior has a vague idea of who this darned Simone is, but the head of a pharmaceuticals giant worth thirty billion dollars isn't allowed to show the teeniest flaw. A Gothic cathedral . . . what a pity.

Joanna has come to Valdeo's head office in Philadelphia with a young associate lawyer who's handling the files—and who carries them around too. The pharmaceuticals company has been a client of Denton & Lovell for seven years, mostly for fiscal issues and takeover bids; she's been working on it for three months, and for two months now Prior has been her direct contact. At their first meeting, Prior turned to her, and with the slow Texan phrasing that he cultivates and the smile like that of a top carnivore, he asked her a question.

"Tell me, Ms. Wasserman, do you know why I chose you from all the dickheads at Denton and Lovell?"

"Let me guess, Mr. Prior. Because I was first in my class at Stanford—maybe; because I'm a young woman—probably; because I'm black—definitely. And also because I win all my cases against the old white guys who were at Harvard with you."

Prior laughed out loud.

"Exactly right, and because you're definitely the only one who would dare give a reply like that."

"In my case, Mr. Prior, I took you on as a client simply because you can tolerate me."

Prior, who can never bear not to have the last word, added, "But don't forget that I also went to Carnegie Mellon."

A tie. Ever since this jousting match, Joanna Wasserman and Sean Prior have pretended to be the best of friends. To speak as equals. Prior makes it a point of honor, this is his big moment of—relative—social and racial diversity, when the multimillion-dollar inheritor takes pride, even revels, in being able to converse without a trace of condescension with a hotshot little black girl from Houston, a scholarship student who deserves affirmative action, the daughter of an electrician and a seamstress (he made sure he had all the details).

Despite the differences between them—thirty-three years, two billion dollars in stock options, and a set of sparkling veneers—they both make profligate use of each other's first names when they talk, and this colors their conversations with a refined touch of venomous hypocrisy. If the English language had such niceties, they would use the familiar "you" singular, rather than the more formal "you" plural. Like a middle-class man claiming to be friends with his gardener, Prior allows himself to believe in this fictitious friendship, but Joanna isn't fooled at all. In Prior's fixed grin she can read the unspeakable Southern characteristics that hover about him, the signs and symbolic nuances that pervade all interracial exchanges; she recognizes the spontaneous gesture that allows a rich white woman with perfect hair to give her black chauffeur her most radiant smile, a devastatingly affected smile that reveals her imperious conviction that this descendant of a slave is beneath her, the poisoned smile that hasn't moved an inch since *Gone with the Wind*, the same smile that, all through her childhood, Joanna saw appear on the powdered faces of her seamstress mother's clients.

One day, toward the close of the twentieth century, when Joanna was waiting for the school bus at the end of the day, a big, shiny black car stopped alongside her, the tinted rear window was lowered, and a classmate offered to give her a ride, with a smile that simply said she'd be happy to spend a few more minutes with Joanna.

"Of course, Joanna," the friend's mother said, "get in, we'll make a little detour to drop you off, it's nothing."

"It's nothing." Joanna understood: the irritated mother had given in to her daughter's insistence. And she stepped into the back of the big German sedan, with her friend. The lady at the wheel was keen to show that she was polite, to make conversation.

"So, Joanna, what do you want to be when you grow up? Not a seamstress like your mother, surely?"

Joanna didn't reply. When she arrived home, she threw herself into her mother's arms, her eyes glistening. She hugged her and then took out her schoolbooks. The arrogance of one sentence had just created the most grateful of daughters and the most hardworking of students.

Twenty years later Joanna knows where she comes from and where she's going. Most of all she knows that for this Hexachlorion lawsuit—in which many of the affected workers are women, almost all of them of color—a black female lawyer as pugnacious as she is will move the goalposts and temper the opponents' aggression. That's what Prior's banking on, anyway. Joanna has even realized that if she was going to be his lawyer, he wanted her to be taken on by D & L, despite what she'd hoped were dissuasively ambitious salary demands; she was immediately allocated one and only one client: Valdeo. Better than that (and a real rarity), the practice made her a partner straightaway.

The wide windows in Prior's office, on the top floor of a tall 1930s building, look out over the Delaware River. In the presence of visitors Prior can't help pacing the room with a satisfied, proprietorial air, and pretending to lose himself in contemplation of the river, his arms crossed and his chin tilted up like Mussolini. The young lawyer always grants him these extended moments of supposedly meditative posturing, not least because she's here with an associate today, and between them they put a fifty-dollar price tag on every minute. She pointed this out to him once, and Prior dredged some decorously cynical words from his memory: if money weren't so overrated we'd value it less...the saying is not his own, but Prior likes to quote. In a managerial world where any literary erudition is incongruous, he has made it a powerful instrument of symbolic domination. And when the threat loomed of a criminal case over Hexachlorion, an insecticide released on the market before all the tests were validated, when the board of directors showed signs of anxiety, Prior masterfully pulverized their precautionary approach: "My dear fellow board members, I often think of that magnificent poem by Ralph Waldo Emerson that ends with these words: 'Do not go where the path may lead, go instead where there is no path and leave a trail.' So yes, in the endless struggle to feed the human race, we will leave a trail."

Hexachlorion... The fact that Joanna is here in this office is down to this active molecule that inhibits certain insects from developing beyond the larval stage. Valdeo synthesized it in the 2000s, the patent has subsequently come into the public domain, and other companies currently manufacture it. But all the evidence now shows that it is highly carcinogenic, even in low doses, and it is also a hormone disruptor. Now that Austin Baker have launched a class action, Valdeo risks having to pay hundreds of millions in compensation.

"Let's talk about the case, if you'd like to, Sean. With sixty-five patients to date accusing Valdeo of imprecaution, this could prove extremely expensive for us."

Joanna is very keen on the word "imprecaution," a neologism that assumes the absence of intentionality. She's also rather taken with that "us," which demonstrates how closely her firm identifies with its clients' interests.

"Tell me, Sean," she continues, "is Austin Baker likely to provide proof that Valdeo knew how dangerous the molecule was and hid the fact from the people working with it?"

"I can't see how they would."

"If you are asked a question like that in court, say anything except 'I can't see how they would.' The way I formulated the question was unreasonable and I would object to it. Start by reiterating that the molecule is harmless."

"Of course it is. Our clinical trials at the time contradict the independent studies that Austin Baker is lining up."

"Perfect. But reiterate it all the same. It'll be one set of experts against another, Sean. Our problem is your former engineer, Francis Goldhagen. He claims that Valdeo chose not to take into account his tests proving that Hexachlorion is harmful."

"We had reservations about his procedures and dismissed his conclusions. We also did some investigating, and his private life proves that he's capable of lying, to his wife at least."

The lawyer sighs. Winning the case with methods like that could damage the practice's image in the medium term. But losing it in the short term is not an option either.

"I wouldn't want to discredit him like that. Valdeo would not come out of it covered in glory, nor would the justice system."

"You know something, Joanna, justice is like a mother's love, everyone's pretty much in favor of it... on the subject of families, Joanna, how's your sister?"

He knows, the lawyer realizes instantly. Obviously. Prior, who's commissioned investigations into her weaknesses, Prior knows that last February her little sister was diagnosed with primary sclerosing cholangitis. He also knows that a young student like Ellen is bound to have taken out standard health insurance before acknowledging, to her horror, that it doesn't cover PSC. Prior believes that Joanna accepted her handsomely paid position at Denton & Lovell only for Ellen's sake. Without the two-hundred-thousand-dollar liver transplant, Ellen would already be dead, and it will now take at least a hundred thousand a year, a hundred thousand dollars, just for her to live what, ten years, maybe fifteen, in the hopes that her waiflike body can withstand the cholangitis and hold out until someone finds a treatment, perhaps. But Prior is wrong. The salary made a difference, of course, but Joanna wanted this career pinnacle, this great mound of money, from whose summit she could survey the full extent of her revenge.

The CEO keeps talking, slipping all the solemnity he can muster into his voice.

"What she's going through is terrible. Please believe me when I say I'm thinking of you with all my heart."

"I'm . . . very touched."

"If your sister needs anything, Joanna, we couldn't be in a better position to help you. Clinics, drugs, new protocols . . ."

"Thank you, Sean. For now, we just need the liver transplant to take. But I'll remember your offer. Could we get back to the class action against Hexachlorion, please. I'm going to ask my colleague, Mr. Spencer, to summarize our planned defense for you."

The young lawyer hardly has time to finish his presentation before Sean signals, with just a tilt of his chin, that he accepts Denton & Lovell's strategy for the defense. He shakes their hands, indicating that as far as he is concerned the meeting is over. When Joanna is about to follow Spencer out of the office, he calls her back.

"Joanna, I wanted to offer you an opportunity. To join our meeting at the Dolder club tomorrow evening, Saturday. You know about the Dolder, don't you?"

Joanna nods. She knows. A very exclusive club even more restricted than its template, the Bilderberg. But while the Bilderberg brings together about a hundred leading figures from the worlds of business and politics, the Dolder comprises only twenty patrons, the elite of big pharma: over the last fifty years, no one has known when these meetings are held, nor what is discussed. It's possible that the price of medicines is negotiated, that tidy arrangements "between friends" are agreed, and long-term game plans determined. The conspiratorial plotters can have a field day. Prior smiles.

"I will introduce you as my personal advisor, which, in my view, you are. The meeting is to be held in the United States this year, so the honor of making the opening speech falls to me, as an American. You'll like the theme, it's 'The End of Death.' Julius Braun—yes, the 2020 Nobel Prize winner—will make a presentation of his work on the phylogenetics of embryos, and there will be two other speakers: what they have to say will blow your mind. My apologies for telling you about this at such short notice, you know how paranoid this sector is. It will be in Manhattan, in the Van Gogh room at the Surrey on the Upper East Side. Could you be there for eight o'clock?"

Joanna casts around for a way to say Yes, it's an honor, Sean, but sadly the invitation comes a little too late and I'm afraid I won't... But she instinctively brings her hand to rest on her stomach in a protective gesture, a primitive gesture. Because there's one thing Prior doesn't know: Joanna is pregnant.

It was exactly seven weeks ago: she did the test in Denton & Lovell's restrooms, between some sashimi eaten on the run and a partners meeting. And when the two little garnet-colored lines appeared on the stick, Joanna felt her chest explode with jubilation.

The man Joanna loves is a newspaper cartoonist. In late October last year a neo-Nazi leader filed a complaint about one of his drawings, deeming it injurious; she represented his newspaper in court and won the case resoundingly. *Keller v. Wasserman* set a precedent: the act of writing, in a cartoon or elsewhere, that a white supremacist lacks gray matter is not an offense but an opinion, a diagnosis even. It was easy. That same evening, Aby Wasserman invited her to dinner at Tomba's, a restaurant that was too expensive for him, and, at the end of the meal, confronted with his heart's irrefutable certainty, he asked her stumblingly what plans she had for the next few centuries. He refrained from telling her he was put on this earth to love her and go wherever she went, even though that was so exactly what he was thinking. Joanna was in no doubt either. He gave her a fountain pen, Here, this is for you, Joanna, it's a Waterman, which isn't far from my own German name, um . . . my name that I'd like you to take, but I'd be happy to take yours too, you know. Joanna accepted the pen, opened it, and right there on the white cotton tablecloth, she wrote Joanna Woods-Wasserman, trying to avoid getting too teary. The manager agreed to let them keep the tablecloth.

They wanted a baby right away, and followed the necessary procedures to achieve this, frequently, at great length, and in many locations. The doctor was sure: It was after Joanna returned from Europe in early March, on that appalling flight when she decided that if she survived, she would marry him as soon as possible—and before their wedding in early April that their gametes had met and immediately agreed to a merger. They will never know how to thank white supremacism. In fact, suggested the Jewish Aby, short for Abraham, if it's a boy, we'll call him Adolf. As a middle name, Joanna moderated, laughing. And she immediately hated herself for being so happy when her sister was preparing to die a long, slow death. But a few ounces of happiness were growing inside her, and they took over everything.

Prior pursues his invitation.

"Joanna? The Dolder?"

Tomorrow evening? Complicated: she was planning on celebrating the end of the first three months of her pregnancy with her parents... On the other hand, meeting the devil to dance with him does have its upsides.

She doesn't have time to make a decision, because a heavy black telephone, a Bakelite antique, starts ringing on Prior's desk. He picks up immediately and snaps irritably, "I asked not to be disturbed... All right... I'll let her know."

Prior turns to Joanna with an intrigued smile.

"This will probably surprise you, Joanna, but there are people waiting for you outside my office. Two FBI agents. I'm still counting on you for tomorrow, if they'll agree to let you go, obviously."

THE MIESEL AFFAIR

APRIL 22, the day that Victor Miesel falls from his balcony, is a Thursday.

Clémence Balmer's lunch at the Rostand has been postponed, and she's preparing to go out for a walk in the nearby Luxembourg Gardens when Miesel's email provokes a small *ding* from her computer. Clémence is fond of Victor: he's a talented author who can give the impression he's improvising, but is in fact a thinker. His books are always constructed, they're both fluid and beautifully written, and never quite the same; Miesel gives Balmer a rewarding reason to do her job. Glory is slow in coming, true, but maybe one day readers will... No one is safe from success. Miesel couldn't care less about it, anyway. His last book, *Failures That Missed the Mark,* ended up on the longlists for the big French prizes, the Médicis, the Goncourt, and the Renaudot, only to disappear two weeks later, when the shortlists were announced: feeling irritated as much as saddened, she called him to console him, but within seconds he was the one consoling her, and he asked her if she was free the next day because he had two invitations for the Odéon Theatre. No, everything glided over him like water off a duck's back.

Clémence downloads the attached document onto her e-reader, an editor's reflex action. But she sees that there's no message introducing the text, and her curiosity is piqued by the title, *The anomaly*—which is harder and more striking than any of his previous titles—so she opens it on the spot, and is awestruck.

Clémence Balmer is a fast reader, it's her job, and she's finished the book in an hour. *The anomaly* is unlike anything Victor has produced before. It isn't a novel, or a confession, or even a succession of unconnected dazzling sentences or brilliant truisms. It's a strange book, thrillingly fast-paced, unputdownable, and between the lines she could see all of Miesel's influences: Jankélévitch, Camus, Goncharov, and so many others. A dark, very immediate text in which even the banter is painful: "God, but stupidity oozes from every corner of a religious mind. Every conviction is a thorn in the side of intelligence. Believers lose their wits in their efforts to see death as just another misadventure. Doubt has made me an autodidact of life, and I have enjoyed every moment all the more for that. I am never overcome by mystical emotions, even when gazing at the glorious glittering around a cloud. On the brink of death by drowning, I try to swim, I cannot in all decency pray to Archimedes. And as I sink today, my eyes open onto an abyss where no theorem holds sway."

Suddenly worried, Balmer decides to call Miesel right away. His cell, then his landline. The police pick up. When she hears what Miesel has done, she's dumbfounded, devastated. She answers the officer's questions and is overwhelmed by genuine sadness as well as glowering anger. The last time she saw Victor, now when was that? Early March, to celebrate that translation prize, they had dinner at the Brasserie Lipp, he had his perennial andouillette, she her Parisienne salad, they drank a Pic-Saint-Loup, and she didn't sense anything, not a thing, didn't decipher the tiniest clue in her friend's words. She rereads *The anomaly* in light of the disaster it foreshadows. She notices that it is signed Victør Miesel, with an ø that is none other than the symbol for the empty set. A tragic witticism.

Balmer contacts those she can. Miesel had lost his parents and had no brothers or sisters. There was Ilena Leskov, of course, the young Russian teacher at Languages East who left him after a stormy, one-year relationship, and by the by, was a great-great-niece of

Nikolai Leskov, whom Victor translated. The young teacher keeps saying *"Boje moï!"* "How terrible!" "How can it be true?" with emphatic conviction, and is in a hurry to end the call. Clémence considers a sentence that she's just read in Miesel's manuscript: "Nobody lives long enough to know just how little interest anybody takes in anybody."

The editor handles everything, calls friends, organizes the funeral (which is nonreligious, naturally), and she arranges for an announcement to appear in *Le Monde*:

ORANGE TREE EDITIONS,
CLÉMENCE BALMER, AND THE WHOLE TEAM
ARE SAD TO ANNOUNCE
THE DEATH OF VICTOR MIESEL,
WRITER, POET, TRANSLATOR,
AND FRIEND.

She writes a long press release for Agence France-Presse, reminding readers of his most prestigious translations and his books that enjoyed favorable critical receptions. She adds that an exceptional text will be published shortly, that Miesel had put the finishing touches to it before his final act. She inserts three extracts from *The anomaly*, and then this woman who doesn't drink pours herself a finger of whiskey and sips it slowly. It's a Scottish single malt, one Victor liked.

The following morning she reads the opening of the book with some conviction to a "select committee," a ridiculous turn of phrase given that the entire publishing company is there, even the two interns. Both commissioning editors approve, the sales director insists on getting the book out as quickly as possible without actually daring to articulate the self-evident necrophilic point: the critics and the general public are going to love this story of a book delivered moments before the big leap. He has an example in mind, it must have been twelve or thirteen years ago, what was the author's name again? Couldn't we at least change the title so that it references the author's tragic end? suggests the bookshop liaison officer. No, we couldn't, Clémence Balmer retorts tartly. A sticker then, or a band? No again. And at least put Victor instead of Victør; it would be a better spelling for data referencing services, right? Wrong.

The book is edited over the weekend, typeset on Monday, and photocopies of the first proofs are sent straight to the press; by the end of the week the final page proofs are with the printer, which starts running the presses the very day that Miesel is incinerated at the Père-Lachaise crematorium. His ashes have not been scattered before the book is sent out to distributors. It's a record, publishing has rarely been this quick to respond since Princess Di's biography. The first Wednesday in May *The anomaly* is piled up in every bookshop. Balmer opted for a print run of ten thousand, to give it a chance, with a simple blue sticker: MIESEL.

It's an instant success. The cultural pages of *Libération* give it the promised double-page spread; *Le Monde des Livres*—conspicuously silent on all his other books—redeems itself with a long, adulatory obit that includes the words "congratulations are due to Orange Tree Editions for publishing Miesel's work"; *La Grande Librairie* exhumes what footage there is of Victor to produce a televised portrait of him; and the radio station France Culture devotes three programs to him. The Miesel affair is underway. Clémence arranges for an urgent reprint of *Failures That Missed the Mark*, and even that novel from five years back, *The Mountains Will Come to Find Us*, whose last remaining copies were in danger of being pulped.

Discussions are organized, and Balmer agrees to take part in some of them. Actors read extracts in bookshops, there's a "Miesel Night" at the Paris literary center, the Maison de la Poésie, where a famous actor who has a fine, deep voice and was "blown away" by *The anomaly* regales a packed house with a complete reading of the book that lasts four hours. Ilena is in the audience, in tears. A May launch isn't ideal for competing in the big literary prizes in the fall, but rumor has it among the juries that Miesel is "a dead cert." There's already talk that he's secured the Médicis.

This same month of May sees the founding of the Society of Friends of Victør Miesel, an eclectic collection of friends and admirers who clearly didn't all know him or even read his books. Victør Miesel now has a plethora of "best friends," from a Mr. T., a dandy with a high pitched voice and a penchant for overtight jackets, to one Salerno—Silvio was it, or Livio?—his "very old friend," whom Clémence has never heard mentioned. This society soon renames itself Frevimi, then "the Anomalists." Ilena is a member, and in an exquisite rewriting of their not very glorious relationship, Ms. Leskov gradually raises herself to the tragic yet dignified status of official widow.

Clémence Balmer watches all this fall into place with detachment and an obscure feeling of distaste. Achieving success at the age of fifty is a little like finally being served the mustard when you're on to dessert, and that's bad enough, but Miesel's posthumous fame upsets Clémence the friend more than his unwarranted invisibility ever did Clémence the publisher. What was it Victor wrote? "Glory is only ever imposture, except perhaps in running races. But I suspect all those who profess to scorn it of secretly fulminating because they have simply had to relinquish any claim to it."

SLIMBOY

FRIDAY, JUNE 25, 2021

EKO ATLANTIC, LAGOS, NIGERIA

THE ITALIAN CONSUL in Lagos stumbles with every step he takes toward the petits fours. Neither Nigeria nor alcohol agrees with him. Ugo Darchini sways and staggers, and when some champagne sloshes from his glass, spattering the exotic wooden floor of this outsize function room at the Eko Atlantic Hotel, he apologizes in a croaky, slurred voice.

Darchini comes over to the French consul by the buffet as a castaway might approach a buoy. Her lemon-yellow dress has a hypnotic effect on him, with its golden spirals that remind him of Gidouille in that film of *Ubu Roi*. Since multicolored dashikis and traditional Yoruban agbadas have replaced Versace suits and Armani tuxedos at these Nigerian receptions, people have had to work hard if they don't want to be invisible. The three

Nigerians who were talking to the French consul abandon her as soon as they spot the Italian, as if he were contaminated with the plague. Darchini's eyes are reeled in by those swirls on the lemon dress, and he feels a wave of nausea.

"*Buona sera,* Hélène. Your outfit is magnificent, it's tapaphysic... pataphysical. Forgive me, I actually only had two glasses."

"Good evening, Ugo, I've been meaning to get in touch to hear your news. I thought you'd have gone home to Italy, after what happened. I know your daughter went back to Siena with her mother."

Ugo Darchini gives a grimace of a smile, but it's no good, Hélène Charrier can't possibly understand, she can't imagine the days spent negotiating with abductors high on meth for the return of his fourteen-year-old daughter, not daring to guess what Renata was going through, terrified one of those nuts would slice off a finger or an ear to get him to hurry up and hand over the seventy thousand dollars. He entrusted the money to Taiwo, a "security consultant," a seriously shady character, but one who was recommended by one of the deputy directors of Eni's oil-prospecting arm. Taiwo had already acted as a go-between two years earlier, when that guy's son was kidnapped. Both sides wore Kalashnikovs slung across one shoulder for the handover with the "area boys" in a side street near the docks in Apapa, opposite an evangelist church with a sign that was flashing "Pray as you go." It was only fifty thousand dollars back then. The price of everything goes up.

And yet everyone from the ambassador in Abuja to the switchboard operator at the consulate had warned him, you be very careful of your daughter when she goes to the international high school, people here survive on a dollar a day, so kidnapping is a business like any other, better than most others in fact. But he just had to do this Lagos job if he wanted to land the Athens posting in a couple of years. Maria insisted on coming with him so that Renata could experience Africa. One time, just one time he hadn't had the heart to forbid his daughter from venturing beyond their guarded, gated community without an armed escort. Just one time.

"They were right to go home to Italy," the French consul sighs, "because I can guarantee it's getting worse and worse in Lagos. Take electricity, you get it for thirty minutes, then it suddenly shuts down, and for hours. I don't know how people keep food in their fridges. Without the generator we wouldn't be able to work at the consulate, and without the tank we wouldn't have any water. And everything's like that, Ugo. *Tutto.*"

Yes, everything's like that. Ugo knows. His first sight of Lagos, from the window on the plane, through the brown haze of pollution, was sprawling square kilometers of slums, millions of rusty corrugated-iron roofs, a gridwork of anarchy, and also that vast traffic jam of thousands of black-and-yellow potato-beetle-like minibuses, vehicles so dangerous that there are efforts—albeit failed efforts—to outlaw them. And every summer, when the torrential rains come and the roads turn into a pestilential swamp, Lagos reminds everyone that its name means "lakes" in Portuguese. For decades the city's been left to its own devices, now so corrupt that foreign roadworks companies refuse all contracts with the city council. Even the country has abandoned the place, and no Nigerian president has set foot in Lagos for five years.

Ugo hears tragic stories every day. The story of the teenage girl who had to cross the expressway to reach the only faucet with drinking water, who was knocked down. Ten trucks ran over her without stopping. The story of the man who had an epileptic fit and collapsed—it was yesterday, his cook Naruma saw him with her own eyes—and passersby left him on the ground, spasming and foaming at the mouth, he might even have died. The story of the old man from the Oshidi slum who threw himself under the tracks of a bulldozer to save three items of clothing, and the vehicle didn't even pause.

If you think you're strong, come to Lagos, and then you'll see.

The French consul puts down her glass and waves to a tall, generously proportioned young black woman in a purple dashiki, who comes over and kisses her enthusiastically.

"Ah, Hélène! I'm looking for the director of Lagos Fashion Week, but I'm not sure where she can..."

"Swahila, allow me to introduce Ugo Darchini, my Italian counterpart. Swahila Odiaka has been our cultural attaché in Lagos for a year."

The woman smiles and shakes the limp hand proffered by the consul. Over by the door there's a flurry of flashbulbs and shouting.

"Oh, it's Slimboy!" exclaims the cultural attaché. "He's giving a concert on Victoria Island in a couple of hours. You've heard of Slimboy, of course, Hélène."

No, Hélène hasn't heard of him.

"*Money not worth it, worth it, worth it...*" Swahila sings, laughing. "Really, Hélène, don't you ever watch YouTube? He had a local following three or four months ago, but it's just gone into hyperspace with his song 'Yaba Girls'—he's had over a billion views in a few weeks. A media explosion, like that Korean guy ten years ago, you know? Surely... Slimboy? And you, Mr. Darchini?"

"I'm so sorry, Mrs. Odiaka," Ugo declines politely, "I've never heard of him either. Verdi and Puccini are more my thing, Paolo Conte in a pinch."

This time—a hint of revenge is sweet—it's Swahila who feigns ignorance.

"'Yaba Girls' has a very hip-hop, R and B rhythm, well, more Afropop actually. It's an homage to his mother, who had a shop in the fashion district in Yaba."

"Come on, follow me," she says, gesturing to them. "Let's go and watch, he's giving a press conference. The minister helped arrange one of his concerts in Paris back in March."

The two consuls follow the cultural attaché, who feverishly weaves through the increasingly compact crowd, all the way to the musician and his girlfriend, all the way to the high-pitched squeals of his fans and the clamoring of the paparazzi.

"Slimboy! Slimboy! A photo please! Give Suomi a kiss!"

The emperor of African pop obeys the photographers, and amid the flashes he kisses the young actress, going down on his knees because he is as tall as his very new fiancée is petite. They pose like this for a long time, docile and cooperative. Maybe that's what happiness is.

Femi Ahmed Kaduna, alias Slimboy, still can't get over it. Three months ago his fame was limited to the Little Lagos that is Peckham in south London, at a stretch to Westchase in the suburbs of Houston, but however many cult Fela Kuti numbers he covered, adding his own special flavor, neither the concert in Paris nor the one in New York right afterward was a great success.

It was during the last hour of the Paris–New York flight, after thinking he wouldn't come out of it alive and making extensive use of the sick bags, that Slimboy got the idea for "Yaba Girls." A song that would use simple words to express his love for the neighborhood where he grew up, for the "needles and scissors" girls, a song of the young Femi's gratitude to his mother, who sold necklaces in the market, his mother who'd prayed for him every day and had just died; it would be an amazing, gentle, melodious song.

And on the flight back to Lagos he decided that for once the music video wouldn't be a parade of powerful motorbikes and outboard motors, it wouldn't feature fabulous seminaked girls dancing on a beach, writhing on a bed with him in a lavish villa; he wouldn't wear gold chains and wouldn't leer as he counted his dollars. No, everyone did that, he wanted something different, so it would show the dignity of ordinary people, work-weary women, shopkeepers, seamstresses, and ironers laughing and dancing while they worked when it was over 110 degrees in the shade, and the only splashes of color would be strips of wax print cotton. And he, Slimboy, would be dressed in white in those dirty streets, singing in English and Yoruba, saying hi to one person, then another, respectfully, humbly even, showing the deference of the kid he'd been during his happy childhood. He, Slimboy, would break the mold of the Afro-rap vibe, he would steer clear of auto-tune, reverb, delay, and other overused effects, and—hovering over the melody—there would be a softly lilting counterpoint provided by a saxophonist. Slimboy had even found the musician, a skeletal old white guy with very little hair left, a Quebecois virtuoso who sometimes played with Drake: he would symbolize the old world handing over the baton to the new.

They filmed the video in two days in the streets of Yaba, uploaded it right away, and the song went global. There are already four remixes of "Yaba Girls," including one by Franks; Slimboy was the surprise guest at the Coachella Festival; he's sung alongside Beyoncé; dueted with Eminem, and been interviewed by *Oprah*. Yes, maybe that's happiness.

After a UK tour in May, though, he did buy a yellow Lamborghini and a massive apartment on the top floor of one of Eko Atlantic's tower blocks, one whose foundation stone hasn't even been laid yet; you can't pursue all things natural indefinitely. And anyway, that's what young Nigerians want, to be sold dreams, they want to drink champagne in a racing car, they want to visit the penthouse with sea views, they want to be told it doesn't matter that they wake every morning in their crummy sheet-metal homes surrounded by old car tires and dead rats, riches and fame are just around the corner, yes, okay, for one in a million, but why should they give a damn, seeing as it's going to be them—it has to be.

The two consuls and the cultural attaché have managed to get close to the stage, where Slimboy is standing. They didn't hear the question very clearly, but the singer clutching his mic seems to be mulling over his answer.

"I like to think," he says, "that Eko Atlantic will be a fantastic opportunity for Lagos and for Nigeria, and that the whole surrounding population will benefit from the construction of the most ambitious city in Africa."

The French consul nods, then sighs: the absurd trickle-down theory still has plenty of life in it. She turns to Darchini.

"So tell me, Ugo, what do you think about this monstrosity that we're helping to launch one tower block at a time by stuffing our faces with canapés?"

The Italian consul purses his lips. Yes, Eko Atlantic, an artificial island claimed from the ocean, is an abomination. It's still just a vast wasteland, but two hundred thousand superrich Lagosians will take refuge in its gleaming skyscrapers, protected from the violence in the megalopolis by guarded bridges and armed security officers. They'll have everything in this fortress, an electrical power station, a water purification plant, restaurants, extravagant hotels, swimming pools, marinas to moor their yachts...

"The African Dubai, as they say," Hélène Charrier adds. "They've even raised it by several meters in anticipation of rising sea levels. And from the top of its luxury tower blocks you'll be able to see Lagos and watch its forty million inhabitants drown, all the way from Kuramo Beach to the open-air sewer of the Makoko slums... I'm sorry, Ugo, I think it's monstrous. And do you know the worst of it? The worst of it is this is tomorrow's world. We've thrown in the towel, and we're each trying to scramble out of this mess in our own way, but no one'll be saved. It's not Lagos that's breaking away from civilization, it's us, all of us, who are getting closer to Lagos."

"You're exaggerating, Hélène."

"How I wish, Ugo."

All at once the sound level of the press conference drops. A journalist has asked Slimboy a question.

"Eze Onyedika from *Punch*. So, Slimboy, they say you're going to sing a new song with Doctor Fake? Is the song in favor of homosexuality? Are you homosexual?"

Silence descends over the room, as dense as a house brick. If Africa as a whole is hell for homosexuals, Nigeria is its ninth circle. There's the law, which threatens them with fourteen years' imprisonment; the police, who hunt them down and extort money from them; and a whole population rejecting them, full of disgust and loathing, bombarded with hatred and rumors by evangelical bishops and priests in the south and Muslims implementing sharia law in the north. Not one day goes by without young men being murdered, lynched;

not one day without some singer, actor, or athlete having to protest—with terror in his voice—that he isn't gay. So yes, three months ago, the very refined Doctor Fake didn't go so far as to broadcast a liking for men but broke the taboo with the harmless yet ambiguous lyrics of his hit song "Be Yourself."

"That's a lot of questions," Slimboy replies. "Yes, I'm going to sing a song with Doctor Fake, it's called 'True Men Tell the Truth.' But a song 'in favor of homosexuality' doesn't mean anything. When I sing 'My Nollywood Girl,' it's about love, it's not 'in favor of heterosexuality.' See the difference? Anyway, I have a scoop for you: I just heard a few minutes ago that I'll soon be recording with Elton John in London. His jet's coming to pick me up in two days."

"But are you gay, Slimboy?" the journalist persists.

"Would you like a date?"

The journalist laughs, and Slimboy delivers his killer shot: "Why don't you ask Suomi that question instead of me?"

The young woman smiles obligingly, and immediately kisses Slimboy on the mouth voraciously—mendaciously. The journalists cheer, but the kiss doesn't drag on because Slimboy gallantly breaks away.

"But," he says, "when I read that people in a village stoned two sixteen-year-olds to death after a preacher denounced them in a sermon, just for kissing . . . I have to say there's something that needs changing in our country. Suomi and I are in complete agreement about that. You can't force people to be something they're not. We need tolerance. We need love. How can anyone think they'll be happier by harming other people?"

There's a hubbub of voices and more questions. Slimboy turns to his anxious-looking manager, who cuts short the press conference. If the singer were listening to his own heart, though, he would tell the story of Tom, his first lover, when he was fifteen years old. Tom, who was burned alive in front of him at the hands of a baying mob, and of how he fled barefoot in the night, distraught, terrorized, his face covered in blood, racing through Ibadan pursued by the hostile crowd, and his subsequent hookups, which were all so dangerous and so brief, and the distress of gays in Nigeria in Africa as a whole, in fact—who've ended up running away, permanently exiling themselves in cold white men's countries, where at least they have the right to breathe. He and Doctor Fake are going to sing "True Men Tell the Truth," but what irony, what a lie, what a betrayal even! Slimboy is very aware that in order to continue living in Lagos, he's had to invent another life for himself, right down to arranging this conniving pact with Suomi, who of course likes women as much as he likes men.

All at once Hélène Charrier becomes aware of a tall black man in a dark suit. He's standing discreetly to one side, watching the young singer. She turns to the Italian consul and points out the man with a tilt of her chin.

"Ugo?" she says, "Do you see that man typing on his cellphone and taking photos? Let me introduce the British commercial attaché, John Gray. I bet that isn't his real name, but I am sure he's in the British secret service. He's not alone. There are two others, men from the consulate's security staff. As well as half a dozen other strange guys I've never seen before. They're MI6, I'm telling you."

"You have a hell of an eye, Hélène. You're not in the French secret service yourself, are you?"

"Don't be silly, Ugo, of course not. And that's proof: if I were, you're thinking I'd say no."

"Definitely. By the way, Hélène, do you know the story of the American spy on a mission in the USSR—oh dear, that ages us! So, anyway, he's in the USSR and wants to give himself up? He hands himself over to the Lubyanka."

"The what?"

"The Lubyanka . . . the KGB's headquarters in Moscow . . . Anyway, he says, 'I'm a spy, I want to hand myself over.' 'Who do you work for?' asks the guy on reception.' 'The United States of America.' 'Okay, go to Office Number Two.' The American spy goes to Office Two and says, 'I'm an American spy and I want to hand myself over.' 'Are you armed?' they ask. 'Yes, I'm armed.' 'Go to Office Three please.' He goes to Office Three and says, 'I'm an American spy, I'm armed, and I want to hand myself over.' 'Are you on a mission?' 'Yes, I'm on a mission,' the American agent replies, getting impatient. 'In that case, it's Office Four.' He goes to Office Four and says, 'I'm an American spy, I'm armed, I'm on a mission, and I want to hand myself over!' 'Are you really on a mission?' 'Yes.' 'Well, then go do your fucking mission! And leave people who are trying to work in peace!'"

Ugo smiles at his own joke.

"Very good," Hélène concedes, although she's already heard it because it's done the rounds of the "swimming pool," the headquarters of French counterespionage. Before she was appointed consul in Lagos, she was the eyes of the senior management team for national security in Kenya and South Africa.

The spooks haven't moved a muscle; all their eyes are pinned on Slimboy.

"Still, it doesn't explain what they're doing here, or when the Intelligence Service started taking an interest in Afro-rap and R and B."

ADRIAN AND MEREDITH

THURSDAY, JUNE 24, 2021

FINE HALL, PRINCETON UNIVERSITY, NEW JERSEY

OUTSIDE PRINCETON'S math department, an elegant glass and reddish-brick building in an already dated modernist style, students have set up trestle tables, erected a large white tent, and lit the barbecue. Indecent quantities of sausages are being used to celebrate Tanizaki's Fields Medal, and the probabilities expert Adrian Miller is painfully aware that he's eyeing his coworker Meredith with something alternating between a tense smile and idiotic sentimentality. The first time Adrian set eyes on Meredith, he thought she was plain ugly. This sort of impression is only fleeting: all the best authors would have confirmed that for him. It's two months since the British topologist arrived, and he now finds that Meredith, with her overthin legs and her overtidy brown hair, her overlong nose and her overdark eyes, Meredith the ever-distant, is irrationally attractive to him.

To drum up the courage to approach her, Adrian has had one beer, then another. When he's sober he can just about look the part—Meredith once told him, not unkindly, that he was "built like Ryan Gosling, but a slightly bald, slightly run-down version"—but right now he just looks like some guy who got drunk. He reckons his chances of success at twenty-seven percent. They could have gone as high as forty percent if he didn't stink so terribly of alcohol, but on the other hand, the inebriation will reduce by about sixty percent the suffering incurred by a rejection. He concluded that with such a high chance of failing, he might as well be drunk.

Most of Adrian's life has been spent calculating probabilities, and occasionally listening to Bach and the Beach Boys. He hasn't raised a family, no child bears his name, unless one obscure theorem can be promoted to the rank of offspring. Meredith is his first love experience in a very long time, in fact at this precise moment he's even thinking rather emphatically: in forever. She's alone under the large acacia tree, graceful in a long, black cotton dress. He tries to walk over to her more or less in a straight line.

"I've been drinking," he offers right away.

"I agree," replies Meredith, who thought he definitely looked shaky.

"And I stink of beer, sorry."

"I can't really tell, Adrian, because me too."

She brandishes the empty bottle in her hand, leans forward in a deliciously unfocused way, and blows her warm, hop-scented breath at his nose.

"Breathe it in, Adrian, that's the smell of irritation and boredom."

Because Meredith is bored at Princeton. She's a Londoner, and she hates this provincial town where the Japanese restaurant—the one that stays open "late"—sets its lamps flashing as early as nine thirty to warn that it's about to close; and this campus that's trying to look like Hogwarts, with its neo-Gothic dungeons and belfries. She can't get used to these students, who think they're God's gift to everything, and who, on the basis that their parents are spending sixty thousand dollars a year in tuition fees, email her at all hours with trivial questions about Gromov's non-prological theories, questions to which they expect immediate answers, when, I mean, really, they could just look at the relevant entry on Wikipedia, which is very well written. She can't stand the teaching staff, who look down their noses at her, given that St. Andrews—where she first studied—obviously is no equal to Princeton, because they're here, in Princeton, QED. Adrian's not like that, and if he were a little less awkward, he would have realized some time ago that she likes him. For a statistician, he's a dreamer. He has green eyes that make him look like a number theorist, even though he has long hair like a game theorist, and wears the Trotskytizing small steel-rimmed glasses of a logician and the holey old T-shirts of an algebraist—the one he's wearing at the moment is especially shapeless and ridiculous. She guesses that he's brilliant. If he were bad at heart, he'd have headed off into finance long ago. Brilliant but shy, and when he stammers "Meredith, I wanted to ask you... um... You do great work on... specifically symmetrical spaces and on—"

"No, Adrian," she interrupts, "not at all. At the moment I'm working on getting conscientiously drunk. I'm delighted to hear that Tanizaki and that sexist pig Browner from Stanford won their Fields Medals on the algebraic geometry-topology interface, a subject on which *I* commissioned basically all their articles, apart from the ones I actually wrote. On top of that, I live in a crappy bungalow in Trenton where the water's cold one day and lukewarm the next, my Toyota hybrid broke down six days ago, something to do with the battery apparently, I broke things off with the love of my life—or that's what I thought he was, anyway—a year ago, and so that makes it, let me work it out, four months since I slept with anyone. Is it the end of June? No, then, six months. Six months... and it wasn't even great. How about you, Adrian, everything okay? House, car, sex life?"

The conversation's hardly started, and it's already taking what to Adrian is an unnerving turn.

"Um... My car hasn't broken down," he starts, as articulately as he can. "I have hot water. I—"

"Well, why do you always go around with a face like a miserable cocker spaniel drowning in its own water bowl? I think I'm going to finish this beer and have another one."

"If you want to get comatose more quickly, Meredith, there's some tequila in the Turing Room, in the cupboard behind the felt pens."

"Wonderful idea."

Meredith puts down her bottle, zigzags across the lawn toward the door to the lobby, and clumsily pushes it open. Adrian follows her, a little anxiously, trying not to look at her butt—or not too much—as she races up the stairs. She stops outside the door to the room and leans against the wall.

"I'm English, Adrian, I warn you, if you try to rape me, I'll lie back and think of the queen."

"You've had too much to drink, Meredith."

"And you haven't had enough."

Meredith turns the door handle and twirls her way into the room, very nearly falling flat on her face, then, feeling giddy, she sits down on a chair.

"Where's this tequila, then?" she asks, looking around.

"I don't know if it's a good idea..."

"Come and sit next to me, and don't talk to me about stochastic processes, I really couldn't care less about that right now, you've no idea."

Adrian does as he's told and watches her, disconcerted.

"Oh and for goodness' sake kiss me, Adrian. You're gagging to do it, and at this precise moment it doesn't bother me either way if you're a rubbish kisser."

"I... Meredith, please believe me... it's not that I don't like you, but I..."

"Okay, fine, it's not very romantic, but what? We can laugh about it later, with our children. Kiss me or I'll start crying. Or screaming. There's a thought! Help!"

"Meredith, please," Adrian says, suddenly very worried. "Please don't joke about that."

"Aha! I've got you. No, come on, I'm teasing. What is it with you men? When a woman takes the initiative, you go to pieces."

Out of nowhere Meredith pulls him to her and smacks her lips to his. They taste of strawberries. She closes her eyes, and they stay like that, pressed against each other, for a little while, not even daring to kiss, until the inside pocket of Adrian's jacket vibrates and rings loudly. He flinches away from Meredith, who's as dazed as he is, then takes out a gray metal smartphone and looks at it in amazement.

"Is that your wife?" Meredith asks—as it happens, she wouldn't care in the least.

"I'm not married."

After three rings the smartphone stops abruptly, stays silent for five seconds, then rings and vibrates again. This time the caller lets it ring once before hanging up. Adrian can't take his eyes off the phone. Now? Really?

"If it's not your wife, it's someone very, very insistent."

"Shit, shit! Really sorry, I absolutely have to... Meredith, I need to..."

He hurries out, runs down the corridors of the department. Ten seconds have passed, and the telephone rings again. Three rings, one ring, three rings. That's the agreed code: he picks up. It's a man's voice, both assured and expressionless, military.

"Professor Adrian Miller?"

"Err... yes," he replies hesitantly.

"Toto, I don't think..."

The voice waits, and waits some more, then Miller utters a deadpan "... we're in Kansas anymore."

"Toto, I don't think... we're in Kansas anymore..." What the hell. Adrian only has himself to blame, the kid with the schoolboy humor that he was twenty years ago, who chose this truncated quote from *The Wizard of Oz*, never guessing that he'd one day have to complete it to confirm his identity. And for twenty years now he's had this smartphone, which is upgraded for him regularly, this smartphone, which in exchange for a thousand dollars a month, he must keep on the whole time, must take with him everywhere, so that in any circumstances—absolutely any, as the present situation proves—he can pick up and instantly be available. It's never rung before.

"Adrian," Meredith yells, "come back and kiss me even if it is your wife!"

"Please stand by, Professor Miller," the voice continues. "A police vehicle will be outside Fine Hall in the next minute, and it will take you to the contact point."

"Outside Fine Hall? You know where I am?"

"Of course, Professor Miller. You're geolocated to within three meters. Once you're on the way, we'll call you back to put you in contact with the operations center."

"Adrian?" Meredith shrieks from the Turing Room. "You're a pain in the arse, Adrian, you're a real pain in the arse."

Adrian runs to the door, Meredith hasn't moved, she's rooted to her chair, her hair awry and her expression furious.

"I'm so sorry, Meredith. This is very important, I . . . I'll explain."

Adrian goes down the stairs four at a time, Meredith screams something involving blood-soaked statisticians and a journey he's invited to make to hell, but he's already in the lobby.

TO UNDERSTAND why Adrian Miller must answer the bulletproof charcoal-gray smartphone on this June 24, 2021, we must rewind to September 10, 2001, the day when, as the youngest postdoctoral researcher on Professor Robert Pozzi's probabilities team, he was celebrating his twentieth birthday at MIT. The following day a case of mad cow disease would be reported in Japan; political declarations would be made in the wake of the suicide bombing targeting Massoud, perpetrated by two Tunisian members of al-Qaida; and Michael Jordan's return to the Washington Wizards would be announced. But more significantly, it would be Ben Sliney's first day of work. He'd just taken up the post of director of operations at the Federal Aviation Administration. Two hours after the coffee and doughnuts of his welcoming do, he grounded four thousand two hundred airplanes, an isolated and unprecedented decision. Some days are just like that.

On September 11, at 8:14 am, an air traffic controller in Boston was concerned when he noticed the transponder on American Airlines 11 cut out. Six minutes later, an attendant on board the flight dialed the only number she could, in the event the American Airlines reservations line. She informed them of a change of course and several murders in the cabin. By the time her identity had been checked it was 8:25, and a supervisor tipped off air traffic control. It was then that Ben Sliney and the air traffic control team saw on their radars that the

AA11 was heading due south, to New York. In the event of a diversion—but let's forget the textbook that instructs the pilot, who in this instance had been stabbed, to enter code 7500 into the transponder—the regulations require an alert to be sent to civil aviation HQ. At the HQ a "special rerouting coordinator" then has to contact a department at the Pentagon, who must refer the incident to the office of the secretary of defense, who informs the president, whose decision has to be passed all the way back down the same chain. Only then can the supervisors at the National Center for Military Command order fighter jets to take off and intercept the plane. And because the number of air bases in a position to respond had dropped from twenty-six to just seven after the Cold War ended, the only two remaining bases on the East Coast were in Otis, near Boston, and Langley, the CIA headquarters near Washington.

This all takes such a long time that on September 11, 2001, it was the supervisor in Boston himself who called Otis military base as an emergency. As it was not his role to do this, Otis insisted that he speak to the military commanders for the northeast region, in Rome, New York. He called them, and was told once again that he wasn't respecting procedure. Nevertheless, convinced by the call and himself acting without authorization from the Department of Defense, Colonel Robert Marr asked the Otis base to prepare to launch fighter jets.

Long before the official conclusion of the 9/11 Commission, the Pentagon knew that on that particular day, every aspect of the chain of command malfunctioned. It set up an internal working group tasked with suggesting a different protocol for emergency situations. And that group subcontracted everything to do with formalization to the Department of Applied Mathematics at MIT. This is where Adrian Miller's name crops up.

At the time, Adrian was a young probabilities expert on the team run by Pozzi, head of "App Math" at MIT. Adrian, then aged twenty, had just defended a dissertation dealing with Markov chains, Kendall notations . . . to make a long story short, he was interested in the statistics of waiting in line. He was especially fond of Little's law, which states that the average number of units in a stable system is equal to their average arrival frequency multiplied by the time they spend in the system. But moving on.

Because everyone at the lab was very busy, and Pozzi always found any contact with the Department of Defense profoundly irritating, it was Adrian who, as part of his hazing, was entrusted with modeling the blockages and finding how to reduce the number of phases and the time taken at each stage. Adrian enlisted the help of Tina Wang, Pozzi's highly intelligent PhD student, for the graph theory element, which was somewhat beyond his capabilities. They worked late, ate terrible food at terrible speed, slept little, aired all their negative views of the Department of Defense, and when they couldn't handle any more, they took Adrian's old Honda and went out bowling at Lucky Strike Boston, which never closed. One night, after an argument about the ergodic hypothesis and stationary distributions, they had a surprise incident that was more sexual than erotic. A good memory, nonetheless.

First and foremost, Adrian and Tina inventoried all the variables that could affect air traffic, and attributed them statistical values. They specified anything that could cause a catastrophe—even simply upsetting traffic flow—and surpassed the Pentagon's expectations. Their model took into account absolutely everything: chains of events, means of communication, language barriers, different units (feet or meters?), pilot error, mechanical failure, technical problems, weather, sabotage, diversions, software piracy, faulty signaling, shortcomings in maintenance, and so much more... The two researchers identified thirty-seven basic protocols, with, in each case, between seven and twenty contingent pathways, in other words nearly five hundred basic situations, and as many responses. When, in December '01, Richard Reid managed to get through security checks with explosives hidden in the soles of his shoes, that was a variant of protocol 12A; the Birmingham–Málaga accident, when the windshield of the cockpit exploded, was an example of 7K; the Airbus that skidded off the landing runway at Halifax because of snow, a 4F; the Icelandic volcano spewing ash and grounding all flights, a 13E; and the depressive German Wings pilot hurling his plane into a mountain, a 25D.

After five months of work, they recorded their recommendations in a top-secret memorandum running to some one thousand five hundred pages under an uninspired title: *Civilian air traffic: diagnoses of crises, optimizing the chain of decisions, and protocols for responses/security.* "T. Wang & A. Miller & *alii,* Department of Applied Mathematics, Graph Theory Department, Probabilities Department, Massachusetts Institute of Technology." In Wang & Miller & *alii,* Alii is the name of the lab's hamster. Total kids.

They left nothing out; if the Pentagon had asked them to present all the possible outcomes of heads or tails, they would have come up with three: heads, tails and the rare incidence of the coin deciding to balance vertically on its edge. But in April 2002, ten days after the report was submitted, the DoD sent it back with a question written in red felt pen: "What if we're confronted with a case that fits none of the situations covered?"

Tina rolled her eyes: How about the hypothesis where the flipped coin stays suspended in the air?

Over the course of five days, they added one final protocol for this "case that fits none of the situations covered." Whereas in all the other eventualities Tina and Adrian recommended there should be a single supervisor—whether civilian or military—to oversee the protocol, Tina decided that "due to the irrational nature of events that would justify such a protocol," this final instance should be entrusted to a brace of scientists. And she wrote down her name and Adrian Miller's. She recommended providing them with bulletproof cellphones dedicated to this protocol, phones that they should keep with them at all times and never turn off. And because Adrian Miller worshipped Douglas Adams's *The Hitchhiker's Guide to the Galaxy,* along with its big question about "life, the universe and everything," to which, after seven and a half million years of calculation, Deep Thought, the second most powerful computer of all time, replies simply "42," this protocol would be number 42.

To look serious or for fun, or because he found being serious fun, Adrian added a word sequence as an initialization code:

Operator: Toto, I don't think...

Supervisor:...we're in Kansas anymore.

WHEN ADRIAN EMERGES from the building, a police car is already waiting for him, just beside the barbecue where the sausages are sizzling happily.

The officer salutes him as if he were a four-star general, and all eyes of the teaching staff turn to Adrian. He responds to the officer with an awkward, sketchy salute, and climbs into the back, not without knocking his head on the roof frame. The car sets off with its sirens blaring and lights flashing. Adrian is driven far away from sex with Meredith and toward the unknown.

So. Someone somewhere in the galaxy has tossed a coin, and it really has stayed suspended in the air.

THE JOKE

EAST COAST OF THE UNITED STATES,
INTERNATIONAL WATERS,
N 41°25'27", W 65°49'23"

MARKLE CHECKS his mic, but it's gone dead. Kennedy has cut off the communication. There's a cracking sound on the line, another very long silence, and then a different, deeper voice comes on.

"Air France 006 Mayday, my name is Luther Davis, commander of special operations for the Federal Aviation Administration. Could you identify yourself again please? Enter squawk code 1234."

Markle makes a face while Gid types in the code. It's not every day that you talk to a commander of special operations at the FAA... The line cuts out again. Then the voice comes back.

"Thank you, this is Luther Davis of the FAA. Could you give me your date and place of birth, Commander Markle?"

Markle sighs and provides the information.

"January 12, 1973, Peoria, Illinois."

"Could you give me the first and last names of every crew member on board the flight?"

"Kennedy, I don't know if you know this but I'm trying to land a damaged 787 . . ."

Another long silence, the line is cut off again, and another voice, a woman's, comes on.

"Air France 006? Kathryn Bloomfield from NORAD. Can you hear me?"

NORAD—aerospace defense. Really? Markle frowns.

"Air France 006 here, what can I do for you, NORAD?"

"For security reasons you need to disconnect your onboard Wi-Fi."

Markle doesn't argue and does as he's told.

"Thank you," the voice says. "Now please ask all your passengers to turn off their cellphones and all other electronic devices."

"We did that a long time ago, NORAD, we hit turbulence and we—"

"Perfect. First Officer Favereaux, in the next few minutes you and the cabin crew will proceed with collecting all, and I mean *all*, devices that enable communication outside the plane: tablets, phones, medical beepers, game consoles, laptops, et cetera. Don't forget augmented reality glasses and smart watches. No exceptions. Commander Markle, we're facing an extremely serious threat of external hacking targeting the navigation system, and any electronic devices could be relaying information... In fact, you can pass on all that information to your passengers, if you feel you need to in order to ensure their cooperation."

"But that will get them worrying..."

"Too bad. Make it clear that all devices will be returned in an hour, when you've landed in New York. Officer Favereaux, if you meet any resistance, emphasize the point about the plane's security and the danger of interference with the plane's instruments. You have full authority to collect all electronic devices. We're following a very specific protocol."

"But... all these devices... where are we going to put them?" Favereaux asks anxiously. "All cellphones look alike, how will we identify them?"

"Use sick bags, write the seat numbers in felt pen, deal with it. Reassure the passengers that they'll get them back on landing."

The copilot gives another vague, strangulated "yes" and gets to his feet. He heads off to pass on the orders to the stewards, while Markle explains the instructions in their entirety over the cabin mic. The copilot expects a wave of protests in the cabin, but—could it be retrospective terror about the turbulence, the threat that's just been announced of electronic hacking, or the indisputable authority of the captain's voice?—the overwhelming majority of passengers comply with his request. The few objectors even find themselves forced by those around them to follow the instructions. It could have been a tricky operation, but amazingly it takes only a few minutes. Once she has confirmation that all communications devices are being held in the cockpit, the NORAD officer picks up where she left off.

"This precautionary measure applies equally to all staff on board. And to you too. Your cellphones and laptops. You have full authority on that plane, Commander Markle. Your orders are to—"

"I'm the captain on this flight, Mrs. NORAD lady!" Markle snaps. "Of course I have full authority on this plane but you're the one who—"

"Commander Markle, we're dealing with a question of national security. We will work through Protocol 42 together."

Markle is lost for words. He's never heard of a Protocol 42.

"Air France 006, your new destination is McGuire Air Force Base, New Jersey. I repeat, McGuire Air Force Base, New Jersey."

Fort McGuire... it was there that in 1937 the German airship the *Hindenburg* caught fire as it attempted to dock with its mooring mast and was completely destroyed. Markle carries out a slow southeasterly turn and resigns himself to announcing to the cabin that, Sorry, folks, but due to major damage, the flight has been redirected to New Jersey. This time a lot of passenger protest; some start booing, particularly as—and this is the ultimate provocation—Manhattan's gleaming skyscrapers are taunting them to the west. Markle could distract them by telling them the story of the *Hindenburg*, but he knows intuitively now's not the time.

New York comes back over the intercom.

"Kennedy Approach again. Commander Markle, I'm putting you in contact with the National Military Command Center at the Pentagon."

Markle doesn't have time to reply before there's another voice, a man's, on the line. His accent is nasal, drawling, very Yankee, very New Hampshire.

"Commander Markle, General Patrick Silveria, National Military Command Center. I'm talking to you under the authority of the secretary of defense. In about three minutes you will be joined by two Navy fighter jets. They've just taken off from the USS *Harry S. Truman* and will escort you into national waters. In the event of an attempt to escape or of any noncompliance with their instructions, they have orders to destroy your aircraft."

This time it's gone too far. Markle bursts out laughing. He finally gets it.

"Commander Markle? This is General Silveria of the NMCC. Are you there?"

Markle can't stop laughing now, to the point of crying. Well, what a huge joke. Holy crap, what a bunch of fuckwit air traffic controllers at JFK, what a pack of moronic aluminum-pushers, he came real close to swallowing the whole thing, NORAD, Protocol 42, and now the Pentagon . . . he picks up the intercom again.

"Howdy there, so-called General Silveria! Is that the best you could do? To be honest, I believed it, but what you said about taking the plane down, that was too much. Do you really think now's the time, after the storm we just came through? And anyway, you messed up, my last flight's the day after tomorrow, not today. But I gotta hand it to you, it's a better parting gift than some lousy carrot cake."

"Air France 006? This is General Silveria from the Pentagon. I'm putting you on the line to the aircraft carrier USS *Harry S. Truman*."

"Yes, and I'm Captain Speaking! Is that you, Frankie? What a shitty fucking Yankee accent . . . you really are . . . thanks to your bullshit, we went ahead and gathered up all the devices from the cabin. Did you want us to be lynched by the passengers, was that the plan?"

Another voice comes over the intercom, higher pitched and with a Texan accent this time.

"Air France 006? This is admiral John Butler of the USS *Harry S. Truman*."

Markle still has a wry smile on his face.

"Hi, John Butler, the Mickey Mouse admiral. It's okay, Frankie, you can stop your little accent show now. It's not even funny anymore."

"Commander Markle? Admiral Butler still. You're currently under the protection of two of our F/A-18 Hornets. One is just behind your aircraft poised to intercept and the other . . . would you look to starboard, please."

Markle rolls his eyes but turns his head. A few meters from the tip of his right wing is a Hornet armed with air-to-air missiles. The pilot waves to him from the cockpit.

"Now, please follow all my instructions."

ANDRÉ

SUNDAY, JUNE 27, 2021

MUMBAI, INDIA

"F*OTOGRAFEI VOCÊ NA MINHA* ROLLEIFLEX . . ." the syrupy bossa nova by Stan Getz, Jobim, and João Gilberto wafts softly around the huge reception lobby of the Grand Hyatt Mumbai. The song is the same age as the man emerging from the elevator, short of breath and with shoulders drooping. When the mirror in the elevator reflected his sixty years back at him under harsh fluorescent light, he looked away.

André Vannier hasn't slept. Not adjusting to the time difference, feeling sad, too many dark thoughts. Before leaving his room, he wrote Lucie a very long email, which he managed to refrain from sending. It was nothing other than a ridiculous message in a bottle, after she'd culled him with a sleepy-voiced "I've moved on," down the line from Paris, where it was still nighttime. He wrote her knowing it was pointless and, more significantly, shall we say, counterproductive. But when the remote-control batteries are dead, we just keep pushing harder. It's only human.

The architect comes out of the international hotel—everything he loathes, no dynamism in the proportions, no elegance in the materials, pompous, stifling spaces—and leaves behind the Arctic of its air-con to venture into the furnace of India's tropical summer. Sounds are suddenly deafening, and the suffocating atmosphere doesn't deserve to be called air. Mumbai reeks of burned tires and diesel running on empty. On the clogged Pipeline Road he hails a dirty-green auto-rickshaw, and the contraption screeches to a stop beside him, with ten horns shrieking. André gives the address for the building site in the Kamathipura neighborhood, suggests a generous fare, and folds himself in three to introduce his tall, still-slender figure into the three-wheeler's cramped space. The rickshaw pulls away swiftly—more horns—and dives into the dense traffic, following a route known only to itself.

"Why do you always take rickshaws?" Nielsen asked the evening before. "Taxis are so much less stressful."

Yes, but Nielsen, with his long, blond hair, his immaculate Hugo Boss suits tailored to his strong, athletic build, and his scant few years in the business, that Nielsen, freshly turned out of the School of Architecture mold—oh, the "since your Grand Mississippi Center project, sir, I've been dreaming of working for Vannier and Edelman"—that Nielsen doesn't know that these minutes spent asphyxiating are Vannier's luxury. What he hopes to find, what he sometimes does find on the sagging rear seat of these tricycles, is himself aged twenty in Sri Lanka, he was there with that adorably deranged Neapolitan girl whose name he can't instantly recall, with her heavy breasts and her dazzling smile, Giulia? Yes, that's it, Giulia, he almost forgot it.

The rickshaw weaves its way through the noisy, stinking traffic toward the Surya Tower site, with a succession of lurching accelerations and shrill blasts of its horn, and André's amazed at the lack of scratches on the fenders of cars, amazed that their side-view mirrors survive. For once the driver isn't one of those exhausted teenagers who've pooled together to buy the machine and work shifts on it in perfect ignorance of the rules of the road, entrusting their fate to Waze. No, he's a stocky, ageless man with large aviator sunglasses, threading his way between trucks and cars with aggressive fluidity, intrepidly crossing the white line and unabashed by the dozens of vehicles powering toward him. The fact that he plows on unharmed in the surging traffic is somewhat miraculous; the translucent plastic Buddha stuck to the handlebars must have something to do with it.

Surya Tower is one of the most ambitious projects secured by Vannier & Edelman, a demonstration of know-how and aesthetics: an eighty-meter building in glass and bamboo, reinforced in strategic places by long lines of steel. The northern facade condenses the water streaming over it and irrigates the plant wall on the eastern side, while the southwestern wall alternates between light wells and solar panels—because *Surya* means sun—and supplies the building with electricity. It will form a symbolic bridge between the museum district and the university district, and will be home to image-hungry start-up companies; every floor is already reserved. No embellishments disturb the tower's simplicity: it is perfection achieved through endless elimination. Even their Chinese competitors were forced to yield.

But an Indian subcontractor lied about the quality of the concrete for the foundations, poor Nielsen didn't realize until it was too late, and the build is now two weeks behind schedule. André Vannier is using his two-day visit to threaten, negotiate, and clinch a deal—and who cares if it's Sunday—before flying to New York and the Ring the same afternoon.

"Moved on": André despises these simple words that Lucie chose with instinctual accuracy, the dead and gone of that past tense, the chilly simplicity; he can sense by extension the "to something better," or "someone better." Lucie was intentionally cruel, because all she wanted now was for things between them to be irreversible, and felt more comfortable reducing what little they'd had in those three months to a banal and short-lived experiment of something new—sleeping with an old man who was still reasonably palatable despite his old skin and his old-school name that no one gives to babies these days. Perhaps he's condemning himself with a fiercer summary than a less severe Lucie would use.

He's known her for three years. It was at a dinner with the Blums. He was bored and was about to leave when a very young woman arrived, Sorry I'm late, had to calibrate the lighting on a scene for a full-length feature. Lucie was a film editor. Despite attempts at discretion, André couldn't take his eyes off her because she was so much his type. He was captivated by the intensity with which she spoke: she never raised her voice, every sentence had a measured, considered quality, she proclaimed her words, and whenever she concentrated and developed a line of thought, a tiny blood vessel throbbed at her temple. He later discovered that she'd had a son, Louis, when she was twenty, and had raised him on her own from the start. It was this responsibility as a single mother, André thought, that produced her total absence of frivolity.

Yes, it would be an understatement to say Lucie had bowled him over. If he'd been twenty years younger, he'd have suggested having a child together. The age difference made everything unrealistic. His daughter Jeanne would soon be Lucie's age. Not long before he'd asked a woman, "Would you like to be my widow?" for a laugh. The putative widow hadn't laughed. And why are his partners so young these days? His friends are aging along with him, but not the women he loves. He's running away, he's scared. He can have dinner with impending death, but not sleep with it.

For two whole years he'd kept seeing her. He couldn't not see her. One miraculous day she'd kissed him, and the miracle had lasted a few months.

The architect draws up a list of the things in the young woman's behavior that gradually annihilated him, and concludes that everything comes down to bodies. Ever since he's been aware of death on the horizon—for a long time, then—he's put desire right at the heart of what he calls love. Lucie clearly located it on the periphery.

When Lucie came home exhausted from long hours spent editing, and he got up with a smile to put his arms around her, he read a reserve in her every gesture—perhaps it was simply tiredness, but once they were in bed he was afraid that the slightest overly intrusive movement would drive her away; he spent his nights far from her, and she ushered him out of what she called her "living space," a term that clearly didn't evoke the Nazi lebensraum for her generation. She slept, and he missed her already. He descended into melancholy, afraid that he might snore and add to her discomfort or—worse still—that he could fall asleep and she might wake to find an old man sleeping beside her, his foul-smelling mouth hanging open.

In the mornings Lucie was up, without kissing him, almost before her alarm had gone off; in the haze of early morning without his glasses, he watched this longed-for body desert the bedroom for the bathroom. He listened to the water flowing, at length, imagined her naked, closing her eyes under the hot stream, and his chest contracted with the pain of it, and perhaps the humiliation.

If he'd been thirty, if he'd had firm, still-immortal skin, skin that fears neither wrinkles nor death, and his hair had still been thick and black, would Lucie have run from her handsome lover for her morning shower? If it had been the good-looking Nielsen, yes, there's a thought, why not Nielsen, and he shudders at the fleeting image of a resplendent Nielsen astride his sweet Lucie. He has his answer, and it crucifies him.

And yet Lucie sometimes put her hand on him, checked the rigidity of that cylinder of flesh, then straddled him. He plied deep inside her, and because this position precluded any kissing, he tried to draw her to him; but she sat back up almost immediately and came, quickly. Everything about her svelte, sweating body meant that his man's pleasure should now follow. André tried to achieve a liberating orgasm straight after by taking her brutally. But neither the infrequency of their couplings nor their frantic rhythm was in any way suited to him.

His longing, his sadness, and his fears gradually made André lose all caution, and more than once he was insensitively insistent, but is there such a thing as sensitive insistence? Denied in person, frustrated physically, he didn't know where to find a second center of gravity. How long did he have left as a man? Age was weakening him, with that wretched six now numbering the decades. If Lucie didn't genuinely desire him today, the years to come wouldn't make him any more appealing.

THE RICKSHAW TURNS into the site and backfires as it zigzags unhesitatingly through the dirt and wooden planks until it reaches the large modular office building topped with the company's impressive V & E sign. André goes up to the spacious room on the second floor where Nielsen is waiting for him. Lucie, with Nielsen? No, it already seems ridiculous.

"The engineers from Singh Sunset Construction are here" is all the young architect troubles himself to say.

"They can wait. Give me a few minutes."

André pours himself a black coffee, sits down facing the window, and casts his eye over the Surya Tower site. It's ten o'clock, the meeting was at nine. Nothing is left to chance now: his indecent lateness, his sandals, his faded jeans and white cotton shirt with its Nehru collar, and his canvas backpack. His site visit was planned long ago, but he and Nielsen decided to tell them that he was coming to India only for their sake.

A little squad of Singh Sunset Construction engineers sits clustered around their boss. Six tight-fitting black suits, six knotted ties, six strained faces. They all get to their feet when André comes into the room. With no hesitation, the architect walks over to Singh; he's never met him but Nielsen sent him a photo. A man with smoothed-down gray hair, a wiry muscular fiftysomething with beady eyes. Before the man has a chance to bow with his hands crossed over his chest in a traditional Indian greeting, Vannier grabs his hand vigorously. Even the Maurice Chevalier accent he's about to use is calculated.

"Good morning, Mr. Singh."

"Very honored, Mr. Vannier, very honored."

"Mr. Singh, we have two hours in which to settle this problem. I need to leave for New York this evening. This is very serious. Very. You understand. First of all, I'd like us to do a site visit together."

"Mr. Vannier, we think that—"

Not waiting to hear, Vannier turns and leaves the room. Everyone follows him. Vannier walks quickly, with Nielsen on his heels and the engineers in single file behind them.

"We had the lab results this morning for the concrete samples from the micropiles," Nielsen mutters quietly to his boss. "In terms of compression resistance, we're a long way off the stipulated C 100/115. We're closer to C 90, even a little less. It's salvageable if we put in more micropiles and forget all about the existing ones."

Vannier nods. Nielsen is his secret weapon in India. A whole month the young man's been here now, a month in which he's run fraught site meetings with suppliers in fluent, technical English, a month in which this boy who looks like a lamebrain Australian surfer has been listening to what's being said around him in Hindi, which he understands perfectly; it's the language of his childhood spent in Goa, in the seaside town on the Indian Ocean where his mother still has a guesthouse. His mastery of this language—can he be in any doubt of this?—was a deciding factor in his recruitment to Vannier & Edelman two weeks after the company won the contract for Surya Tower.

When they reach the foundations, Vannier opens his bag and takes out a laptop, a satellite box, and a laser telemeter. He hooks up some wires, checks some data, orients the telemeter five times, ten times, recalculates, and tilts it again toward the top of a micropile, then another, while the Singh Sunset men sweat in the sunshine. He draws out the process, making it longer than necessary, then packs everything away with meticulous care, in no hurry, and they all return to the modular base camp.

Vannier sits down and gestures for them all to do the same. He lets a few seconds trickle by before speaking in suddenly accent-free English.

"Mr. Singh, a mistake was made, and it already has consequences. Now is the time to set it straight, any later will be too late. Architecture's a game, a cunning game but still a game, we won't talk about this. Construction isn't about playing but about making things together... Do you understand? Together..."

Singh nods his head.

By midday Vannier has secured everything he came to secure. Singh Sunset Construction has committed to a new schedule, and the modest fine imposed on them by Vannier & Edelman is intended only to cover expert and lawyer fees. You don't shoot your horse midstream. The new drilling will start the same afternoon, the new concrete will be pressure-injected overnight, when it's coolest. Given the urgency, Vannier insists not only on the standard C 115 but on X S2, which withstands salt water. With the heat, it will be dry in a week, and load-bearing in three.

While the Singh Sunset engineers start arguing over the new timetable, Vannier gives an Indian-style bow, and he and Nielsen leave the room.

They walk away from the site, buy a couple of iced Kingfishers from a street vendor, and head toward the docks. Vannier still has three hours before his flight to New York.

"By the way, André, how's Lucie?" Nielsen asks with sudden concern. "Did she finish the von Trotta she was working on?"

Vannier smiles. It's more of a grimace. Then he prevaricates, is elusive, realizing he's hiding their breakup, as if admitting it to Nielsen would make it all the more definitive. He's humiliated, and for the first time ever he feels old and is ashamed of the injustice life is doing him.

Lucie's definitely gone, and the architect repeats the formula to himself: "moved on." *Sic transit.* André can already tell that, all things considered, spending every day missing a woman who's no longer there will be less painful than relentlessly desiring one who's sleeping beside him but is light-years away from him in the tepid indifference of the shadows.

On the United flight to New York, Vannier rereads the same short book that he gave Lucie, *The anomaly*, by Victør Miesel, an author he'd never heard of two months ago. He tries to work, but can't help rewriting his desperate email for the tenth time. His wings are clipped. He hadn't anticipated anything of this vertiginous fall from grace.

This suffering—which he expressed, he exhibited—is what exasperated Lucie, what finally condemned him, but he proved incapable of compromise. Confronted with the pain of failure, he blames himself and curses his impatience. He thought he was a good lover, tender and skilled, he dreamed he could keep her with sex, could become synonymous in her mind with exquisite pleasure. Which was why, stupidly—because there's nothing more stupid than desire, which is the very essence of life, if Spinoza is to be believed—André kept trying to lure her back to a bed that she'd ended up avoiding.

"Your desire's oppressive. You've managed to kill mine," Lucie told him, and she asked for a "break," which of course wasn't one.

Miss Plato versus Dr. Spinoza. And Spinoza lost. Checkmate.

André doesn't write any of this, no, the email he's writing is, beyond any doubt, absurd. "I would have liked the two of us to walk the longest possible path, together, and even the longest of possible paths." He hates all these words but still writes them, and sends them. What time is it in Paris? It's Monday already. She's still asleep.

With melatonin taking effect, he eventually succumbs and has no dreams. When, still sleepy, he goes through customs at JFK, the officer scans his passport, studies him closely and keeps him back for a few minutes while a man and a woman come over to join them.

They're young, smart casual, the man in a black suit, the woman in a gray one, and they look like what they are: FBI or CIA. They even produce their bluish cards and their golden marshal's badges, on which a judge with a Playmobil face holds scales and a sword.

"Mr. André Vannier?" the woman asks.

He nods, and she shows him a photograph on a phone screen.

"Do you know this person?"

It's Lucie. Lucie sitting in a small room with yellow fluorescent lights. She's frightened, terrified, yes: everything about her posture and her eyes says so. Something's not right in this picture of Lucie.

"Yes, I know her. Of course. It's Lucie Bogaert, she's a friend. Has something happened to her? Isn't she in Paris?"

"Our only orders are to ask you to follow us, Mr. Vannier. Someone from the French consulate should have been here to greet you. He'll join us where we have to take you. You have the right to refuse, but then we'll just wait for him together in the detention area."

Vannier nods his head. Obviously, he doesn't refuse.

They come out of the airport and walk over to a black limousine; there's a man waiting beside it. He takes Vannier's case and puts it in the trunk. They climb into the back. They've hardly had time to sit down before the man knocks on the tinted glass screen between them and the driver. The car sets off, and it's then that André notices the windows are tinted too—they're completely opaque.

"Please turn off your cellphone and hand it to me," the woman continues. "Apologies, procedure."

André obeys. He's frightened too. Both for Lucie and for himself.

THE FIRST FEW HOURS

THURSDAY, JUNE 24, 2021

McGUIRE AIR FORCE BASE, TRENTON, NEW JERSEY

A Boeing 787 with a damaged fuselage is parked at the end of runway 2, not far from a group of U.S. Air Force Black Hawk helicopters and gray, twin-engine propeller planes. Three armored vehicles are in position beside the long-haul Boeing. A warm night with a smell of the sea settles over the wasteland, overrun with broom and sage.

Over by the buildings, there's a constant choreographed flow of military trucks. In a mixture of crisis mode and discipline, hundreds of soldiers are setting up something unidentifiable in a vast hangar recently vacated by the impressive Lockheed C-5 Galaxy cargo plane that was being serviced there. Silhouetted against the huge sliding doors are three tiny figures. Something in the bearing of the woman, wearing a misfired copy of a Chanel jacket, and one of the men, in a dark *Men in Black*–style suit, leaves little room for doubt: they're in the security services. The third person is more unusual: his hair is long and on the greasy side, a pair of round steel-rimmed glasses keeps slipping down his nose, and his holey T-shirt announces "I ♡ zero, one, and Fibonacci." He also smells of sweat, a little, and beer, a lot.

Adrian Miller may well have drunk two bottles of water, but his head's still spinning. As soon as he stepped out of the police car, the two agents came over to introduce themselves, and Miller immediately forgot their names, both the guy from the CIA and the woman from the FBI. He now proffers his hand limply, making no pretense of energy.

The CIA guy shakes it reluctantly, stiffly even, making as little contact as possible, as if touching the viscous fin of some slightly rotten bottom-feeder fish.

"I have to confess, Professor Miller, I didn't picture you so . . . so young."

The FBI woman, a thirtysomething Latina with delicate features and sharp eyes, appraises the mathematician in silence. At first, she thinks he looks like John Cusack, let's say a somewhat flabby, poor man's John Cusack, then she thinks better of it: no, not even that. Still, there's a combination of amazement and surprise in her voice when she speaks.

"We know your report by heart, Professor Miller. Remarkable work. We have high hopes for what your experience can offer us. I imagine you and Dr. Brewster-Wang have dealt with Protocol 42 before."

Adrian Miller mumbles an inaudible "no." He's had so little contact with Tina Wang that he didn't know a Brewster had come into her life, and no, he's never dealt with a Protocol 42. So far as he knows, not one of the events envisaged in the "low probability" protocols has come to interfere with air traffic: no extraterrestrials, to which three protocols are assigned—"Encounters of the third kind," "War of the worlds," and "Unknown intentions"—each with a dozen variations, including Godzilla to keep Tina happy; no airborne invasions by zombies or vampires—or any rapidly spreading airborne epidemic, like a coronavirus or a hemorrhagic fever such as Ebola—to which five further protocols were dedicated; as for a hypothetical destructive form of artificial intelligence taking control of air traffic—whether acting autonomously (Protocol 29) or remote-controlled by a foreign power (Protocol 30)—that hasn't yet happened, although it's increasingly plausible.

But Protocol 42... it simply *can't happen,* not Protocol 42. Miller takes a sip of water and makes his opening gambit.

"You know, Ms.... I'm sorry, I forgot your names."

"Senior Agent Gloria Lopez. And my opposite number from the CIA, Marcus Cox."

"Well, Senior Agent Gloria Lopez, to be totally honest, Protocol 42 is... how shall I put this..."

Adrian Miller takes another sip of water; he can't find the words. He can't in all decency admit that it was just a naughty math-geek joke that's already cost the taxpayer half a million dollars, and that's if you're counting only the twenty years when the State has paid two pranksters to carry bulletproof cellphones twenty-four hours a day, cellphones that should never have received a call. He looks at the Boeing, a great aluminum cigar now lit up by powerful floodlights.

"Do you know exactly why we're here? What's so special about this plane? Apart from the hail damage to its windshield and its crumpled nose."

"It's a radome," the CIA agent corrects him. "The aircraft's nose. It's called a radome."

"We don't know very much, Professor Miller," the woman interrupts them. "And Professor Brewster-Wang's chopper is about to arrive. It's that black dot over there, to the north."

"Yes, actually, could you sign the bottom of this page, Professor Miller," Agent Cox adds, opening an envelope. "It's a confidentiality agreement: all the information you're given from now on will be classified. If you refuse to sign this, you'll be brought before the military tribunal for breaching national security. And, thanks to 18 U.S. code section 79, it would be considered high treason if you violate it after signing it. Thank you for your cooperation."

SINCE KING ARTHUR and his knights, if not before, military types have liked gathering in the round, most likely because circles profess equality while doing nothing to hide the true hierarchy. The McGuire base therefore has its statutory big round table in the middle of the underground command center, where the lighting is harsh and the walls are lined with large screens: several of them show images of the grounded 787, shot from every angle by a battery of cameras.

Tina and Adrian felt safer sitting next to each other, so that they could jointly confront the good dozen multistar generals and men and women from every imaginable agency, all with their names and credentials in Plexiglas name-holders. Besides the FBI and the Department of Defense, there are representatives of the State Department, the U.S. Air Force, the CIA, the NSA, NORAD, the FAA, and still other acronyms that Miller's never heard of. He and Tina also qualify to be identified by their titles, and their first and last names above a mention of the Massachusetts Institute of Technology—where neither of them still works.

Tina Wang hasn't changed much, although her outfit is more sensible than the Goth look favored by the PhD student she once was. She's had time to tell Adrian under her breath that she's stopped teaching, that, yes, she married a Georg Brewster, a physicist she met in the cafeteria at Columbia, and—smiling deviously—that she would have struggled to recognize Adrian, seeing as he no longer really looks like Christian Slater in *The Name of the Rose*. She thinks he now has something of a balding Keanu Reeves about him, but keeps this to herself.

A powerful voice booms above the hubbub. This tall, slim man doesn't need to trot out his results from West Point, nor his war exploits in Homs and Mogadishu: his crew-cut white hair and muscular, willful features, along with the three black stars embroidered on his collar, are as good as a résumé. In this room, with its civilized wood paneling, his gray-green camouflage combat fatigues are of little use to him.

"Ladies and gentlemen, I'm General Patrick Silveria of the National Military Command Center, and I have full authority to represent the Department of Defense. This situation must remain secret, and the president has opted not to change his schedule in Rio, but rest assured that he's being given constant updates. I'll do the rounds of the table: on my left is General Buchanan, who commands the McGuire base and is our host for these few days. I imagine no one knows Professors Miller and Brewster-Wang to my right: they're mathematicians, and we're indebted to them for the crisis protocols we've been following since 9/11."

The two in question give awkward waves amid a murmur of approval.

"Professor Miller teaches at Princeton," Silveria continues, "and Professor Brewster-Wang is a consultant for NASA and Google. They will have complete free rein to apply Protocol 42, and I will coordinate the operation. Before anyone points out that the CIA isn't authorized to operate on national territory, I'd like to make it clear that the protocol requires the cooperation of all agencies."

While an officer hands each participant a tablet and a thick dossier labeled "Classified Information," Silveria goes on to introduce the senior FBI agent and all the others, from the CIA special agent to the NSA's head of digital surveillance—early thirties, with the irritating face of a geek who's set up a social network—and all the way to a small woman with a soft, clear voice and short, snowy hair, despite being barely forty: Jamy Pudlowski of Special Operations Command, PsyOps, a specialist in psychological operations. Each in their own way, they are necessary to the smooth running of Protocol 42. It's all coming back to Miller: the government agencies involved, the rank of each person around the table, even the agenda for this meeting... nothing that he and Tina Wang hadn't specified in their report.

"Our team will be receiving a lot of reinforcements in the next few hours," Silveria says. "Right now, many people from a variety of disciplines are on their way to the base and will help us deal with the situation. How many agents are the FBI's PsyOps sending us, Special Agent Pudlowski?"

"More than a hundred. We're also working out of our offices in New York."

"Thank you. You have before you an up-to-date account of what we know of the situation. The 787 on the tarmac is the reason we're all here: it opened communication with Kennedy Airport at exactly 19:03 hours today, June 24. It identified itself as flight Air France 006 from Paris to New York. The plane reported significant damage and was rerouted to this base within minutes. The captain states that he is David Markle, and the copilot Gideon Favereaux, and you each have a full list of passengers and crew. I'm going to hand things straight over to Brian Mitnick of the NSA. A word about the tablets, Brian?"

The man from the National Security Agency stands up. On his feet he looks even more boyish, particularly as he's tinkering with a slender black rectangle with adolescent zeal.

"Hello, everyone, you have in front of you a tablet like mine. Yours is personal and unlocked. On the welcome page you'll find a plan of the Boeing 787. Click on each seat and a name will appear in a pop-up window, seat by seat, including the crew. The NSA is updating your tablets in real time as we get the data for each person on the flight. If and when there's a link to another page from an image or a fragment of text, it will be highlighted in blue. Click on it and the page will appear. To go back, click on the 'back' arrow. It's very simple. Now, please look at the display screens."

With a flick of his finger, Mitnick scrolls through photos of Markle and Favereaux, then the cabin stewards. While Mitnick is having fun with his toy, Silveria takes over again.

"Protocol 42 has been set in motion because today's Air France 006 flight already landed at JFK more than four hours ago, at the scheduled time of 16:35 hours. But it was a different aircraft, with a different captain and copilot. On the other hand, an Air France Boeing 787, with the same reference Air France 006, with exactly the same damage as this one, piloted by the same Commander Markle, copiloted by the same Favereaux, and manned by the same crew and with the same passengers, in other words the exact same plane as this one you see here, this same plane, then, landed at JFK Airport, but at 17:17 hours on March 10. Precisely one hundred six days ago."

The whole room is a cacophony, but the CIA agent brings the racket to an end by raising his hand.

"I don't understand," he says. "The same plane landed twice?"

"Yes. I repeat: it's the same plane. One of the maintenance technicians has confirmed it: he worked on this same 787 nearly four months ago. He says that the damage is lighter, as if the plane spent half as much time in the hail, but he incontrovertibly recognizes some of the impacts on the windshield, some of the damage on the radome, et cetera. I now have a live link to the pilot."

A touch of feedback buzzes through the command center.

"Good evening, Captain Markle. General Patrick Silveria here again. I'm with the crisis staff. Could I ask you to introduce yourself once more? And give us your date of birth again."

Markle's voice reverberates around the room. It's weary.

"David Markle, born January 12, 1973. General, the passengers can't take much more. They want to disembark."

"We're going to evacuate them in the next few minutes. One last question, Captain Markle: What day is it and what time is it?"

"My instruments aren't functioning but it's March 10, and my watch says 8:45 pm."

Silveria cuts the call. The luminous clock says the date is June 24, and the time 22:43. With no warning, the image of an intubated patient on a hospital bed now appears on the largest of the screens.

"This photo was taken ten minutes ago by an FBI agent in room 344 of Mount Sinai Hospital. This man is also called David Markle. He was the pilot on flight Air France 006 on March 10. That particular David Markle is dying of pancreatic cancer, diagnosed a month ago."

Silveria turns to Adrian Miller and Tina Brewster-Wang, who are still silent.

"I hope you understand why we've implemented Protocol 42, and can tell us what the next step should be."

. II .

Life Is a Dream, They Say

(JUNE 24–26, 2021)

Existence precedes essence,

and by quite a distance.

—*The anomaly,* Victør Miesel

THE MOMENT WHEN

THURSDAY, JUNE 24, 2021

McGUIRE AIR FORCE BASE, TRENTON, NEW JERSEY

THE PASSENGERS trundle toward the hangar in single file between two columns of armed soldiers in yellow anticontamination suits. They walk through a radioactivity detector and an antibacterial airlock before arriving in dribs and drabs under the huge dome; soldiers in a row write down their first and last names and their seat numbers. Very few of them make any protest. Irritation and then anger have given way to exhaustion and anxiety. Only one incensed lawyer finds the energy to hand around her business cards.

Inside the hangar, soldiers have set up showers, mobile toilets, hundreds of tents, and some long tables. They serve hot meals, and some of the passengers try to rest on the mattresses provided in the tents, but everything reverberates under the steel vault; children shriek, arguments break out. Dozens of soldiers patrol the building, filter every move; in the northern corner, a medical unit has the use of a laboratory in a sterile tent, and a team of twelve nurses take saliva samples from all the passengers; in prefabricated units in the eastern corner, the newly arrived PsyOps psychologists start their one-to-one interrogations, following a questionnaire hastily put together by Miller and Brewster-Wang. Protocol 42 has been substantially elaborated in the last few hours.

On the western side, the hangar is dominated by a huge metal platform five meters above the ground. The task force team has moved into one of the rooms overlooking the hangar, and through its floor-to-ceiling windows they can watch the noisy, chaotic hive of activity. Their tablets constantly display new information. The NSA has geolocated most of the passengers and crew members from the Paris–New York flight of March 10. Around one hundred of them are already under house arrest with police surveillance. Biologists compare their DNA with that of their counterparts being held in the hangar: they are absolutely identical. The plane grounded at McGuire is an exact replica of the one that landed just under four months earlier.

Mitnick, the NSA geek, projects onto a screen two images of the cabin.

"What we're looking at side by side are videos from the camera in first class: on the left is the image from the first plane from March 10, on the right the one from the plane that landed today. If I pause it... On the time codes for the images it's 16:26 and 30 seconds... the two images are the same. We're right in the middle of the turbulence. And now image by image..."

Up on the screen, at 16 hours 26 minutes 34 seconds and 20 hundredths, the videos diverge, and the split screen becomes a game of spot the difference: on the left a passenger watches her glasses fly off, while on the right they stay on her nose, here an overhead locker opens, whereas there it stays shut. And most noticeably, it's dark on the left, while the cabin on the right is illuminated by radiant sunlight. The first plane is still making bumpy progress through the terrible storm of March 10 when the second emerges into the calm skies of June 24 at 18:07.

There is such an uproar that Mitnick has to shout to be heard.

"There," he says in a gleeful, overexcited voice. "That's when it all happens—at 16 hours 26 minutes 34 seconds and 20 hundredths... and this extraordinary fact just keeps going. We chose three cameras from onboard the Boeing 787: one at the front, one in the center, and one at the back. There are twelve meters between each of them. At 900 kilometers an hour, which is 250 meters per second, the Boeing covers these twelve meters in one twenty-fifth of a second and—what a miracle!—these cameras take twenty-five images per second . . . do you follow?"

Mitnick gets no response, so he keeps going.

"I'll split the screen in three. On the left the video from the first camera, in the middle the center camera, and on the right the camera at the back. So, at 16 hours 26 minutes 34 seconds and 20 hundredths, sunlight suddenly floods into the cabin according to the first camera, but on the next image it's at 16 hours 26 minutes 34 seconds and 24 hundredths. And on the third camera the sunlight appears at 16 hours 26 minutes 34 seconds and 28 hundredths."

"And? What does that mean?" Silveria asks.

Mitnick is exultant.

"There's a discrepancy of one twenty-fifth of a second between each camera. It's as if our second plane appears out of nowhere through an unmoving vertical window. Before the window, there's the storm, once it's come through it, the sky's blue. According to our observation satellites, this window was at precisely N 42°8′50″, W 65°25′9″, but the plane reappeared today a little further southwest, and there's about sixty kilometers between the two."

"What do you conclude from this, Mitnick?"

"Oh, me? Nothing, nothing at all. It's just another fact to put into the mix for the eggheads from Princeton," he says, turning to the two mathematicians.

"It operated a little like a photocopier, then?" Tina Brewster-Wang asks. "A scan taken in one place and a copy delivered somewhere else, like a sheet of paper coming out of a machine?"

Mitnick hesitates. The concept had struck him as too absurd to put forward.

Silence is returning. Air-conditioning units have not yet been installed, and a clammy heat hangs over everything. A message buzzes on the cellphone of the man from National Security. He reads it and sighs.

"The president of the United States is insisting that the NSA check whether there was a Russian or Chinese ship near our Atlantic coastline on March 10 . . . that could have carried out a time travel experiment . . ."

A peevish despondency washes over General Silveria. He leans his head against the window, gazes out over the hangar filled with harsh light.

"Where the hell did this plane come from?" he sighs. "You must have a theory, Professor Brewster-Wang? A professor without a theory's like a dog without fleas."

"Really sorry, right now I don't have any fleas."

"We hope to track everybody down within forty-eight hours," Silveria continues, "including foreign passengers who've returned to their own countries since March 10. Between now and then you'd better come up with an explanation for us."

"We need to expand the scientific team," suggests Adrian. "Quantum physics, astrophysics, molecular biology . . . the team needs to be on the premises by dawn."

"We'll give you a list of scientists in thirty minutes," Tina Brewster-Wang adds. "Two or three philosophers as well."

"Really? Why?" Silveria asks.

"Why should scientists always be the only people woken in the night?"

Silveria gives a shrug.

"Don't be afraid to name anyone you like, I have full authority to kidnap every Nobel winner in the field. The exact wording is 'to ask them to cooperate at the express request of the president of the United States.'"

"And find us a hypothesis room too," Tina continues. "A really big communal work room with lots of different spaces, several tables, some easy chairs, sofas, blackboards, chalk, well, you get the picture . . ."

"The boards will be white and interactive, will that be okay?" Silveria asks without a trace of irony.

"And anti-sleep pills too."

"We'll pump you full of modafinil. We have hundreds of boxes of it . . ."

"We'll need a specialist in continuity in space," Adrian pitches in, "she can help with graph theory."

"Why 'she'? Do you have someone in mind?"

Adrian has someone in mind.

"Professor Harper, from Princeton. Meredith Harper. A few hours ago, she and I . . . as it happens, we were talking about Grothendieck's topoi in geometry."

"I'll send a military vehicle for her right away. Is she . . . reliable? In terms of national security?"

"Absolutely. Particularly as she's English. Is that a problem?"

General Silveria has his doubts.

"There are thirteen English people on this damn plane anyway. So long as she's not Russian, Chinese, or French. And we're going to be collaborating with the British services anyway."

"And a coffee machine, a real one, that makes espresso," Adrian adds.

"Don't ask the impossible," the general replies with a grimace.

SHORTLY BEFORE 11:00 PM, a swirl of gray smoke rises in the northern corner of the hangar, a harmless plume at first, but it gradually becomes blacker and denser. A man's voice cries "Fire!" and a wave of panic spreads through the crowd: Passengers race toward the closed doors, jostling the soldiers guarding them. Teams of security officers surge forward to help the soldiers.

The fire is quickly brought under control, but Silveria reaches for the mic.

"This is General Patrick Silveria. Please don't give in to panic. I'll come down and give you the explanations you deserve."

A rising hubbub fills the room.

"What can you possibly tell these people?" Tina Brewster-Wang asks as the officer prepares to climb down from the platform. "I don't recommend you tell them that they all already exist in duplicate somewhere in the world and they darn well shouldn't be on this earth at all . . ."

"I'll improvise. Who knows what we're all doing on this planet, anyway?"

While Silveria is at the mic in front of the two hundred passengers, launching into his misleading explanations concerning national security, piracy, and public health, the soldiers examine the damage: the fire started under one of the mattresses and quickly spread through the whole tent. A deliberate act.

Thirty meters away, a narrow metal door with access to the outside has been forced with a crowbar. During the panic, the soldiers guarding it relaxed their vigilance. After another ten minutes a five-meter gap is found, where the perimeter fence has been torn open by a vehicle. It was gray, as indicated by flakes of paint;

but the parking lot close to the hangar, and from which it must have been stolen, has more than three hundred vehicles in it.

A passenger has escaped and vanished into the night.

AT MIDNIGHT the list for the multidisciplinary team is ready: Nobel Prizes, Abel Prizes, Fields Medals—either actual or potential winners. Thirty minutes later, the FBI start ringing doorbells, interrupting all sorts of nocturnal activities, although sleep is the most common. The "express request of the president of the United States" and the flashing lights piercing the darkness do their job. And it's not yet one in the morning before a choreography of cars, helicopters, and jets is bringing the scientists to McGuire Air Base.

Meredith is here too, recognizable from her smell of vodka and toothpaste. She's clearly been hauled out of bed, and when Adrian launches into a—muddled—exposition of the situation, her anger is already long gone. She listens, frowning, and looks out at the crowd below without a word.

"Don't you have any questions?" Adrian asks, amazed.

"Would you have any answers?"

Adrian shakes his head, disconcerted, and hands her a modafinil. To stop you sleeping, he wants to say, but she's already swallowed it without any protest.

"You should have told me you were a secret agent, Adrian."

"That's . . . that's not exactly true. Um . . . come, I'll take you to the control room."

"Tut-tut. Princeton mathematician, what an off-the-wall cover for a spy . . ."

When Adrian opens the door, Meredith stands open-mouthed at the scene.

"Oh, Adrian, I love it," she whispers. "We're in *Dr. Strangelove*."

Each new piece of information on the screens confirms the impossible. The plane on the runway is in every way identical to the 787 that landed on March 10. Granted, that aircraft has been repaired, and granted, the passengers have aged: this very evening in Chicago people are celebrating the six-month "birthday" of a baby that, in the hangar, is a screaming two-month-old. In the one hundred six days that separate the two landings, of the two hundred thirty passengers and thirteen crew members, one woman has given birth and two men have died. But genetically they're the same individuals. Silveria is taking stock of the figures with a select committee, and completely ignores the mathematicians.

"And the interrogations?"

"We're adding to the questionnaire devised by Professors Wang and Miller," replies Jamy Pudlowski, the woman from Psychological Operations. "We're introducing faulty details to produce reactions that will confirm identities. At least initially, the passengers' names must remain secret."

The man from the NSA is waggling his tablet again.

"We're monitoring social networks for alerts on keywords, from 'Boeing' to 'McGuire.' When this story explodes, we'll be able to identify who's posting and to limit the spread of information. But this isn't China or Iran, we can't block the internet. For now, only one page, attributed to a soldier at the base, mentions the plane, and we've erased it. Thank God..."

"On the subject of God..." says Pudlowski.

The word "God" has the gift of creating silence. The woman from the FBI shakes her head, and under the lights, a narrow lock of black disrupts the arrangement of her white hair.

"Well... God is likely to prove a problem. In our country, as in many others, there'll be talk of an act of God. Or of the devil. We won't be able to stop outbursts of superstition and the reckless behavior of visionaries. I've taken the initiative of summoning a committee of spiritual leaders from all religions. The president's religious advisors are all evangelists, we can't be criticized for limiting ourselves to them. On board that plane there were Christians, Muslims, Buddhists... Time is against us, and religious individuals are unpredictable by nature."

"You have carte blanche, Jamy," the general says. "With its nine-billion-dollar budget, I'm sure your bureau can achieve something."

"What about the French, the other Europeans, the Chinese, and all the rest... what do we do?" Mitnick asks. "Should we contact their embassies?"

"To tell them we're illegally detaining their citizens? We're not going to do anything. We'll wait for a decision from the president. Anything else?"

At the back of the room, Adrian raises his finger shyly.

"We need a code to distinguish the people on the first plane that landed in March from those on the second: one and two? Alpha and beta? Or colors: blue and green, blue and red?"

"Tom and Jerry?" suggests Meredith. "Laurel and Hardy?"

"Excellent ideas, but no," Silveria says decisively. "Let's make it simple: March for the first one, which landed in March, June for the one that landed in June."

TIME IS ALL-IMPORTANT, Blake knows that. Fifteen minutes in the hangar are all it takes for him to exploit a chink in the security setup, another seven and he's driving toward New York in an old Ford F-150 pickup, the most unremarkable vehicle there is, "borrowed" from the parking lot at the air base. Always have just a backpack as luggage. Of course, he didn't give the cabin crew the disposable cellphone he'd bought in Paris, and obviously he avoided the DNA test. He reaches New York at two in the morning, throws away the Australian passport he used for his outward journey, parks the pickup in a dark street, cleans all traces from the steering wheel and seat, before setting fire to it in spite of these measures, to be extra sure.

It's an archetypal summer's night, sweltering even, and Blake—who's astonished to see on a newspaper that the date is June 24—at least finds the temperature logical. In a twenty-four-hour cybercafe, he scrolls through the news for the last few months, learning that on March 21 a certain Frank Stone was assassinated in Quogue; someone carried out his contract. He wants to check his secret bank accounts, but the codes have changed. He visits the Facebook page for his Paris restaurant, then Flora's page. In a photo posted on June 20, a man who looks confoundingly like him has his daughter on his knee and a bandage around his forehead, and Flora has captioned it: "The dangers of horseback riding—and that was just the box stall!" He studies his own forehead: no scar, no bruising. Just for a moment, Blake considered the lazy but crazy explanation of amnesia. It's no longer an option.

His pragmatism wins the day, as it always does. He needs to get back to base: he takes a taxi to JFK, then uses cash and a new identity to buy a ticket on the next flight to Europe. The New York–Brussels plane takes off at 6:15. At nine o'clock on Saturday evening he'll be back on European soil, and there's a bus to Paris every hour. Blake has many hours to sleep, and if not to understand, to think.

SEVEN INTERVIEWS

EXTRACTS FROM the interview with David Markle

CONFIDENTIALITY: Top secret / PROTOCOL: Number 42

INTERVIEW CARRIED OUT BY: Officer Charles Woodworth, PsyOps, SOC

DATE: 2021/06/25 / TIME: 00:12 / PLACE: Joint Base McGuire-Dix-Lakehurst

SURNAME: Markle / FIRST NAMES: David Bernard / CODE: June

DATE OF BIRTH: 01/12/1973 (48 years) / NATIONALITY: American

CREW POSITION: Captain / SEAT: CP 1

Off. CW: Day 2, twelve after midnight. Hello, Captain Markle, I'm Officer Charles Woodworth, Special Operations Command, U.S. Army. You're David Bernard Markle, born January 12, 1973, in Chicago, Illinois. With your permission, our entire conversation will be recorded and followed up by the NSA.

DBM: Okay. I was born in Peoria, not Chicago.

Off. CW: Thank you for that correction. You started your career with Delta Airways in 1997. You moved to Air France in March 2003. You spent three years working short-haul on Airbus A319s, 320s, and 321s, then long-haul on A330s and A340s, and you now fly Boeing B787s. Is that right?

DBM: Yes.

Off. CW: Captain Markle, could we come back to your last flight, would you describe the cumulonimbus and go over the turbulence again, please?

DBM: At about 4:20 pm New York time, we were south of Nova Scotia and had to fly through a cumulonimbus that wasn't indicated on the weather charts. It was a monster, on a wide front, peaking at more than 15,000 meters—it was unusual for March. We dropped—I'd say a thousand meters—at an angle of at least twenty-five degrees. We hit a wall of hailstones, righted the bird, and then after five or six minutes we suddenly came out of the cloud to a clear sky.

Off. CW: Did you go to elementary school when you lived in Peoria?

DBM: Excuse me?

Off. CW: Please answer the question, Captain Markle. Do you remember the name of the school?

DBM: Kellar Primary School. Are you going to look at your tablet the entire time?

Off. CW: It's the protocol: these questions are deliberately personal. Your answers are verified in real time. Do you recollect the name of any teachers there?

DBM: It was fifty years ago. Wait, yes . . . Mrs. Pratchett.

Off. CW: Thank you, Captain. [. . .] Do you paint or play a musical instrument in your free time?

DBM: No.

Off. CW: Do you have constant, pleasant, melodic sounds in your ears?

DMB: No.

Off. CW: Do you have headaches, migraines?

DBM: No.

Off. CW: Inflammation of your eyes or sinuses?

DBM: Yes, sometimes. What kind of questions are these?

Off CW: I'm just following a protocol, Captain Markle. Do you have itching or burning on your face?

DBM: No.

Off. CW: Do you recognize the young woman in the photo that I've just been sent, now showing on the screen in front of you?

DBM: I think I do.

Off. CW: Could you tell me her name?

DBM: I think it's Mrs. Pratchett.

Off. CW: It's Pamela Pritchett, not Pratchett, taken fifty years ago. She's now eighty-four, and still lives in Peoria.

DBM: I'd like to speak to your superior. And call my wife, she must be seriously concerned.

Off. CW: Soon, Captain Markle. Have you had any medical tests recently? [. . .]

END OF INTERVIEW 06/25/2021 at 00:43

EXTRACTS OF the interview with André Vannier

CONFIDENTIALITY: Defense-secret / PROTOCOL: Number 42

INTERVIEW CARRIED OUT BY: Lt. Terry Klein, PsyOps, SOC

DATE: 06/25/2021 / TIME: 07:10 / PLACE: Joint Base McGuire-Dix-Lakehurst

SURNAME: Vannier / FIRST NAMES: André Frédéric / CODE: June

DATE OF BIRTH: 04/13/1958 (63 years) / NATIONALITY: French

PASSENGER POSITION: Economy-class cabin 2 / SEAT: 11 B

Off. TK: Day 2, ten after seven. Good morning, I'm Officer Terry Klein, Special Operations Command, U.S. Army. Are you Mr. André Vannier, born April 13, 1958, in Paris?

AFV: Yes.

Off. TK: Mr. Vannier, for security reasons I'm recording our conversation.

AFV: I'd like to contact my associate. We're working on a build in New York. I need to let him know I'm being detained here.

Off. TK: I can't promise anything for now, Mr. Vannier.

AFV: Very well, in that case, I insist that you contact the Quai d'Orsay.

Off. TK: Kay who, Mr. Vannier?

AFV: The French Ministry of Foreign Affairs. And ask your boss at Special Operations Command, he's bound to know Armand Mélois.

Off. TK: I'll transmit the information. Could you describe the flight for me, particularly the turbulence? [. . .]

INTERVIEW ENDS 06/25/2021 at 07:25

EXTRACTS FROM the interview with Sophia Kleffman

CONFIDENTIALITY: Defense-secret / PROTOCOL: Number 42

INTERVIEW CARRIED OUT BY: Lt. Mary Tamas, PsyOps, SOC

DATE: 06/25/2021 / TIME: 08:45 / PLACE: Joint Base McGuire-Dix-Lakehurst

SURNAME: Kleffman / FIRST NAMES: Sophia Taylor / CODE: June

DATE OF BIRTH: 05/13/2014 (7 years) / NATIONALITY: American

PASSENGER POSITION: Economy-class cabin 1 / SEAT: 6 C

Off. MT: It's quarter to nine in the morning on day 2. Hi, Sophia, my name is Mary, I'm an officer in the security forces. Are you doing okay this morning?

STK: Yes, ma'am.

Off. MT: You can call me Mary, you know. Did you manage to sleep? Did you have some breakfast?

STK: Yes.

Off. MT: You need plenty to eat. You guys had a very tiring flight yesterday. I'm going to ask you some questions and I'm going to make a note of all your answers on this tablet I have here. And I'll record our whole conversation. Is that okay, Sophia?

STK: Did I do something wrong?

Off. MT: Not at all, Sophia, don't worry. Afterward you and I can go take a look at the games that were set up in the night, because there are nearly thirty kids here, you know. And you could watch cartoons too. Okay?

STK. Yes. Could I play on an iPad? I have one, but it was taken.

Off. MT: You'll get it back soon. How old are you, Sophia?

STK: I'm six, I'll be seven in two months.

Off. TM: That's great. Which date exactly?

STK: May 13.

Off. MT: And May 13 is in two months, is it?

STK: Yes.

Off. MT: What presents would you like?

STK: Another frog. So Betty's not all on her own anymore.

Off. MT: Who's Betty?

STK: She's my frog. She's waiting for me back home.

Off. MT: I'm going to show you a picture that your mommy took. Do you recognize your home?

STK: Yes...

Off. MT: Can you tell me who's in the picture?

STK: Yes, they're my friends from school, that there is Jenny, he's Andrew, Sarah...

Off. MT: Yes, Sophia. You see, I'm writing down everything you tell me, it's important. It's a birthday party, can you count the number of candles on the cake?

STK: Yes . . . I can see seven candles.

Off. MT: Thank you, Sophia. You must have been sick to your stomach on the plane, right?

STK: I sure was, it jumped around a lot.

Off. MT: Do you ever get the feeling you can hear music?

STK: No, ma'am.

Off. MT: You can call me Mary, you know, Sophia. And do you sometimes get headaches?

STK: No, not really.

Off. MT: And are your eyes sore?

STK: Na-ah.

Off. MT: Well, that's good. And does your face get itchy on your cheeks or your forehead?

STK: No.

Off. MT: Were you traveling with your mommy and your little brother Liam?

STK: He's my big brother.

Off. MT: Yes, I'm sorry, I got that wrong. And what about your daddy, is he not with you?

STK: No. He stayed in Europe.

Off. MT: Did you have a nice vacation in Europe?

STK: Yes. Did I do something wrong?

Off. MT: Of course you didn't, Sophia, not at all. Your daddy's in the army, isn't he?

STK: Yes. He didn't do anything wrong either, right?

Off. MT: Of course not, Sophia. Aw, come on, don't cry. Have a Kleenex. You shouldn't worry. Really not. Would you like me to ask your mommy to come and talk with us?

STK: No.

Off. MT: Look, I have some paper and coloring pens. Do you like drawing, Sophia? Would you draw a picture for me?

STK: What should I draw?

Off. MT: Whatever you like, Sophia.

INTERVIEW SUSPENDED 06/25/2021 at 09:02

INTERVIEW RESUMED 06/25/2021 at 09:09

Off. MT: Thank you so much, Sophia. That's a beautiful drawing. You made it all black. Did you notice there were colored pens too?

STK: Yes.

Off. MT: Who's this tall man here?

STK: That's my daddy.

Off. MT: And who's that next to him?

STK: That's ME.

Off. MT: You're all scribbled out. Why is that?

STK: [*silence*]

Off. MT: Is that your mouth there?

STK: [*nods her head*]

Off. MT: What about Mommy, is she not here?

STK: No.

Off. MT: Would you mind telling me some more about your drawing, Sophia? And I'm going to ask another lady to come join me, to listen to what you say, if that's okay. Is that okay, Sophia?

STK: Yes. [. . .]

INTERVIEW ENDS 06/25/2021 at 09:19

EXTRACTS FROM the interview with Joanna Woods

CONFIDENTIALITY: Defense-secret / PROTOCOL: Number 42

INTERVIEW CARRIED OUT BY: Lt. Damian Hepstein, PsyOps, SOC

DATE: 06/25/2021 / TIME: 07:23 / PLACE: Joint Base McGuire-Dix-Lakehurst

SURNAME: Woods / FIRST NAMES: Joanna Sarah / CODE: June

DATE OF BIRTH: 06/04/1987 (34 years) / NATIONALITY: American

PASSENGER POSITION: First-class cabin / SEAT: 4 B

Off. DH: Day 2, seven twenty-three. Good morning, Ms. Woods, I'm Lieutenant Damian Hepstein, Special Operations Command, U.S. Army. Our conversation is being recorded, with your permission.

JSW: Well, I don't give my permission.

Off. DH: Ms. Woods, a refusal to cooperate in a situation of national security will be viewed as suspect behavior. Are you Joanna Woods, born June 4, 1987, in Baltimore?

JSW: Lieutenant Hepstein, I'm protected by the Fourth Amendment from any arbitrary detention. I'd like to call my office.

Off. DH: I can assure you that the situation justifies the restrictive measures that have been placed on your movements.

JSW: Lieutenant Hepstein, no judge has signed a detention order, or if they have I'd like to see it. We can't be detained like this, it's a case of habeas corpus.

Off. DH: I understand, Ms. Woods, but everything will be explained in the next few hours.

JSW: I'm collecting data for a federal class action, maybe even an international one. Forty-seven passengers have already agreed to be represented by my firm . . .

Off. DH: That is your right. Could I ask you a few questions, Ms. Woods?

JSW: I don't think so, no. And I'd like to talk to your boss. [. . .]

INTERVIEW ENDS 06/25/2021 at 07:27

EXTRACTS FROM the interview with Lucie Bogaert

CONFIDENTIALITY: Defense-secret / PROTOCOL: Number 42

INTERVIEW CARRIED OUT BY: Lt. Francesca Caro, PsyOps, SOC

DATE: 06/25/2021 / TIME: 07:52 / PLACE: Joint Base McGuire-Dix-Lakehurst

SURNAME: Bogaert / FIRST NAMES: Lucie / CODE: June

DATE OF BIRTH: 01/22/1989 (32 years) / NATIONALITY: French

PASSENGER POSITION: Economy-class cabin 2/ SEAT: 11 C

Off. FC: Day 2, seven fifty-two. Good morning, I'm Officer Francesca Caro, Special Operations Command, U.S. Army. Do you need an interpreter, Ms. Bogaert?

LB: No.

Off. FC: Ms. Bogaert, our conversation is being recorded for security reasons. Do you understand what I'm saying?

LB: I speak English, I just said.

Off. FC: Are you Lucie Bogaert, born January 22, 1989, in Lyon?

LB: Where? No. Not in Lyon. In Montreuil.

Off. FC: Thank you for that correction. What is the reason for your trip to the United States, Ms. Bogaert?

LB: It's a personal reason . . . Please, I have a little boy, he's ten years old, I really have to call him. They've refused to give me back my phone.

Off. FC: I'm so sorry, you'll be able to contact him very soon.

JB: I should have called him yesterday. He must be worried. Do you have children?

Off. FC: Don't get upset, Ms. Bogaert.

LB: No one's telling us anything. We've been held here for hours . . .

Off. FC: I need to ask you a number of questions.

LB: Promise me you'll get in touch with Louis. This is the number to call.

Off. FC: Yes, Ms. Bogaert. Could you tell me about your flight, and describe the turbulence? [. . .]

INTERVIEW ENDS 06/25/2021 at 7:59

EXTRACTS FROM the interview with Victor Miesel

CONFIDENTIALITY: Defense-secret / PROTOCOL: Number 42

INTERVIEW CARRIED OUT BY: Off. Fredric Kenneth White, PsyOps, SOC

DATE: 06/25/2021 / TIME: 08:20 / PLACE: Joint Base McGuire-Dix-Lakehurst

SURNAME: Miesel / FIRST NAMES: Victor Serge / CODE: June

DATE OF BIRTH: 06/03/1977 (44 years) / NATIONALITY: French

PASSENGER POSITION: Economy-class cabin 2 / SEAT: 15 H

Off. FKW: Day 2, twenty after eight. Mr. Miesel, I'm Officer Fredric Kenneth White, Special Operations Command, U.S. Army. For security reasons, with your permission, our conversation will be recorded. Are you Victor Serge Miesel, born June 3, 1977, in Lorient, France?

VSM: I was born in Lille, not in Lorient.

Off. FKW: Thank you for the correction, Mr. Miesel.

VSM: Can you explain what's going on?

Off. FKW: I'm sorry. What's the reason for your visit to the United States?

VSM: I have just won a translation prize for a novel.

Off. FKW: You're a translator? I can see that you're an author.

VSM: I . . . I also write novels, and short stories. And, anyway, translations are works of literature, translators are authors. But... Why are you asking me these questions?

Off. FKW: Could you describe your flight for me, especially the turbulence?

VSM: The plane dived down, we were shaken around a lot, the noise was terrible, we all thought we were going to die, and it all suddenly stopped. That's it.

Off. FKW: Are you working on a book at the moment?

VSM: I... I'm translating a fantasy novel by an American author, a story about teenage vampires...

Off. FKW: But are you working on a more personal book, a book by the title *The anomaly*?

VSM: *The anomaly*? No. Why do you ask?

Off. FKW: Do you ever paint, Mr. Miesel, or play a musical instrument?

VSM: No.

Off. FKW: Do you hear constant, pleasant, melodic sounds?

VSM: No.

Off. FKW: Do you have headaches, migraines?

VSM: No.

Off. FKW: Inflammation of your eyes or sinuses?

VSM: Wait... you're pulling my leg! Do you think you're in *Close Encounters of the Third Kind*?

Off. FKW: I don't understand, Mr. Miesel.

VSM: I've seen Spielberg's film twenty times, I know it by heart: you're asking me the questions that François Truffaut asks Richard Dreyfuss, almost word for word. What kind of idiot wrote this questionnaire?

Off. FKW: I don't know what you're talking about. This is the protocol followed by National Defense in this sort of situation.

VSM: What sort of situation? Do you think I met extraterrestrials? Next will you ask me if my skin itches or I have sunburn on my forehead and cheeks?

Off. FKW: Um... Yes... So, do you feel itching or burning on your face? [. . .]

INTERVIEW ENDS 96/25/2021 at 08:53

EXTRACTS FROM the interview with Femi Ahmed Kaduna, aka Slimboy

CONFIDENTIALITY: Defense-secret / PROTOCOL: Number 42

INTERVIEW CARRIED OUT BY: Off. Charles Woodworth, PsyOps, SOC

DATE: 06/25/2021 / TIME: 09:08 / PLACE: Joint Base McGuire-Dix-Lakehurst

SURNAME: Kaduna / FIRST NAMES: Femi Ahmed / CODE: June

DATE OF BIRTH: 11/19/1995 (25 years) / NATIONALITY: Nigerian

PASSENGER POSITION: Economy-class cabin 2 / SEAT: 14 D

Off. CW: Day 2, eight after nine. I'm Officer Charles Woodworth, Special Operations Command, U.S. Army. You are Femi Ahmed Kaduna, you were born November 19, 1995, in Ibadan, Nigeria.

FAK: Yes. But in Lagos. Not Ibadan.

Off. CW: What's the reason for your visit to the United States, Mr. Kaduna?

FAK: Everyone calls me Slimboy. I'm the front man in a band. The other musicians arrived yesterday. We're playing in New York tomorrow. You can't hold me here like this.

Off. CW: I understand, Mr. Kaduna.

FAK: Slimboy . . .

Off. CW: What's the date of your concert, Slimboy?

FAK: Tomorrow, like I said. At ten pm at the Mercury Lounge.

Off. CW: Which means the date is . . . ?

FAK: The twelfth of March . . .

Off. CW: I'm going to play you a song: "Yaba Girls." Put the headphones on, please.

INTERVIEW INTERRUPTED 06/25/2021 at 09:15

INTERVIEW RESUMES 06/25/2021 at 09:19

Off. CW: Do you know that song?

FAK: No. It's not bad. "Yaba Girls"? Yaba's a neighborhood in Lagos. Is that a Nigerian group? Strange, I don't recognize it.

Off. CW: Mr. Kaduna, do you hear recurring pleasant, melodic sounds?

FAK: Obviously, I'm a musician. [. . .]

INTERVIEW ENDS 06/25/2021 at 10:07

DESCARTES 2.0

FRIDAY, JUNE 25, 2021

HYPOTHESIS ROOM, McGUIRE AIR FORCE BASE

Tired people are argumentative. Exhausted people a lot less so. It's six o'clock in the morning when Adrian, Tina, and their first twenty experts settle into a command room. By seven o'clock, with the rate dictated by helicopters arriving at McGuire, there are forty of them. The sofas and interactive boards have been installed, and a soldier is plugging in the espresso machine.

It takes a minute to reveal the situation. Then come ten minutes of questions, and Tina and Adrian fall back on repeating the unbelievable: the people in this hangar are the self-same ones who already landed in the same plane one hundred six days earlier. The dialogue between Adrian Miller and Riccardo Bertoni—who's in the running for the 2021 Nobel Prize in Physics for his work on dark matter—summarizes the general mood:

"Are you jerking us around, Professor Miller?"

"If only."

At nine o'clock, when Tina Brewster-Wang is still running interdisciplinary meetings in the Hypothesis Room, Adrian comes back to talk to the task force. Meredith comes with him, as well as a tall thin guy with exuberant gray hair and steel-blue eyes. Silveria points to a conference call screen featuring familiar faces.

"Professor Miller, we have the president of the United States live, along with the secretaries of state and defense."

"This phenomenon is extraordinary, Mister President," Adrian starts the conversation, then clears his throat before adding, "but, as Arthur C. Clarke said, any sufficiently advanced technology is indistinguishable from magic. We've reached ten hypotheses, seven of them are jokes, three have caught our attention, and one of those gets support from most of us. Let's start with the simplest."

"Please, yes," says Silveria.

"The 'wormhole.' I'll let the topologist Meredith Harper explain it."

Meredith picks up a black pencil and a sheet of paper from the desk and folds the paper in two. She gets the distinct feeling she's playing the schoolroom scene from a very low-budget sci-fi movie, but hey.

"Thank you, Adrian. Let's imagine space can fold back on itself like a sheet of paper... but in a dimension that's beyond our scope, none of the three dimensions that we know. If our universe really does operate according to string theory, then hyperspace could be in ten, eleven, twenty-six dimensions. In this model, every elementary particle is a string that vibrates differently from every other, and its dimensions are folded back on themselves. Are you with me?"

The American president sits openmouthed, showing a marked resemblance to a fat grouper with a blond wig.

"Once space is folded over, then, we make a 'hole' in it..." Meredith pierces the paper with the tip of the pencil and puts her index finger into the tear, "...and we can get from one point in our three dimensional space to another very easily. That's what's called an Einstein–Rosen bridge, a Lorentz wormhole with negative mass..."

"I see," says the president, frowning.

"This respects the laws of classical physics. We're not exceeding the speed of light in our Einsteinian space. But, by opening up a vortex in hyperspace, we can travel between galaxies in a fraction of a second."

"The idea's common in fiction," says Adrian who thinks Meredith is being too abstract. "In Frank Herbert's *Dune,* and plenty of others. And it's also used in films like Christopher Nolan's *Interstellar.* Or the spaceship USS *Enterprise* in *Star Trek*..."

"*Star Trek*! I saw those, yes," the president exclaims suddenly.

"Usually—well, in a manner of speaking," Meredith continues, "usually you travel through time and space instantaneously, and there's no reason for anything to be duplicated. Here, though, we have these two planes..."

"It's like the USS *Enterprise* popped up in two points in space," Miller enthuses, "with two Captain Kirks, two Mr. Spocks, two—"

"Thank you, Professor Miller," Silveria says, "we get the picture... So, what's the second hypothesis?"

"We call it the 'photocopier' theory, we've been working on it with Brian Mitnick of the NSA."

Mitnik nods with a little curl of his lip, like a good student who's quietly proud to get a mention.

"As you know," Miller continues, "the bioprinting revolution has started..."

"Excuse me? Could you be clearer?" Silveria asks, anticipating the president's irritation and taking on the role of the simpleton himself.

"We can use 3D printing to make biological matter. Nowadays we can make a mouse-sized human heart in the space of an hour. The resolution has doubled in ten years, and printing speeds have too, as has the size of objects that can be reproduced. If we follow exponential curves in each of these areas, and if we're conservative ab—"

"I *am* conservative," interrupts the president, and Miller wonders briefly whether it's a joke.

"Then," the mathematician pursues his train of thought, "in less than two centuries, we'll be able to scan something like this plan in a fraction of a second and print it just as quickly, with atomic-level definition. But a couple of problems: One, where was the printer? Two, where did the raw materials come from to make the plane and its passengers?"

"The point is..." Meredith intervenes, "this image of a 'photocopier' presupposes an original and a copy. And with our desktop photocopiers, what comes out first is always the copy."

"I see," Silveria thinks out loud. "The 'copy' plane landed on March 10. It's the 'original' that just landed yesterday. In that case, why treat the members of the two groups differently, on the grounds that the first plane..."

"...came out of the 'photocopier' first," Meredith concludes.

"I wanted to mention the last hypothesis," Miller resumes. "It has quite broad support, but it's also the most shocking."

On the screen, the president is shaking his head, then knitting his brows to prove that he's concentrating.

"Are you talking about an act of God?" he asks.

"Um, no, Mister President... no one's raised that hypothesis," Adrian replies, surprised.

Silveria mops his brow.

"Let's hear the third theory, Miller."

"We call it the Bostrom hypothesis, which is named after Nick Bostrom, a philosopher who teaches at Oxford. At the turn of the century, he—"

"That's a long time ago," the president sighs.

"At the turn of *this* century," Miller clarifies, "in 2002, to be precise. I'll hand over to Arch Wesley from Columbia University, he's a logician."

The tall guy with the wild hair walks over to a whiteboard and writes out an equation:

$$F_{sim} = (f_p f_i N_i) / ((f_p f_i N_i) + 1)$$

and then turns to the screen with a genial smile and a good dose of excitement.

"Good morning, Mister President. Before explaining this equation, I'd like to start by talking about 'reality.' Any reality is a construction, and even a reconstruction. Our brains are sealed away in darkness and silence inside our skulls, their only access to the world is via the receptors of our eyes, ears, nose, and skin: everything that we see and feel is transmitted to the brain by electric cables, our synapses . . . our nerve cells, Mister President."

"I got that, thank you."

"Of course. And the brain reconstructs its reality. Based on the number of synapses, the brain carries out ten million billion operations a second. A lot less than a computer, but with more interconnections. But in a few years we'll be able to simulate a human brain, and that program will achieve a degree of self-awareness. Eric Drexler, the nanotechnology specialist, conceived of a system the size of a sugar lump capable of reproducing one hundred thousand human brains."

"Stop with all your billions already, I don't understand any of it," says the president, "and neither do my aides. Move along with your demonstration, please."

"Okay, Mister President. I'm going to ask you to imagine superior beings whose intelligence is to ours what ours is to an earthworm's... Our descendants, perhaps. Let's also imagine they have computers so powerful that they can re-create a virtual world in which they can bring back to life very precise replicas of their 'ancestors' and watch how they evolve in different scenarios. With a computer the size of a very small moon, the history of the human race from the birth of *Homo sapiens* could be simulated a billion times. This is the digital simulation hypothesis..."

"Like in *The Matrix*?" asks the president, baffled.

"No, Mister President," Wesley replies. "In *The Matrix* machines exploit the bodily energy of real humans, real flesh-and-blood slaves who are kept imprisoned. They make them live in a virtual world. In our hypothesis it's the other way around: we're not real living beings. We believe we are humans when we're actually just programs. Highly evolved programs, but programs all the same. As Agent Smith says in *The Matrix,* Mister President. Except that Agent Smith knows that he's a program."

"So right now I'm not sitting at a table drinking my coffee?" asks Silveria. "The things we feel, smell, and see... are simulated too? It's all fake?"

"It doesn't alter the fact that you're at this table drinking a cup of coffee, General," Wesley replies, "it only alters what the table and the coffee are made of. It would be easy: the maximal sensory bandwidth of a human isn't very wide—simulating every sound, image, touch, and smell would be only a negligible expense. Our environment itself isn't too complicated to counterfeit, it all depends on the level of detail. 'Simulated humans' wouldn't notice anomalies in their virtual environment, they'd have their houses, their cars, their dogs, even their computers while we're at it."

"Like in the British series *Black Mirror,* Mister President," Adrian whispers.

The president frowns, and Wesley keeps going.

"In fact, the more we learn about the universe, the more it seems to be based on mathematical laws."

"With all due respect, Professor," Silveria interrupts, "couldn't an experiment be used to demonstrate that you're talking garbage?"

"I'm afraid not," Wesley says, amused. "If the artificial intelligence that's simulating us states that a 'simulated human' is going to observe the world on a microscopic level, it just needs to supply that individual with enough simulated details. And in the event of any errors, it would just have to reprogram any 'virtual brains' that might have noticed an anomaly. Or maybe just rewind by a few seconds, with a sort of 'undo,' you see, and relaunch the simulation in such a way as to avoid any problems..."

"What you're describing is ridiculous," the president explodes. "I'm not some kind of Super Mario and I'm certainly not about to explain to the American people that they're programs in a virtual world."

"I understand, Mister President. But on the other hand, a plane that appears out of nowhere and is an exact copy of another plane, with all the passengers, even down to the tiniest ketchup stain on the carpeting, is also unbelievable. Will you allow me to explain the formula I wrote out?"

"Go ahead," the president spits out, furious. "But make it quick."

"I'll lay out the general idea. I'd like to demonstrate that it's fairly probable that we are some kind of simulated consciousness. There are only three possible fates for a technical civilization: it can of course die out before reaching technological maturity, as we're so magnificently demonstrating with pollution, climate change, the sixth extinction, et cetera. I personally believe that, simulated or not, we're going to die."

The president shrugs, but Wesley keeps going.

"That's not the question. Let's imagine that, in spite of everything, one civilization in a thousand doesn't destroy itself all on its own. It reaches a post-technological phase and becomes equipped with unimaginable computing powers. And then let's imagine that, among all the civilizations that have survived, only one in a thousand feels an urge to simulate its 'ancestors' or 'competitors' of those ancestors. So, that one-in-a-thousand technical civilization could single-handedly simulate, say, a billion 'virtual civilizations.' And by 'virtual civilizations,' I mean in each instance hundreds of virtual millennia during which there would be a succession of millions of virtual generations giving birth to hundreds of billions of equally virtual thinking beings. So, for example, in fifty thousand years of existence, fewer than one hundred billion *Homo sapiens* have walked the earth. To simulate *Homo sapiens*, in other words us, it's a simple question of computing power. Do you follow?"

Wesley doesn't even look at the screen, on which the president is rolling his eyes.

"Here's the important point," he continues, "a hypertechnical civilization can simulate a thousand times more 'false civilizations' than there are real ones. Which means that if we take a 'thinking brain' at random, mine or yours, it has nine hundred ninety-nine chances in a thousand of being virtual and one chance in a thousand of being a real brain. In other words, the 'I think therefore I am' of Descartes's *Discourse on Method* is obsolete. It's more like: 'I think therefore I'm almost certainly a program.' Descartes 2.0, to use the formula of a certain topologist in the group. Are you following me, Mister President?"

The president doesn't reply. Wesley studies his face, still wearing its furious, stubborn expression.

"So you see, Mister President," he concludes, "I was aware of this hypothesis, and until today, I estimated the probability that our existence was just a program on a hard drive as one in ten. With this 'anomaly,' I'm now as good as certain. Apart from anything else, it would explain the Fermi paradox: if we've never met any extraterrestrials, then it's because they haven't been programmed to exist in our simulation. I think we're even dealing with some sort of test. To take the idea further, it may be precisely because we can now envision the idea of being programs that the simulation is offering us this test. And we'd better get it right, or at least make something interesting of it."

"Why's that?" Silveria asks.

"Because if we fail, the entities running this simulation could just shut it down."

TABLE 14

FRIDAY, JUNE 25, 2021, 8:30 AM

HANGAR B, McGUIRE AIR FORCE BASE

CLOSE ENCOUNTERS, really? Now back from his interview, Victor is hovering between anger and unbridled laughter. The future feels so uncertain that the writer wants to make a cool, detailed catalog of what's happening in this hangar. Hangar, such a strange word. Like coat hanger and not far from hangman, and here they all are hanging in the balance. He's taken out his notebook and a pen, and is trying to cut himself off from the shouts and noise. He jots down: *An attempt at exhausting an improbable place*. Wait, no. Why walk in Perec's shadow? Why does he never break free of influences and tutelary figures? Why, when he's not afraid of being an impostor, is he just a little boy on a quest for accolades?

He looks at the page thoughtfully, and writes, *Airplane mode.*

"The date: March 11, 2021.

"There are lots of things in this hangar. For example: about a hundred ocher tents, a field hospital, rows of long tables, an improvised basketball court, dozens of prefab units, public toilets, metal barriers, in double rows, an 'information' center with no one to give information, an 'ecumenical space' indicated by a sign in six languages, four water fountains, and plenty more besides.

"The weather: too hot and too humid for the time of year.

"Draft inventory of everything strictly visible: firstly, the letters of the alphabet, A to E, on one wall of the hangar, a capital H for 'Hospital,' the words 'Air France' (on the cabin crew's bags), brands on passengers' clothing, 'U.S. Air Force' on the ground, 'Danger' and 'High Voltage' on electric fuse boxes. Slogans on the walls: 'Aim High, Fly-Fight-Win,' the motto of the U.S. Air Force, along with the Seventh Bomb Wing's motto 'Mors ab alto' and the recruiting line 'Do something amazing.'"

Victor writes unhurriedly, mechanically. Having read a lot, translated a lot, and seen too much nonsense beneath surface prettiness, he would think it indecent to inflict yet more inanity on the world. He really couldn't care less that extravagant prose emerges from the simple "displacement of a pen on the page," he doesn't believe he is "all-powerful in the face of every sentence," he has no intention of "closing his eyelids to keep his eyes open," and—in this soulless place—he certainly won't "withdraw from the world to mark it with his own turmoil." Besides, he doesn't trust metaphors. The Trojan War must have started like that. Still, he knows that it would take only one of his sentences being more intelligent than he is for this miracle to make a writer of him.

Victor watches all these disparate lives, all these shifting anxieties in the outsized petri dish of the hangar—it really is a funny word—but can't decide on which one to focus his attention. He surrenders to the fascination of lives other than his own. He'd like to choose one, to find the right words to describe this creature, and succeed in believing that he has come close enough to it not to betray it. Then move on to another. And another. Three characters, seven, twenty? How many simultaneous stories would a reader consent to follow?

There are a few other passengers at the same table as him, number 14, and also the captain. The man reminds Victor of his father. The same gray-green eyes, the same aquiline nose, the same long inlets at his temples, which will end up winning their battle with the thick gray hair, the powerful torso. The writer instinctively reaches into his pocket, feels the smooth edges of the red brick. Victor also has a photograph of his late father in his wallet, a picture taken from an album, from the days when there were albums, when too many photos hadn't yet killed photos. The man in the photograph is twenty years old, with a swaggering smile and a direct expression. He once laughed and told his son, "I was young in those days, I don't know when everything started to slide." Yes, in the dawn light, Captain Markle looks like this father whom Victor himself resembles so little.

Only the day before, his uniform was still proving a draw for the most frightened, who were reassured by that Air France blue, and the most infuriated, looking for someone to blame. But he's no longer the object of all hostilities. Seeing him sharing in the general exasperation, everyone eventually acknowledged that he was benefiting from no favorable treatment and had access to no privileged information. In order to demonstrate this, or simply for the sake of comfort, he's changed into a business suit. On the ground, David Markle is no longer the one and only master after God, but just a nice-enough guy you might end up feeling sorry for, a General Dumouriez abandoned by his troops, but a friendlier version, in all fairness. This morning, along with a dozen other passengers and with no explanation, he was made to take a battery of medical tests.

Also at table 14 is the tall Black man with the beautiful, deep, and melancholy eyes. His short-cropped hair follows geometric patterns worthy of the Alhambra's tessellations. He says "johnny" for journey, "yuwa" for you are, and "vishon" for vision: a Nigerian singer and guitarist. He may well have a concert tomorrow evening somewhere in Manhattan, he's understood that there's no point going on about it and he too has stopped making a fuss. But he has managed to reclaim his twelve-string Taylor that had been kept in a locker in the cabin, and he's playing it as he composes a song with a gentle rhythm.

I remember your eyes of yesterday

The way you smiled in a dazzling way

The guitar makes a rich, rounded sound, his voice is husky and warm. A slim boy, the professional name he's given himself suits him well. He smiles at Victor.

"It's a long time since I sang acoustically, with no effects."

He strums a chord and keeps going:

But beautiful men in uniform forbid you . . .

"Beautiful men in uniform?" Victor asks, pointing to the soldiers guarding the doors.

"Yes. That's most likely going to be my title."

And he continues, almost whispering:

The way to the light, way to the light, way to the light.

There's a murmuring from the far end of the table, "'Tis but thy name that is my enemy," and Victor immediately recognizes Shakespeare. "Thou art thyself, though not a Montague."

Juliet Capulet is here; she's little more than a girl, rehearsing her lines:

What's Montague? It is nor hand, nor foot,
Nor arm, nor face, nor any other part
Belonging to a man. O, be some other name!
What's in a name? That which we call a rose,
By any other word would smell as sweet.
So Romeo would, were he not Romeo called,
Retain that dear perfection which he owes
Without that title...

She is intense, even in the way she hesitates, and knows that she'll be able to cry when she needs to. The audition is next week, she tells Victor. They'll have to let us out once they've done their tests, they are doing tests on us, aren't they? You can't just hold people like this, this is a free country, I mean there are laws.

"Yes, there are laws," says a young woman with delicate features and black skin, her hair scooped back by a silver barrette. The lawyer has gathered fifty signatures for a class action covering half a dozen complaints—arbitrary arrest, discretionary detention, illegal confiscation of property, refused access to a legal advisor for more than forty-eight hours, etc. How to bill each passing minute when she can't get hold of her office? How to put a figure on her own pain when she can't hear Aby's voice and imagines he's worried out of his mind? Wouldn't putting a price of just two thousand dollars per person per day on the damages and considerations of detention be a gift to the U.S. Air Force and the government?

How does the story go again? Oh yes. The devil comes into a lawyer's office and says, "Hello, I'm the devil. I have a deal for you." "I'm listening," says the lawyer. "I'm going to make you the richest lawyer in the world. In exchange, will you give me your soul, your parents' souls, your children's souls, and the souls of your five best friends?" The lawyer looks at him in amazement and says, "Okay. What's the catch?"

The young woman makes a face. No, really, she's not the despicable man in the joke. But in this environment, you have to kick them hard in the wallet, it's the only thing they understand. She scrounges yet another sheet of paper and a colored felt pen from a little girl and starts writing yet another letter. The child's mother, a blond woman, seems unsure.

"My husband works for the army, I wouldn't want to make any trouble for him."

"That definitely wouldn't happen, ma'am. Didn't you tell me your husband was a war hero, that he was wounded in combat? That makes him untouchable, and plus, by signing this class action, you'll make it impossible for the army to intimidate him or threaten him. It would be an obstacle too far for justice. We're stronger if we're united. We can't stay locked in here any longer. You have two children with you, right? There will be significant psychological damage, especially for them."

"Psychological damage?" The woman picks up on these words.

She looks over at her little boy, who's given up asking for his tablet and has fallen asleep at the table, then at her daughter, who's scribbling strange dark figures with terrifying, long, thin limbs, figures made up of endlessly crossed-out black lines.

Victor can't help noticing that, here at table 14, the most significant person is a young woman. Thirtyish, brown hair, slim as a reed—and he immediately hates himself for the cliché. She reminds him of that other woman he met a few years ago at the translation conference, the one who transfixed him and whom he's never seen again. Nostalgia is a scoundrel. It allows us to believe life has some meaning. Victor sits down next to her, irresistibly drawn: it is characteristic of attraction to want to constantly reduce distances.

He tries to exchange a few words. No, she's like everyone else, she doesn't know anything, she gives a weary pout and goes back to her book. She's with someone: an elegant sixty-something man who can't be her father, Victor has surmised from the man's attentive thoughtfulness, and also from his expression when he—Victor—tried to engage her in conversation. A hint of feral anxiety that he didn't succeed in hiding. The two men introduce themselves. An architect. Victor knows his name, but not his work. That world of concrete and glass bores him. Sometimes, during a translation, a technical term—"architrave" or "clapboard," perhaps—appears; he has to research it and then immediately forgets it. Victor studies him, and although he doesn't think him ugly, he can already see the old man breaking through his soft-skinned hands and his lined brow. He is most likely only as old as she makes him. What does she see in him? What can he know about a woman's desire for a man?

The architect stands up, asks the young woman whether she'd like a coffee, because the army have now set up dispensing-type machines. She shakes her head, and he walks away, slowly. Victor guesses that this is a delicacy on his part, a way to give her some space. The claustrophobic situation is oppressive enough without him stifling her with his attentions.

Oh look, the book she's leafing through is by Coetzee. Victor hasn't read it.

Is it any good? Victor asks. What? The Coetzee? Yes, she says, but not as good as *Disgrace*. I agree, Victor replies, that's his best, isn't it? A masterpiece, she confirms, and turns away. Victor realizes that he's bothering her, he doesn't persist, goes back to his notebook, and, without irony, writes the word "disgrace."

E PUR, SI MUOVE

SATURDAY, JUNE 26, 2021, 9:30 AM

SITUATION ROOM, THE WHITE HOUSE,

WASHINGTON, DC

JAMY PUDLOWSKI and her team are in the underground crisis room at the White House, where they have brought together a dozen male individuals all convinced that, thanks be to God, they were born into the right religion: two cardinals; two rabbis—one Orthodox, one Reform; an Eastern Orthodox priest; a Lutheran pastor; another Baptist; a Mormon leader; three learned Muslims, one each representing Sunnism, Salafism, and Shiism; a Vajrayana Buddhist monk, and a Mahayana one. And there's a lot of coffee on the table, even though Pudlowski managed the feat of sleeping during her forty-minute helicopter flight.

The head of Psychological Operations is worried. The direct route hates a pothole, and the obscure professes hatred of the inexplicable. The immutability of the law keeps crashing up against the constantly shifting cosmos and the advancement of knowledge. Where in the Torah, the New Testament, the Koran, or any other text can anyone identify the least sentence, ambiguous sura, or obscure verse that predicts or justifies a plane looming out of the azure skies and turning out to be in every way identical to one that landed three months earlier?

When the peoples of the Americas discovered—at their cost—the existence of Christopher Columbus, and later the swarms of conquistadors whose forerunner he was, the Catholic Church must have found some explanation for their existence in their texts. Sure enough, according to Paul, the Gospel had been "heard to the ends of the earth," but how the devil did Noah's three sons—Shem, Ham, and Japheth—populate the whole world, what route did those damn boys take to spawn as far afield as the West Indies? Were these new men the lost tribes of Israel, the very ones cited in the fourth book of Esdras, the apocryphal apocalypse mentioned by Tertullian? In the end someone came up with a formula in John's Gospel to fit the bill: Jesus had "other sheep that are not of this fold."

Jamy Pudlowski is Roman Catholic by her father and Jewish by her mother. In January 1960, a female Ashkenazi doctor from Boston fell madly in love with a goy police officer from Baltimore, and nothing went smoothly from there. Little Jamy grew up between two sets of grandparents who didn't have a kind word for each other, German Jews on her mother's side, Polish Catholics on her father's, and their serial disputes shaped a questioning child. From doubting, Jamy moved on to skeptical, before becoming downright intractable about any form of religious conviction. Still, she was baptized—in secret—by her Pudlowski grandparents, but refused to take her first communion, or to have a bat mitzvah the following year. She has hardly any strong political convictions either, though she votes Democrat anyway.

During the interview that was meant to open the doors to PsyOps for her, the woman in charge of recruitment had asked Jamy her religion, to which the psychologist had replied: "I don't have one." The woman had pursued the point. "So you're an atheist then," she'd asked, fiddling with her pen as if she had a box to check on an imaginary questionnaire. Jamy Pudlowski had shrugged, "I don't give a damn. To me God is like bridge—I never think about it. So I don't define myself by the fact that I don't give a damn about bridge, nor do I align myself with people who talk about the fact that they too couldn't give a damn about bridge." Her answer had hit home. Six years later, at not yet forty, she was running a department of Psychological Operations at the FBI, before then taking over the same role at SOC while maintaining close links to her former employer.

Jamy Pudlowski has specialized in religious issues, and she's learned to recognize each of the men present in this room today. Being the only representative of her sex, naturally Pudlowski starts by saying, "Ladies and gentlemen..." in the hope that one of them will pick up on the irony, but no, of course not, so she points to the big screen on which the president appears, surrounded by the same people as he was the day before, but also by his spiritual advisors.

"Mister President, obviously please speak up whenever you'd like to. Thank you, everyone, for being here. I'm Jamy Pudlowski, senior officer of Special Operations Command of the U.S. Army. You're here because you all represent the overwhelming majority of religions practiced on United States territory."

Pudlowski then introduces each prelate in the room, not allowing any of them time to complain that they were woken at dawn, hastily expedited to the White House, and brought to this crisis room.

"I'm going to explain a situation to all of you, and then formulate a number of simple questions. I'm not asking you for ethical answers, but theological ones. I'll clarify what I mean. You know that some laboratories can now produce organic matter with 3D printing, using stem cells to generate artificial biological structures such as muscles or hearts, that won't risk being rejected by patients. And—"

"Yes, we've already reached a unanimous agreement," the Orthodox rabbi interrupts. "Including with our Catholic and Muslim friends."

The cardinals nod, and the Salafist imam agrees, "'The committee of the Islamic Fiqh Academy authorizes genetic engineering on condition that it saves lives."

"Thank you, gentlemen. I'm going to ask you to imagine that a person could be completely duplicated."

"What do you mean by completely?" the Lutheran asks.

"Reproduced with infinitesimal precision. This new individual has the same genetic code as the original, but it goes further than that."

"Like a perfect carbon copy, you mean?" asks the Mormon leader.

"Yes," Pudlowski smiles, "a carbon copy."

"Is this speculative?" asks one of the Buddhists with an Eastern gentleness that borders on cliché.

The head of Psychological Operations pauses at some length; she wants to take her time.

"No, my question isn't theoretical. We have taken an individual in for questioning who has turned out to be indistinguishable from another person, whom he, in fact, claims to be. Their meeting has taken place. It was mind-blowing."

"Like a twin?"

"No . . . They both have the same personality and the same memories, so much so that they're both convinced they're the original. Their two brains are coded in the same way, on a chemical and electrical level, on an atomic level."

There's a restless ripple around the room. The words "blasphemy" and "scandal" are uttered, along with others that are more scatological than theological.

"Who's to blame for this disgrace?" the Baptist asks, summarizing the mood.

"We don't know," Jamy Pudlowski replies. "We're not asking your ethical opinions. But these individuals do exist."

"Was it Google?" asks a cardinal heatedly. "They've been—"

"No, Your Eminence, it wasn't Google."

"But ma'am," the prelate retorts, "Google bought shares in an Israeli 3D printing company and—"

"No, Your Eminence, it's not them. My first question would be: According to law, is this . . . being a divine creation?"

Pudlowski isn't at a loss for words, her rhetorical hesitation is intended to encourage discussion: there's confusion around the table, and the Salafist is the first to lean toward his mic.

"Allah gave man and animals the gift of procreation, and Allah gave man reason, which allows him to invent these objects. But the Prophet—peace and Allah's blessings be upon him—also says in the Pilgrimage: 'O humankind! A parable is struck, so pay heed to it: those whom, apart from God, you deify and invoke will never be able to create even a fly, even if all of them were to come together to do so.' That's what the parable says: man cannot create life, even the life of a fly."

"I understand, but we're dealing with much more than a fly here, dear friends," Jamy Pudlowski sets the record straight.

The Sunnite gets to his feet and says, "In the hadith of Sahih al Bukhari, Abu Sa'id al-Khudri—may Allah be satisfied with his works—reports that the Prophet—peace and Allah's blessings be upon him—said, 'There is no being created, except that Allah created it.' That's what matters."

"So, according to you, these beings were created by God."

"I won't repeat the parable of the fly," the Salafist replies. "If Allah didn't want this being to be created, he would not have allowed it to exist."

"I see," Pudlowski says, "I see..."

Then she falls silent, waiting in vain for something from the Catholics or Protestants. Meanwhile the traditional rabbi hesitates for a moment before launching into his opinion:

"There *are* creation myths in the Talmud. It says in the Sanhedrin tractate that Rava—blessings be on him—created a man using magical powers. The tractate doesn't say who..."

"Sorry, but who is Rava?" asks Pudlowski.

"He was a rabbi of the fourth generation... Either way, Rava sent the man he created to Rabbi Zera, who asked him a question, but when the man gave no answer, Rabbi Zera deduced that he wasn't created by God, that he was a golem, and he ordered him to return to dust."

"In other versions," the Reform rabbi adds, "the man that Rava created can talk, but can't reproduce. Later in the Sanhedrin it also says that Rav Hanina and Rav Oshaya create a sheep and then eat it... none of it's very clear... it must be read as a parable. To show man's evanescence and God's omnipotence."

"But, please, let's get back to the Koran," the Shiite sighs. "The Arabic word for create, *khalaqa,* that is used in the Koran means 'made from nothing,' and this—we all agree—is something that only Allah can do. Even your rabbi Rava uses earth as his starting point. But in this case that you've described to us, ma'am, this... being... wasn't created from nothing, was it?"

"Almost certainly not," replies the woman from the SOC. "But we know nothing about the... the process of... fabrication."

The Reform rabbi makes the most of a brief silence to interject.

"We must remember Maimonides's teachings," he says. "God gave man his soul, gave him *nephesh*, but if God gave man laws and precepts, then it's because man has free will, he has good tendencies and bad."

"I don't see the connection between free will and what we're discussing," the Orthodox rabbi says irritably. "We're being asked for a theological stance and of course you—completely off topic, as usual—can't resist trotting out your Maimonides!"

"Well, I like that! I'm not 'trotting out' my Maimonides!"

"Please," Pudlowski soothes, "please understand me: I'm asking you this question about creation because I categorically wouldn't want this man to be said to have been created by Satan."

"Satan doesn't create!" the Salafist says indignantly.

"Absolutely not!" agrees the Orthodox rabbi, and the two Protestants shake their heads.

"God created Satan," says one of the cardinals, making a sketchy sign of the cross. "He created him in order to tempt men, and in the Garden of Eden, Satan incarnated himself as the serpent, the wiliest of God's creatures. But Satan wouldn't be able to create."

"Ah," Pudlowski says naively. "And yet I feel like I've already heard the words 'spawn of Satan.'"

"That's just an abuse of language, a popular vulgate," the Salafist says with a smile, while the Shiite, at the far end of the table, sniggers and spits an indignant question: "A vulgate? But I seem to remember your theologian Muhammad Al-Munajjid described Mickey Mouse as the 'spawn of Satan.'"

"Mickey Mouse?" pipes up the president of the United States, who hadn't yet said a word.

"Al-Munajjid is not 'our' theologian, as you call him," sighs the Salafist. "He's simply a respected scholar. His precise expression was 'soldier of Satan,' and his words were misrepresented by infidels and apostates to poke fun at Islam."

"He did announce a fatwa against Mickey Mouse, though," the Shiite continues ironically. "And Al-Munajjid has nothing against slavery, or against sexual relations with slaves."

"That is *ijma* and therefore the opinion of Muslim scholars," the Salafist retorts with some annoyance. "Muhammad Al-Munajjid is simply repeating it and I—"

"Ha! Along with the fact that homosexuals can be burned?" the Lutheran asks.

"Hmm," says the Reform rabbi, rolling his eyes. "Need I remind you what Luther said about homosexuals?"

"Gentlemen, gentlemen," Pudlowski intervenes authoritatively. "We're getting away from the subject. I consider the first question to have been dealt with: our man is not a creature of the devil. Okay?"

"He is a creature of God alone, and we're all in agreement," the Orthodox rabbi says in a pacifying tone.

The Buddhist monks have been silent so far, but one of them, infuriated, now speaks.

"On the subject of your 'creatures of God' ... We've let you argue it out, but the origin of the world is only ever relative. It's an endless cycle, with the universe fluctuating between different states: periods of creation, which are Brahma's privilege, times of stability when Vishnu dominates, and periods when Shiva destroys everything, and this may happen quickly or slowly. And then everything can begin again. To us, your question has no meaning of any kind. All sentient beings have the presence of Buddha in them and can achieve enlightenment. You won't ever see Buddhists screaming at 'spawn of Satan.' We welcome this new creature. And, as ever, we send a message of peace."

"A very fine message of peace, I have to say," replies the Sunnite, "when people of your faith are massacring our Rohingya brothers in Myanmar, under the banner of that fanatic, Wirathu..."

"But... that's not my Buddhism... And, first of all, who destroyed the Buddhas of Bamiyan? Answer me that. And in Sri Lanka who—"

"Please," Pudlowski interrupts gently. "I know you all mean well, but—much to my regret—we can't solve the problems of the planet in this room. This man is therefore a creature of God or a creature who feels the presence of Buddha. That's something we've established. I have another request, about a concept: the soul."

"The soul?" the Sunnite asks.

"Yes. I can't define it for you, but it's an essential principle, isn't it?

"It's essential, but complicated," says the Sunnite. "May I expand on that?"

"I'm listening..." Pudlowski sighs.

THE MEETING LASTS two hours, two hours at the end of which nothing has been settled, and a tired Jamy Pudlowski brings it to a close. Allowing a week, a month even, would resolve nothing.

"Gentlemen, please. Can we agree on a common position? And even draft a declaration, something as unanimous as possible, and of course temporary, but one that would protect this person from any criminal act inspired by a misreading of sacred texts?"

"That's the best solution," says one of the Buddhists.

"Absolutely," agrees the Reform rabbi. "We can cite the fine words from Leviticus nineteen, verse eighteen, where God commands us to love our neighbor as ourselves."

"Or the words of the Gospel of John, chapter thirteen, verse thirty-four," says the Lutheran pastor, "when Jesus tells his disciples to love one another."

The Salafist leans forward and concludes, "'Do it well,' said the Prophet—peace and Allah's blessings be upon him. 'Allah loves those who do good.' And if we welcome these creatures without tormenting them, we cannot be doing evil."

"Good," says Jamy Pudlowski. "Thank you all. I owe it to you to give you a significant piece of information: we're not dealing with just one 'duplicated' being, but several. Two hundred forty-three to be precise."

"Two hundred forty-three?"

She doesn't allow time for them to react before adding, "My friends, we will meet again tomorrow morning, and you will then be supplied with all the details. In any event, I don't imagine this changes anything fundamental about the debate. I will draft a report of this meeting, and will submit to each of you an ecumenical decision that transcends individual religions."

Pudlowski thanks each participant at length, then takes her leave. Once in the helicopter returning her to the air base, she calls Adrian Miller.

"So," asks the mathematician, "did it go well?"

"Pretty well," Pudlowski sighs. "Pretty well."

A phone vibrates. A text from the POTUS.

"Great job!" the president writes.

HANGAR

SATURDAY, JUNE 26, 2021

HANGAR B, McGUIRE AIR FORCE BASE

"BUT THEY'RE DANCING!" exclaims Silveria from high up on the platform.

In the northern corner, a space has been cleared between the tables, and, yes, the passengers are dancing. Teenagers and children, but not exclusively the young, are jigging to Ed Sheeran's "So Tired of Being Me," midway between R and B and dancehall, but Silveria is far from an expert, and neither Pudlowski nor Mitnick, who are standing beside him, is in a position to offer help.

It's such a long time since he danced. Two years ago, with his daughter, when they were first on the floor at her wedding? Maybe. They danced to Louis Armstrong that day, with him crammed into his suit and her spilling exuberantly out of her white dress. Silveria was just back from Afghanistan; he laughed as he twirled around with Gina, and Gina laughed as she twirled in her father's arms, and twirling along beside them were all the disgusting images of war inside his head. Even with his eyes closed, even after three beers, even wrapped in the sweetness of his daughter's fruity perfume, Silveria's world was a less and less *wonderful* one. In spite of everything, as he waltzed with her, driving away the blood and the dust and the desert, he was spitting in the face of every demon in hell.

"Who let them put music on?" Silveria asks peevishly.

"It's kind of a good idea," says Jamy Pudlowski. "We're already screening movies for the children, and we're going to hand out board games, chess, and playing cards. It should help reduce tension."

"Let them dance, then."

The general looks at the clock: it's two in the afternoon, and he's as exhausted as if it were nightfall. From the platform where he's standing, the hangar has been transformed into a village of tents in sand camouflage and white prefabricated units, a temporary settlement that smells of rancid fat and disinfectant. Military logistics are doing their best to adapt to these ill-disciplined civilians. The soldiers know the bare minimum, which is as good as saying nothing, and their only instruction is not to give any clue as to the date. Most of them are firmly guarding the doors, but some have been given permission to take care of the children. Silveria has brought in three times as many troops, and thinking his men jumpy, has replaced their pistols with Tasers.

Yes, Patrick Silveria is tired, yet he's gliding in a rare state of fulfillment. For the first time in his life, he's asking himself questions that don't revolve around why he ended up becoming General Silveria, recipient of the Air Force Cross, the Purple Heart, and the Legion of Merit. As a child he'd wanted to be a doctor to cure his dying mother; as a teenager he'd tried to become an actor, and then he started studying theoretical physics. But the wind kept changing against him. He hadn't managed to secure a scholarship for Lawrence University, his father had been diagnosed with the leukemia that killed him, and the beautiful Myra had left Patrick for an old man of thirty-five. So out of defiance, he had taken and passed the entrance exam for West Point, becoming the only person in his year to not have a single military connection in his family. Ever since, he has constantly explored what people call fate: what if, aged eighteen, he'd been given the supporting role in that police drama on Broadway; what if Hannah hadn't gotten pregnant so quickly; what if, during the April offensive in 2003, he hadn't managed to bring down that bastard MiG-25 over Mosul? He now has his answer: this fateful path existed only so that one day, from high up on a steel platform in a Lockheed Galaxy hangar, he could stand surrounded by Nobel Prize winners, resting his hands on the red lead–painted guardrail, looking out over this crowd of people who have appeared from nowhere.

"I'm heading down into the lion's den," Silveria says decisively.

"There were the beginnings of a riot earlier," says Pudlowski. "They'll tear you apart..."

"Maybe that's what I want."

"And I nearly forgot," says Mitnick, "there's a lawyer among the passengers...Joanna Woods. I'm no legal expert, but her file looks serious, even if it is a little...colorful."

"Colorful?" Silveria asks, surprised.

"She's writing her requests on the coloring paper we've given the kids, and using their felt pens too."

The general sighs. A good dozen lawyer jokes come to his mind, including an excellent one about the difference between a tick and a lawyer, but he keeps them to himself. They wouldn't even relax the atmosphere.

"If you feel like negotiating, Miss Woods is in the first row, table 14, with the captain."

Silveria just stares at Mitnick in amazement.

"General Silveria," Mitnick continues, "if you looked at your tablet a little more often, you'd know that we've set up hundreds of high-definition surveillance cameras on the walls, and just as many directional mics. There are also various interfaces: facial recognition and speech analysis in every language, complete with simultaneous translation. Click on a passenger's name, and the script comes up live. The bouquets of dried flowers on the tables are miracles of electronics. The tents are listening devices too."

"Congratulations. Nothing in the bathrooms while you were at it?"

"We discussed it, but in the end no."

Not one feature of Mitnick's face moved. Silveria wonders whether he has a deadpan sense of humor or is being utterly serious.

"Seeing as you're so hot on this, Mitnick, you must have an image of the passenger who ran away..."

"No. We didn't install the cameras and mics till yesterday morning. He'd already escaped. We know that he boarded the flight in Paris under the name Michaël Weber. It's a cloned identity, he was traveling with an Australian passport, but that Michaël Weber lives on the Gold Coast, he's a school bus driver and he's never left his town. We wanted to take fingerprints from his seat on the Boeing, but it's made of fabric. If we eliminate the DNA of all the other passengers, we still have to consider the DNA of staff who prepared the meal trays. Imagine, in spite of all this, that we succeed in identifying his: at best we would know the color of his skin, eyes, and hair, and in a pinch whether he's susceptible to various diseases, but we couldn't exactly create a profile and go looking for him on social media. We shouldn't wait for a miracle."

"And images from the plane?"

"He reserved seat 30 E, which isn't in range of any of the security cameras, and even during the boarding process we can't find a single shot that shows his face. We interviewed the people near him in the cabin, but no one really noticed him. We've had an Identi-Kit image made of him: thick glasses, long hair, a moustache—details that draw the eye and deflect it from what really matters. And he wore his hood up during the flight."

"Surveillance images from Charles de Gaulle Airport?"

"It was back in March: most of them have been wiped. On the few that are left, we can't see anything at all. With this level of invisibility, we must be dealing with a professional."

"And the breakout from the hangar?"

"He forced a door during the little panic created by the beginnings of a fire, which he probably started. No prints on the handle or the iron bar he used. At midday the pickup he stole was found in New York, burned out. A pro, like I said."

"Keep looking. Even an ant leaves a trace."

"A winged ant doesn't really, though," Mitnick countered with a grimace.

MEREDITH'S QUESTIONS

SATURDAY, JUNE 26, 2021, 7:30 AM

McGUIRE AIR FORCE BASE

"I REFUSE TO BE a program," Meredith rants. "Adrian, if that theory is the right one, then we're living a sort of cave allegory, but to the power of *n*. And it's unbearable! I could just about cope with the fact that we only have access to a surface reality, with no hope of achieving real consciousness, but for that surface itself to be an illusion, it's enough to make you top yourself."

"I don't know that 'topping yourself,' as you call it, is appropriate for a program," Adrian says in measured tones, handing her the third coffee of the morning.

But Meredith is furious, completely beside herself, even though it's probably an undesirable side effect of the modafinil that she's taking every six hours to stop her from sleeping. Adrian is confronted with a tide of questions to which she doesn't appear to want answers. She leaves nothing out.

"Is the fact that I don't even like coffee written into my program? And my hangover yesterday, when I became a tequila sponge, was that simulated too? If a program can feel desire, can love, and can be hurt, what are the algorithms for desire, love, and pain? Am I programmed to be angry when I realize I'm a program? Do I have free will, despite all this? Is everything planned, programmed, and inevitable? What dose of chaos is included in the simulation? *Is* there even any chaos? Is there no way of proving that, actually no, phew, we're *not* in a simulation?"

Tricky, Adrian wants to reply, to find an experiment that would invalidate the hypothesis, given that the simulation would be clever enough to provide a result that proved the opposite. And yet they've all been doggedly trying to think of an experiment for thirty hours now. The astrophysicists in particular have been attempting to watch the behavior of the highest-energy cosmic rays. They believe it would be impossible, simply by applying the "real" laws of physics, to simulate them one hundred percent accurately. Anomalies in their behavior could prove that reality isn't real. For now, it's not achieving anything.

Adrian loathes this idea of a simulation, bearing in mind that he adopted Karl Popper as the leading light of his epistemology studies—the stalwart Popper, who felt a theory could be attributed no scientific weight if there was nothing to refute it . . . But Adrian can look at this question from every angle as much as he likes: all things being equal, the simplest explanation is often the right one. The simplest but the most uncomfortable: this plane's appearance can't be a bungle in the simulation—it would have been so easy to "erase" it, to rewind by a few seconds. No, it's obviously a test: How will billions of virtual individuals react when confronted with their own virtuality?

But Adrian doesn't have time to put forward his arguments, because Meredith is off again.

"Are we living in a time that's just an illusion, where every apparent century actually lasts only a fraction of a second in the processor of a gigantic computer? And what does that make death, other than a simple 'end' written on a line of code?

"Did Hitler and the Holocaust exist only in our simulation or in some of the others too, were six million Jewish programs killed by thousands of Nazi programs? Are some programs configured to be rapists? Surely paranoid programs are a tad more discerning than the rest? And isn't this bonkers hypothesis the most elaborate conspiracy theory devised by the most enormous imaginable conspiracy?

"How perverse do you have to be to design programs simulating such stupid beings and others simulating individuals far too intelligent not to suffer from being surrounded by the first category, and programs simulating musicians and others, artists, and still others, writers, who write books read by yet more programs? Or books that nobody reads, for that matter? Who designed the programs for Moses, Homer, Mozart, and Einstein, and why are there so many programs with no particular qualities, which shuffle through their electronic existence not adding anything—or only very little—to the complexity of the simulation?

"Or maybe, or maybe," Meredith gets even more irate, "are we simulations of a Cro-Magnon world devised by Neanderthals, the race of *sapiens* who, contrary to popular belief, were the ones who *actually* succeeded fifty thousand years ago? And now they want to see what those hyperaggressive African primates could have achieved if the poor things hadn't been wiped out? Well, it worked, they have their answer now, Cro-Magnon humans are so irretrievably moronic that they've ravaged their virtual environment, destroyed their forests and polluted their oceans, reproduced themselves beyond all reason, burned up all the fossil fuels, and basically the whole species will die of heat and stupidity in less than fifty more simulated years. Or hang on, this isn't any better or worse, but what if we were a simulation set up by the descendants of the dinosaurs, who were never killed off by a meteor, and they're having a laugh watching a world run by mammals? Or are we living in some faked carbon biology conceived around a double helix of DNA in a world simulated by extraterrestrials whose life-form is based on a triple helix of sulfur atoms? And could we even, could we even be simulated by other beings who themselves are no less simulated in a bigger simulation, and all these simulated worlds slot into each other like nesting tables?

"Hey, what do you think, Adrian,"—at this point Meredith is choking with rage—"here's another idea that's not as ridiculous as all that: Is there a non-afterlife after our non-death? That's true, actually, isn't it? What would it cost them—if they're *so* superior to us and *so* brilliant—to add phony heavens to their simulation as compensation for all those compliant and deserving little programs who submitted to the diktats of every faith? Why wouldn't they have come up with a Paradise for good Muslim programs who always eat halal food and piously turn toward Mecca to pray to Allah five times a day? A heaven for Catholic programs who went to confession every Sunday? And a heaven for the followers of Tlaloc, the Aztec god of water, all those victims sacrificed at the top of pyramids who come back to Earth, metamorphosed into butterflies?

"And what if there were also thousands of hells, for the shameful heretical, faithless, or free-thinking programs, a thousand Gehennas where these emancipated individuals would be burned mercilessly in unending virtual torment, attacked by red demons and devoured by monsters with ferocious jaws? And better still, why wouldn't these genius practical jokers have imagined that every religious program was praying to the wrong god? And once they die—surprise, surprise, mate—are you a Baptist/Buddhist/Jew/Muslim? You should have been a Mormon, you moron! Come on then, off to hell with the lot of you!

"I mean, after all, the Aztec gods created the world several times, and destroyed it several times: Ocelotonatiuh had humans eaten up by jaguars, Ehecatonatiuh transformed them into monkeys, Quiauhtonatiuh buried them under a flood of fire, and Atonatiuh drowned them and turned them into fish."

These are the questions Meredith is pondering, or perhaps her program is, having dredged up all that remembered information about Aztec gods. Besides, without wishing to denigrate monotheism, the malfunctions of this world are much better explained by endless conflict between gods, plural.

MEREDITH SUDDENLY feels like having a coffee, even though she doesn't like it; she battles with the recalcitrant machine—the fuckwits, they even programed faulty machines in their simulation—and when the frothy black liquid finally starts to flow, she turns to the silent Adrian.

He gazes at her with a vermillion enchantment in his heart. He really does like everything about her, her pink cheeks when she gets carried away, that bead of sweat on the tip of her nose, and the way she wears baggy shirts over her extremely slim body. Perhaps all this enthusiasm for her is also programmed? He doesn't give a damn. Maybe life begins the moment we know we don't have one.

What difference would it make for them, after all? Simulated or not, we all live, feel, love, suffer, create, and die, each leaving our own tiny trace in the simulation. What point is there in knowing? We should always favor mystery over science. Ignorance is a good traveling companion, and the truth never produces happiness. We might as well be simulated and happy.

Meredith drinks a mouthful of bitter coffee and smiles.

"Thanks for arranging for me to be here, Adrian. My anger's in direct proportion to the intensity of what we're going through. I'm over the moon to be on board, and with you."

The English topologist bursts out laughing, and at this precise moment, she too couldn't give a damn about being simulated, and neither is her happiness a side effect of modafinil. She starts singing to the tune of "(I Can't Get No) Satisfaction":

I can't be no simulation
No, no, no
'Cause I cry and I cry and I cry!
I can't be no, no, no

She dances and spins to the Stones' melody, and because Adrian is still awkward and silent, brimming with emotion, she takes his hands and pulls him along with her.

"Come on, Adrian, don't stand there like a lemon! *I can't be no simulation!*"

It's fantastic, thinks Adrian, it's fantastic how much I like this woman.

In a flash, he draws her to him, he's about to smother her in his arms, light-headed with tenderness and longing, about to kiss her, when General Silveria comes into the room.

"Professor Miller," the general says, not in the least embarrassed, "there's a helicopter waiting for you on the tarmac. You're leaving for the White House right now. The president's expecting you."

A FEW PRESIDENTS

SATURDAY, JUNE 26, 2021, 11:00 AM

THE WEST WING, THE WHITE HOUSE, WASHINGTON, DC

THE PRESIDENT is pacing around the Oval Office in a state of volcanic excitement, his eyes pinned on the sunbeams on the thick beige carpet. He does a full counterclockwise circuit of the room, under the indifferent gaze of a Winston Churchill in bust form, although the Washington framed above the fireplace seems hardly any more attentive.

There are four people waiting in chairs, facing the presidential desk: the special advisor, the secretary of state, a scientific advisor, and lastly Adrian Miller, captivated by the majestic eagle in a panel of the *Resolute* desk, Adrian, to whom the head of protocol gave a clean, perfumed white shirt as soon as he arrived: And we'll take the opportunity to give your T-shirt a quick wash, Professor Miller.

"I don't feel like calling that little French asshole," the president sulks, going back to sit down.

"We're holding sixty-seven French nationals," says the special advisor. "And it's an Air France flight. We're going to have to call him, Mister Pre—"

"No and no. First, I'm going to call Jinping. How many Chinese do we have?"

"About twenty, Mister President. But we'll call the French president right after."

"Yes, we'll see. Jennifer, pass me China. And Professor Muller, in a few minutes I'll put you on the line to Jinping, right?"

The President turns to Adrian Miller, who reminds him vaguely of that actor in *Forrest Gump*, what was his name again? But with something more teenaged about him.

Adrian doesn't reply. The exhaustion of sleepless nights is taking its toll, and he's a little dazed to realize, this is nuts, it's nuts, I'm in the Oval Office with the president, I'm going to talk to the Chinese president, and I'm wearing a white shirt.

"Professor Muller, I'm talking to you..."

Tom Hanks, there, that's it, thinks the president. He reminds me of Tom Hanks.

"Yes, Mister President," Adrian acknowledges. "It's Miller, Mister President."

"I was saying, I'll hand you Jinping, you can explain for him."

"Should Professor Miller answer all his questions, with no exceptions?" asks the special advisor.

The president raises his eyebrows, looks for a response from the secretary of state, who nods and says, "Tell him everything you want to, Professor. We don't know much, anyway."

"Mister President, I have the Chinese president for you," says a woman's voice.

Eleven thousand kilometers away, in the conference room of the West Building Compound in Zhongnanhai, a hand picks up.

"Hello, President Xi," says the President. "It's very late, I'm so sorry."

"I wasn't asleep, dear president."

"Well good, good. I'm calling you about an extremely important matter. We've been confronted with an unprecedented situation. The whole world is confronted with it, and that's why you're the first person I'm calling. I'm with my scientific advisors right now. They're here to assist me at any time. Here's the thing: two days ago, an Air France plane landed on U.S. soil. A plane that already landed three months ago."

"Really? Planes often land several times," says the Chinese president, stifling a laugh. "Especially with regular flights..."

"It's more complicated than that. I'll hand you over to one of my scientific advisors, Professor Adrian Muller from Princeton University."

Adrian gets up, takes the handset that the president passes to him, and stammers, "Professor Adrian Miller, Mister President..." then tries to be clear and brief as well as exhaustive.

He is met by incomprehension on the other end of the line.

"The plane landed twice?" asks the Chinese president, "*Twice?*"

The conversation goes on for some time, and Adrian answers questions about the cumulonimbus clouds, DNA tests on the passengers, the conditions in which they're being held...After presenting the facts, he moves on to the different hypotheses, trying to explain the inexplicable. In the face of the Chinese president's astonishment, he often has to go back over things. After a long fifteen minutes, the president insists on having the list of Chinese nationals being detained at McGuire Air Base.

"You can bet they have it already," mutters the scientific advisor, shifting in her seat. "They know where every Chinese person is at any given moment, so, surely the ones that boarded a Paris–New York flight in March..."

"We'll let our special services handle any contingent problems," the Chinese president concludes, "say goodbye to your president for me, and tell him I'll call him back within an hour."

Then the man from the Middle Kingdom hangs up, and Adrian does the same and goes back to his chair. The American president sits motionless, apparently stunned. The mathematician studies this unsophisticated man, and reaffirms the soul-destroying notion that by accumulating our individual obscurities, we rarely achieve collective brilliance.

"They're bound to be out there arresting the 'doubles' of their nationals already," the secretary of state thinks out loud.

"We've contacted President Macron, Mister President. He'll be on the line in a minute," says the special advisor.

"I have a problem with the French, and that guy in particular. Whatever. Jennifer, pass me the arrogant little jerk."

The telephone vibrates, the president drinks a glass of water and picks up with a forced-looking smile.

"My dear Emmanuel, it's so good to talk to you. I hope you're well, and your charming wife too. I'm contacting you about an extremely important situation . . ."

Eleven thousand kilometers away, Xi Jinping looks briefly at the night closing in peacefully over the Lake of the Middle Kingdom in the new Forbidden City. He had hundreds of ginkgo trees planted all along its banks, so that he can gaze at them and meditate. He's always been fascinated by these primitive trees. Their ancestors existed millions of years before even the dinosaurs appeared, and will outlive the human race. A plant version of a memento mori. Then Jinping goes to sit at the conference table again. A dozen or so people are seated around it, both military and civilian, all silent. They listened to Miller's explanations, taking only a scant few notes. These are the blackest of black swans, improbable events like this with unfathomable consequences.

Screens around the presidential conference room are showing images taken by the brand-new Yaogan 30-06 satellites, deployed all around the globe. The definition is excellent: the number on the Air France Boeing can clearly be seen, as can the long procession between the plane and the hangar, and the nonstop aerial ballet of helicopters. The faces of each passenger also appear: for two days now the Ministry for State Security has been gathering all possible information about them, with no less efficiency than the NSA.

"That's it," Xi Jinping summarizes glumly. "They're in the same shit that we were in last April with the Beijing–Shenzhen flight from January. They're holding two hundred forty-three people at their base on the East Coast... Compared to how many already from the Airbus?"

"There are three hundred twenty-two of them, Comrade President," says a general. "Most of them are still at the Huiyang military air base."

"Should we tell the Americans about that flight?" asks a woman in civilian dress.

"Not right away. Maybe never. They haven't asked for any of the fifteen Americans on board. They're not missing anyone."

"So, they think so too . . ." says another four-star military man, "the simulation hypothesis is the most prob—"

"Yes, they think so too," interrupts the president.

The president of 1,415,152,689 programs.

AS ADRIAN LEAVES the White House, the head of protocol catches up with him in the corridor, and hands him a black tote bag with an American flag on it.

"Your T-shirt's in there, Professor Miller. We washed it and took the liberty of . . . mending it. I will also say that I had to type 'Fibonacci' into a search engine to understand your 'I ♡ zero, one, and Fibonacci.' Very funny, if I may say so. You can keep the shirt, of course. You'll also find a sweatshirt with a White House logo on it. The president insisted on autographing it for you personally."

Adrian doesn't have time to get a word in before the head of protocol adds a straight-faced, "Don't worry, Professor. We gave him a water-based pen, it'll come out in the first wash."

"THE PEOPLE HAVE THE RIGHT TO KNOW"

ARTICLE IN THE *NEW YORK TIMES*,

SUNDAY, JUNE 27, 2021

USAF DENIES HOLDING FRENCH AIRLINER AND ITS PASSENGERS AT McGUIRE AIR FORCE BASE

An Air France Boeing 787 was forced to land at Joint Base McGuire-Dix-Lakehurst, New Jersey, early Thursday evening. Passengers and crew are being kept isolated in a huge hangar adapted to accommodate them. Despite our repeated requests, neither the army nor the airline will provide any explanation for this incident.

JOINT BASE McGUIRE-DIX-LAKE-HURST, JUNE 26. Retired couple John and Judith Madderick, aged 65 and 66 respectively, could not believe their eyes. On Thursday evening they were eating their dinner in their garden in Cookstown, New Jersey, when an airliner escorted by two fighter jets landed at the McGuire Air Force Base a mile away. John and Judith are used to the comings and goings of Super Hercules and AWACS aircraft, but in thirty years of living here they do not remember a single civilian aircraft landing at the base.

Other witnesses, including a member of the armed forces, have confirmed that the aircraft is a Boeing 787 flying under the Air France banner.

Airforce spokesman Andrew Wiley denies that any information is being withheld, but confirms that the McGuire base is completely sealed off, and guarded by soldiers from the combat arm of the Eighty-Sixth Infantry Brigade, who arrived on site during the night of Thursday, June 24. All unauthorized personnel are banned from visiting. Armored vehicles have been positioned at the two remaining entry points to the base, compared to the usual seven. These vehicles carry out checks on the base's 4,000 military staff, whose cars are admitted one at a time, causing traffic delays on local roads.

According to a source who works for Kennedy Airport air traffic control, a damaged Boeing 787 entered national air space Thursday, giving an incorrect code for an Air France Paris–New York flight. The aircraft was immediately rerouted on orders from NORAD and diverted to a military base on the East Coast.

According to civilian staff at McGuire base, who have asked to remain anonymous, more than two hundred passengers as well as the crew have disembarked and been accommodated in a specially adapted building. Significant movements have been observed since their arrival. The Boeing itself has been parked up in another hangar, but not before witnesses were able to take a number of photographs that prove that it is a 787-8. Some images posted on social media were quickly blocked.

Speaking for Air France, Director of Communications François Bertrand has said that none of their planes is missing. The French airline company has also supplied a list of the twenty-three Boeing 787s that it uses on half a dozen routes, including some under the banner of KLM. All twenty-three aircraft are accounted for. Records show that Boeing has delivered 387 Boeing 787-8s around the world, and Air France is their second-largest European client. Boeing also handles maintenance of its aircraft and indicates that none are missing. Furthermore, no airport on the East Coast has reported an incident concerning a commercial flight.

Reference numbers on the 787 are legible in the few images of its fuselage, and they correspond with those on a plane usually used on Paris–New York flights. Air France has acknowledged that one of its Boeings, with this same reference number, has been grounded. For "security reasons" it was sequestered by the American authorities on the morning of Saturday, June 26. It is currently at Kennedy Airport, where it will undergo numerous tests. This aircraft sustained damage in turbulence experienced during the "storm of the decade" back in March. This major weather event caused substantial damage to many aircraft and oceangoing vessels.

The identity of the aircraft forced to land at McGuire remains a mystery. Sources close to the military authorities confirm that its occupants—totaling more than 200 people—are still being held in the huge hangar at the base. International civil aviation law allows the detention of civilians without trial only under certain circumstances, strictly defined in national legislation. Terrorism is one instance, but more significantly, medical precautions can enforce the quarantining of passengers and crew. Nevertheless, this procedure can be implemented only on the orders of the president, after consultation with the Centers for Disease Control and Prevention. Kenneth Logan, director of the CDC, responded to questions on this subject by saying that his agency is aware of no problem relating to an epidemic in the United States.

A further surprising fact is that neither the seizing of this aircraft two days ago nor the detention of its occupants has produced any reaction. The White House, speaking through its newly appointed director of communications, Jenna White, has said that no American or foreign nationals are being arbitrarily detained. On average more than one-third of passengers on Air France's Paris–New York flights are French, but when the French Embassy was contacted, it denied that any French nationals were being held against their wishes at McGuire base. The French Embassy declined to comment further on the story.

Anja Stein,
Bureau of Investigative Reporters

SATURDAY, JUNE 26, 2021, 11:00 PM

McGUIRE AIR FORCE BASE

GENERAL SILVERIA puts the remote control down on the table, with the *New York Times* article still up on the screen.

"The article will be online in an hour. Don't ask me how the NSA did it, but we've been offered the scoop. There it is: just two days. We couldn't exactly hope that a great big Boeing and its two hundred passengers would go unnoticed for long."

"Rumors circulate super-quick on the web," says Brian Mitnick. "Five hundred mentions already and climbing. As agreed with Air France, we've gone into their reservation system and destroyed the original file for the passengers on the flight on March 10, and replaced it with a fictitious list. We're currently altering the majority of flight comparison sites, eradicating traces of all trips. Even though there's no information yet in circulation about the plane's passengers, there are references to the arrests taking place across the country."

"Technically they're not arrests, they're 'requisitions related to national security,'" Silveria corrects.

"And where are all these people actually being taken?" asks Adrian.

"The FBI and the NSA are bringing them here in discreet black vans," the general snaps irritably. "Which isn't very clever of your two agencies—Jamy, Mitnick—if I may say so."

"If I may comment as well, General," replies the man from the NSA, "it's not very clever to be keeping them all together in Hangar H. Some of them have recognized others... they now all know that they boarded the same Air France plane back in March... They're imagining the worst, a virus or a terrorist incident..."

"The FBI has brought in psychologists for temporary duty in anticipation of the confrontation," says Jamy Pudlowski. "These people need to be prepared for when they meet their... doubles."

"Of course," Silveria sighs. "We can't gun down the two hundred forty-three people in Hangar B... It's a hell of a shame, I agree, Mitnick, but that's the way it is."

"CNN, CBS, and Fox are sending a little team of journalists with satellite trucks, sandwiches, and hot coffee. And Elaine Quijano on *CBS Evening News* just had on a rabbi and a pastor as her last guests. They revealed that the White House had summoned representatives of major religions to discuss the 'nature of the soul,' and that the world can expect an important announcement."

"It was the Reform rabbi who talked, for sure," Jamy Pudlowki says with a grimace. "He couldn't help himself. He just loves a TV studio. And there's more: despite all our insistence on complete secrecy, NBC has just announced not only that several renowned scientists have disappeared, but also that some of them have been brought together here..."

"Journalists have two enemies: censorship and information," Mitnick says sententiously. "This is just the beginning..."

"It's not the beginning, it's the end," says Silveria. "Meetings between the March and June passengers will start as soon as possible. And tomorrow evening, so Sunday evening, or Monday morning at the latest, the army can entrust all these lovely people to the FBI. Do you have a problem with that, Jamy?"

"Not at all, General. I know no problem that can resist the absence of a solution."

. III .
Song of Oblivion

(AFTER JUNE 26, 2021)

No author writes the reader's book, no reader reads the author's book. At most, they may have the final period in common.

—*The anomaly,* Victør Miesel

ENCOUNTER OF THE SECOND KIND

SUNDAY, JUNE 27, 2021

RUE LA FAYETTE, PARIS

SOMEONE PINCHES his cheek, and Blake wakes in a chair made of cold steel. He's bound, gagged with tape, and naked—a professional job: although the ties aren't cutting off his blood supply, he can't move a muscle. He recognizes the plain, functional interior, he's in his own apartment on rue La Fayette. He even recognizes his restraints, the extra-tough webbing that he bought back in April. He just about remembers that when he walked into the one-bedroom apartment he felt the sharp sting of an injection in his neck and immediately collapsed.

The room he's in was once a bedroom, it still has a small bed and leads to a bathroom with a large enamel tub. It could smack of deliberate design if the main aim weren't practicality. He can't turn his head, but even so he grasps that the entire room is covered in transparent plastic. Blake March—let's call him that—has a strong suspicion he knows what this means. To his right, completing this setting that wouldn't be out of place in the series *Dexter*, are thirty or so gleaming surgical instruments: scalpels, lancets, electric saws, scissors, and files. He recognizes them too. Some have never been used, such as the cranial drill, which he did go to the trouble of trying out on marrow bones. He's not terrified, but that may well be the very relaxing side effect of the midazolam that was injected into him.

It takes him several seconds to identify the man behind the visor in an all-in-one coverall, the man standing in front of him, watching him come to. His eyes open wide in stupefaction. Stupefaction is a weak word.

The two men eye each other for a long time. Blake June studies his prisoner. For three days now he's been thinking, pondering, without finding an explanation. But the absurdity of it didn't preclude his pragmatism, and he set his trap. There was no other option. The fly never asks to see the spider.

Blake March suddenly starts to struggle, groan, and moan, muttering something through the tape, but Blake June doesn't remove it.

"I'm not going to make any speeches," he says flatly into March's ear. "You don't understand what's going on, and neither do I. That doesn't matter. I'm you and you're me. That's one too many, there can't be two of us. You understand that."

He picks up a pencil and notepad, and sits down at the computer, which is on.

"All the access codes for my bank accounts have been changed. By you, obviously, because I do it every three months. Do you know the system for remembering the codes... Nod for 'yes.'"

Blake March obeys. His thoughts jostle frantically, and he even wonders whether he's having an incredibly realistic dream.

"I'm going to log on to my accounts now in front of you and dictate numbers and letters to you, you will confirm them by nodding. The first mistake you make I'll rip off one of your fingernails, the second, I'll crush your index finger. I don't know who you are, but you must have the same memories as me. Do you remember the Amiens contract a couple of years ago? Nod for 'yes.'"

March nods. He remembers... a typical Albanian gig, but either the client didn't have the connections, or they frightened him too much. It was so hideous he almost didn't take it. Shattered kneecaps, broken elbows, fingers cut off, tongue cut out, penis removed, eardrums pierced, and the best saved till last, acid in his eyes. To secure the other half of the 70,000 euros, the man had to be kept alive.

"You'd do exactly the same in my shoes," June says. "And you *are* in my shoes."

March screws up his eyes, watching him. Blake June's smile isn't cruel; more embarrassed. He didn't enjoy Amiens. Too much, it was too much.

"If there are no mistakes, and I can get into all the accounts, we can talk about the future, about what we can negotiate between us. Do you understand?"

March nods, and June remembers Al Capone's words: you can get much farther with a kind word and a gun than you can with a kind word alone.

"Okay then, let's get started. Bank number one, First Caribbean Investment Trust."

March nods. He closes his eyes, concentrates and thinks about half a dozen flamingoes flying across Europe.

"First character. Letter? Okay. Lowercase? Uppercase. Before L? No. Before T? Okay. L M N O P Q R... R? Perfect."

Blake writes down R.

"Second character. Letter? No. Number. Yes. One. Two. Three. Four. Five. Six."

A nod.

"Six. Yes?"

A nod. Blake writes a 6 after the R.

Fifteen minutes later, Blake June has accessed all his accounts and changed them all again, still using the same method. One sentence for each of the three accounts, easy to transliterate. For the First Caribbean Investment

Trust it was "Remember 6 pink colored birds!" which doesn't mean much, but is written "R6pcb!" and you just have to remember six flamingoes. Then for Latvijas International Bank: "They fly through black skies from Venice to Paris." "TftbsfVtP." Et cetera.

He's also found out the username and passwords for his site on the dark web, and even the code for his cellphone, which had also been changed. He's read through his old messages, and discovered that he—well, "Joe"—had dinner several times with someone called Timothée, about whom he currently knows nothing. But June isn't curious enough to take the tape off March's mouth. He's not worried that his captive will cry for help because they both know the room is soundproofed—all four walls, the floor and ceiling. But he doesn't want to let in the tiniest doubt on his part, he doesn't want a moment's hesitation.

When March sees June stand up, he needs no explanation. He would obviously do the same himself. He closes his eyes, he just wants it to be quick. June walks behind him, unhurried, and injects a dose of propofol into his neck; he passes out within seconds. No pointless suffering, Blake doesn't hate himself that much. A minute later, an injection of curare stops March's heart. Sleep and death are twin brothers. Homer was already saying that in his day.

Blake—there's no longer any ambiguity there—cuts the webbing straps and holds the body before it slumps to the floor. His victim is already naked, and he's carefully folded away his clothes—they're his size, after all. He puts the body into the bathtub, with its legs in the air and its head down, turns on the shower, slices open the body's neck and lets it bleed out. He dips the fingers in acid to destroy the prints. Then he carefully carves up the body with the bone saw, making sure not to leave any clearly identifiable human parts, such as a hand or foot. He's a little lacking in experience. On the back of the corpse, on his back, he sees a mole that he's never noticed before. It's an irregular shape—one to watch. When he cuts up the penis, his penis, he can't suppress a shudder of disgust. Three hours later he's filled about a hundred hermetically sealed freezer bags. All that's left is the head.

Shit. The Band-Aid.

Blake almost forgot the dumb pony-riding head injury. He peels off the adhesive square on March's forehead; the wound is already healing. Using a scalpel, he makes a small cut in his own skin, just enough for the future scar to be plausible, he disinfects the Band-Aid and puts it on his own forehead. Then he puts March's head in the acid bath he's prepared in a bowl: the skin disintegrates, giving off a wreath of nitric vapor.

It's seven in the evening. He'll finish this tomorrow. He cleans the bathroom, removes the plastic sheeting, which is hardly spattered with any blood, and folds it carefully—an unnecessary precaution, because, after all, if this particular blood were ever found in his apartment, it's his anyway. He piles up the freezer bags in the bathtub. There's less of it than he would have expected. Eight small cases, four trips.

From a burner phone, he sends a message to a secret recipient: "Eight logs, Total Clignancourt." Instant reply: "Okay. Wednesday, 3 pm." Day minus two, hour minus two: Francis will be in his 4x4 to meet him at the Total gas station near Porte de Clignancourt tomorrow, Monday, at 1 pm.

Then Blake goes out and locks the door. He knows he'll notice that Quentin and Mathilde have grown, a bit. There is a life after death, particularly other people's.

MONDAY, JUNE 28, 2021, 9:55 PM

ÉLYSÉE PALACE, PARIS

EVERYTHING'S READY, Emmanuel. Five minutes. We have news channels, Facebook Live, and a live YouTube link. With a one-minute broadcast delay in case of problems."

"What about Washington? I can't have him stealing the limelight from everyone."

"He'll be later than us, he's still rehearsing his speech."

"The guy rehearses his speeches? He always looks like he's freewheeling to me. Putin? Xi Jinping?"

"I don't know."

"Mister President?" a man's voice asks.

Macron turns to Grimal, the assistant director of counterespionage, a small, bald man who's still looking anxiously at his cellphone.

"Was that Mélois? When will he be back from the States?"

"It wasn't him, Mister President," says Grimal. "The ministerial plane has just taken off from McGuire base. But I do have some information."

"Make it quick, Grimal."

"The Airbus maintenance team noticed something strange ten days ago. When they were servicing another China Airlines Airbus in Dubai, they found a section of the airfoils with the same serial number as the ones on a plane used for an internal Chinese route from Beijing to Shenzhen. But that's completely impossible. At first the manufacturers suspected it was a pirated copy, but our satellites picked up an air traffic anomaly on the Beijing–Shenzhen line in April: an unidentified aircraft was redirected to Huiyang military base. According to the secret services, the Chinese have also been treated to a, how shall I put this, duplicated plane... and they pulled the whole thing to pieces and recycled the parts."

"And the passengers? The crew?"

"That's all we know."

"Do the Americans know about this?"

"No indication that they know anything at all."

The two men fall silent, as the director of communications comes over to them.

"Emmanuel?" she says, "Twenty seconds."

The president sits down, and the makeup artist corrects a sheen on his forehead.

"Ten..."

The dir comm finishes the countdown in silence. The president looks into the camera, and the autocue starts to roll.

"Men and women of France, my dear compatriots, I'm making this announcement to you now, just as the American president is now doing in Washington, the German chancellor in Berlin, the Russian president in Moscow, and many other heads of state around the world.

"An exceptional event took place on Thursday. The rumors circulating in the press and on social media are partly accurate. These are the facts: last Thursday an airplane appeared in the sky just off the East Coast of the United States..."

The French president keeps talking for five minutes and then—very unusually—hands over to his scientific advisor. To avoid compounding the incomprehensible with the eccentric, the mathematician has pared back his mad-scientist look, swapping his unsettling purple ascot for a narrow beige silk scarf, although he couldn't resign himself to unpinning a silver spider from the lapel of his jacket. He puts forward the hypotheses, an animated sequence is inserted for added clarification, and then he mentions the Élysée Palace website, where more detailed explanations can be found, and live chats have been organized.

In Blake's house, as is most likely the case all over France, there is absolute silence. Although Flora does whisper a That's nuts. That's totally nuts.

Joe doesn't say anything, but Flora wasn't expecting him to comment. The president thanks his advisor and addresses the nation again.

"My dear fellow citizens, in August 1945, after the Hiroshima bombing, when the world tipped into the nuclear age and fear of annihilation, the writer Albert Camus wrote: 'We're being presented with a new source of anguish here, and it has every chance of being definitive. Humanity is perhaps being offered its last chance. And, yes, that could be a good pretext for a special edition. But it's more likely to be a topic for some reflection and a great deal of silence.' We must take inspiration from these fine words.

"And that is why, men and women of France, the days and weeks to come must be a time for thinking but also a time for finding peace. Scientists will want to interpret, they will want to understand, they will want to explain, and that is their role, but it is inside ourselves and ourselves alone that each of us will find answers.

"Thank you for listening. *Vive la République, vive la France.*"

"That's nuts," Flora says again. "Can you imagine, Joe, if there were two of you?"

A MAN WATCHES A WOMAN

MONDAY, JUNE 28, 2021

HANGAR B, McGUIRE AIR FORCE BASE

"MR. VANNIER?" Jamy Pudlowski says a second time to the architect who's standing by the one-way mirror of the control room. Lined up on the platform behind them are dozens of units, half cubes of steel and tinted glass with a single glazed door. A few meters below them is the hangar's small multitude in all its noise and agitation.

"Do you understand the situation, Mr. Vannier?"

"Insofar as that's possible, yes."

"Have you been shown the video with images from the cameras on both planes? The moment of divergence? And the short animated film made by the NSA putting forward the hypotheses? Have you been told that there's another 'you' here in this hangar? Along with two hundred forty-two more 'doubles,' to be precise."

André Vannier's only reply is to put his hands on the guardrail and study the crowd. He thought he'd be able to spot 'himself' straightaway, but he's searching in vain for his own figure. He's even afraid that he's seen himself without recognizing himself.

"Come with me," says Jamy Pudlowski, and she takes him into one of the units, simply furnished with an oval table, four chairs, a camera, and a screen on the wall. The presence of windows and the ocher-and-claret colors of the walls remove a prisonlike feel from what is effectively a large cell. While Vannier sits down, Pudlowski scrolls calmly on her tablet.

"I see that your company, Vannier and Edelman, applied to be considered for the new FBI premises in Washington. Shame, the project was abandoned, lack of funding."

"We did put together a proposal, yes. You know everything."

"Sadly, no. For example, we didn't know that you knew the French director of counterespionage. With a friend like that, you would never have secured that job... France is an ally, but you can't be too careful."

"What matters is taking part," Vannier sighs. "Mélois and I attended the same *grande école,* I went into architecture, he diplomacy."

Pudlowski moves her finger, and the screen shows a general view of the room.

"We're filming illegally," she says, and adds by way of an excuse, "but the circumstances are exceptional."

Vannier looks at the camera positioned in the center of the room and realizes that she's already recorded everything so far. Pudlowski nods, embarrassed.

"High-definition cameras and directional mics," she says, more comfortable talking about the equipment. "The NSA have installed . . . quite a few. Passengers or members of the crew can get up and walk about, and the cameras are dedicated, they automatically follow them."

She types something quickly, and the image of the other André, the "June" one, immediately appears. Another drumming of her fingers, and the screen divides in two: Lucie is in the second half.

Vannier is enthralled. Knowing something isn't the same as living it.

"He" and Lucie are sitting idle at a table, talking. One last tap of Pudlowski's finger and they can be heard, and their words appear, transcribed onto the screen. "Americano?" André June asks, making a face. "A merry car, no?" the subtitles say idiotically. The system has a way to go yet, André March reassures himself . . .

"I'll leave you for a moment, Mr. Vannier," says the woman from the U.S. Army's Special Operations Command, getting up and leaving him alone facing the screen.

Captivated, flabbergasted, he studies this other André, his wrinkles, his gray eyes like milky sapphires, his sparse hair, and his withered cheeks with the beginnings of a white beard. André looks into the mirror to shave every morning, and the two of them have ended up taming each other. Here, though, the camera is incorruptible, there's no indulgence in its high definition, no courtesy in its angle: this is an old man he's seeing. A tired, worn, unattractive man. He scours "his" face for the immutable seal of youthfulness that he sometimes believes he incarnates, but can't find it. Old age is in every detail, like a straitjacket of filth. He thinks he looks bloated too, fatter. He should go on a diet. So, aging definitely doesn't simply mean you used to love the Stones and start preferring the Beatles.

There's an angel sitting next to this man. The light pays homage to her. It's still the Lucie of early March, a Lucie whose hair isn't yet short, whose eyes are still tender, a Lucie who's still his, whom he hasn't yet driven away. When this other André takes Lucie's hand, he feels no jealousy; fascination overrides everything. He watches the André he was then get up and head for the coffee machine, and—because he thinks him slow and stooped—he instinctively straightens his back and clenches his fists till they hurt.

As he stands in this connected cabin where he's being watched by the NSA, not that he cares about that at all,

André can think only of Lucie and this other him, and definitely not of any practical issues. Not for a moment does he consider Vannier & Edelman, which really can't become Vannier, Vannier & Edelman; nor does he think about his daughter Jeanne, who now has two fathers, probably two too many, but it may well have its advantages; he doesn't worry about the apartment in Paris that he will have to share, or the house in the Drôme...

No, he's not yet thinking of any of that. He's running aground on the disaster laid before him by the screen. He wishes he could take his eyes off them, but it's a giddying whirl. Here in this small room, a great weight is crushing his chest, he's short of air. They're not a couple, far from it, rather an attentive and anxious old man quivering with love, and a distant young woman. This André is still caught up in the wonder of the early days, still reading Lucie's reserve as caution, her tepid responses as signs of a certain wisdom. But André March now grasps that he never stopped worrying about frightening her away, about startling this adorable swallow that had consented to fly alongside such an old crow. Fuck it, love—the real kind—can't be a ball of fear in your heart. He was never relaxed and, of course, this anxiety held within it their demise.

The André in the hangar returns, carrying two coffees; he smiles, and it's the smile of an abject creature, but Lucie doesn't look up from her book. The other André watching the screen is only too familiar with this detachment, this ability she has for being absent. Look at him, fuck it, forget your damn Romain Gary collection and turn your beautiful eyes on this rather ancient man instead, give him a bit of attention and tenderness. But no, nothing. Not everyone gets the chance to witness their own downfall from afar, to pity themselves without actually feeling self-pity.

A smirk of pain twists his lips. Deep down, he feels sorry for this earlier André. He knows what the poor man still has to live through, the humiliation and frustration. Age was always a contributory factor, but no one should ever love someone who feels so little love for them. Why was it so complicated?

As he sits watching the screen, André March breaks away from Lucie, as a dead leaf breaks away from a tree, or rather as a tree might abandon a dead leaf. Ten cruel minutes of detailed observation are worth months of painful loss. Up on the platform, André—who loathes himself for still loving Lucie—is already glad that he loves her less.

A movement in the crowd: several agents in civilian dress have ventured into the hangar, and everyone clusters around them, bombarding them with questions. One of them comes over to Vannier and slips a note to him. Vannier looks at it but doesn't seem to understand, presses Lucie's hand, and she smiles at him. Then he agrees to follow the man from the bureau.

From his windowed room, a disabused André watches a tired André walk away. He then notices a man at the far end of the table, a short, slight, dark-haired man in his thankless forties cramming a small black notebook with writing, a man who occasionally, sneakily, eyes Lucie. André March immediately recognizes something in the man's eyes, that distinctive distraction whose only cause is the turmoil produced by attraction. Just another butterfly caught in the web that Lucie weaves in all innocence. Suddenly realizing who the man is, André is incredulous: it's Victor Miesel. But he's meant to be dead! Was he on that flight, then?

What was it he said again? Hope is the hallway to happiness, its accomplishment is the antechamber to unhappiness, or something like that. So, Victor Miesel is in that hallway, hoping to catch Lucie's attention. Perhaps the aphorism even came to him when he was thinking about Lucie? The man gets up, and he too goes over to the drinks machine—what is it with all of them that they love that revolting mixture so much?—and Lucie doesn't look up as he walks away. André's infuriated with himself for feeling relief. But this annoyance reveals the gulf that's opening up.

"Mr. Vannier?"

André jumps and turns around; Jamy Pudlowski is leaning against the door. How long has she been watching him? There's a tall, stooped fiftysomething man standing beside her in that awkward way people have when they're burdened by a body too big for them. The man comes toward him and proffers a hand from slightly too far away.

"Jacques Liévin, from the consulate. Commercial attaché."

His voice is expressionless, his gesture hesitant. André smiles at the fear sweating from the man's every pore: Liévin might as well be forming a cross with his fingers, or wearing a necklace of garlic. He realizes that Liévin has just been talking with the André from the grounded plane, and that—in his opinion—this second André is nothing short of a monstrosity.

"Quite a business, isn't it, Mr. Commercial Attaché?" André asks playfully. "What do you think: am I the original or the copy?"

"I... A French military plane will be landing at McGuire in a few minutes, France is sending about twenty... agents, and Mr. Mélois from counterespionage is coming in person. Then all the French nationals are to leave with him. He asked me to come and say hello to you first."

"Was that 'you' singular or plural? I mean are you saying hello to me *and* me?"

"Are you ready, Mr. Vannier?" Pudlowski interrupts, unamused by the game. "We can arrange for you to meet your 'double.'"

"I insist on being left alone with him. It's a private conversation, even if it is between me and myself..."

"The... your... the other Vannier asked for that too. But you're the first of the French passengers to... meet face-to-face, and the Ministry of Foreign Affairs has given me instructions to stay with the two of you the whole time. I have to submit a statement..."

"A statement stating the state of our relationship, would you say?" Vannier scoffs.

The architect points to the camera. The FBI agent makes one simple action and the green light immediately goes out. The indicator's off, at least, Vannier thinks. He catches the man from the consulate surreptitiously staring at someone over to the left: on the far side of the wall of glass is another André, a disoriented André who snatches open the door and comes in.

They stand looking at each other without a word for a long time. It's so disturbing: neither André is the one in the mirror. Nothing is familiar anymore, the inverted features make this other André a stranger, hostile. One is about to speak, but a gesture from the other delays the moment. André March turns to Liévin and Pudlowski, both standing there awkwardly. Pudlowki nods her head, and Liévin leaves the room with obvious relief. With the door closed, they study each other. Sartorial originality has never been André's strong point: they're wearing the same jeans, subtly more worn in one case; the same familiar and reassuring gray-hooded sweatshirt used for long flights; the same sturdy black walking shoes. Oh, actually no, not exactly the same, André June notices. The two Andrés still say nothing. But they surely won't be satisfied with this for long. An Indian proverb says that those who beg in silence die of hunger in silence.

"New shoes?"

"Two weeks ago."

They're both surprised by the voice too. A higher timbre than either André thought, and not as gentle. He's always heard himself "from the inside." At conferences and in interviews he slows his delivery, enunciates carefully, and deepens the tone. Now he can hear his real voice.

"Jeanne?" André June asks after another pause.

"She's fine. She doesn't yet know, obviously."

"Lucie? Lucie and me?"

"We split up."

Then André March corrects this—you can always lie to yourself but what's the point of lying to *you*?—by saying "She left me. Too little desire on her side, and too many frustrations on mine. And probably too many expectations, too much impatience. You suspected that, didn't you?"

"Well, forewarned I'll be twice the man."

For a moment, just for a moment, André March has an idea, to win back this earlier Lucie, this Lucie from

March who hasn't yet rejected him. But he screws up his face, and it already melts into a smile. He managed to attract her when he was not as young and not as good-looking as all the others pursuing her, and never knew what his assets were. Competing with himself would be a novelty. But then again... one André is a thirty-year age gap, two Andrés and it's a senior living facility. She's bound to run for the hills, it's obvious. He'd do better to wish André June good luck.

"I have just one piece of advice," he adds. "Be gentle and attentive but at the same time pretend not to care too much. And don't want her the whole time. You already know that but haven't yet accepted it. I remember now."

We so rarely have an opportunity to coach ourselves.

André June wants to take this lightly, but a knot is forming in his stomach. Within the hour he'll be with Lucie again; how to tell her that their fate may already be sealed? Or how to hide the fact from her?

"And work?" André June asks, uncomfortable talking about Lucie.

"A problem with concrete at Surya Tower. It's been dealt with. And do you remember a few months ago I was thinking of going part-time, retiring even? I'm a bit fed up with it, you know that."

André March waves to the commercial attaché through the window; the man was pretending to stare at the metal floor but immediately sees the gesture and comes in.

"Did you say, sir, that France can offer a second identity?"

"Yes. A new identity for which one of you?"

"For me," André March says, and then turns to June and adds, "you can go back to work. That'll be better. I spent my whole time there for the three months that Lucie and I were together. Spending my time waiting for her would have driven me crazy. Because—you'll find out soon enough—Lucie works a lot. You need to be busy. I'll bring you up to speed on the latest progress at each build. I'll go down to Drôme. I like it there. Actually . . ."

March's voice trails off and he frowns.

"Let's be pragmatic about this," he says, turning to the commercial attaché. "What's the government saying about practical considerations? I've heard that there are about seventy French people involved in this. They're not going to share their apartments and split their savings. Could it be said that there's been a . . . natural disaster? Get onto . . . insurance companies? The concept of virtual disasters might start featuring in their terms. What if I decide to retire, then what happens? Would I be taking my . . . my double's retirement? Given the generosity of complementary pension schemes, I doubt they'd double the contributions I've made! Unless there's a government order."

The man from the consulate looks out of his depth. He peers at his cellphone, his lifeline.

"Ah, I just heard that Mr. Mélois's arriving any minute."

"It's just the sort of problem he'll love," André June laughs.

"By the way, the other house, the old coaching inn in Montjoux that I couldn't make up my mind about, it's still for sale," says André March. "I'll buy it, whether or not we can get this idea of a 'virtual disaster' to work. We'd have a house each, ten kilometers apart. The friends who used to come to stay for vacations can share themselves between the two of us. We'll see which of us is nicer."

SOPHIAS' WORLD

MONDAY, JUNE 28, 2021

CLYDE TOLSON RESORT, FBI ANNEX, NEW YORK

A TALL, VERY LANKY blond with blue eyes, a kid fresh out of FBI training, stands stiff as a flagpole in front of another man sitting at a desk, a sporty, Black forty-five-year-old who's lost the battle against baldness. Special Agent Walker hardly even looks up at Cadet Jonathan Wayne.

"Cadet Wayne. How's your course going? Don't answer that. Your file says you're from Alaska."

"I'm from Juneau, Special Agent Walker. A little town on the Pacific Coa—"

"And you just finished Quantico."

"Yes, Special Agent Walker."

"Stop calling me Special Agent Walker. Call me Julius..."

"Yes, Julius."

"Actually, no, keep calling me Special Agent Walker."

"Of course, Special Age—"

"I see that you and your father used to hunt grizzlies. You have experience of wild animals. Have you already worked in the field?"

"No, Special Agent Walker."

Julius Walker puts down the file he's perusing, concerned. He turns to Senior Agent Gloria Lopez, who's standing next to him, holding a coffee in a paper cup.

"Gloria," Walker sighs, "it's reckless to give him this mission."

"It's an opportunity to test his abilities in the field, Julius. Plus he'll have Cadet Anna Steinbeck as his partner. She already has one month under her belt, and she's proved completely satisfactory."

"Two cadets together? When the mission's danger level four?"

"We're snowed under."

Special Agent Julius Walker looks back at the cadet and hands him a black file.

"Cadet Wayne, your mission is to capture this wild animal without injuring it..."

The tall blond boy opens the file...and his eyes widen with amazement.

"But...it's a frog!"

"It's a toad. She's called Betty, why wouldn't she be? Bring her to us in her terrarium."

"I..."

"Should have left already, Cadet Wayne."

"One last thing," Gloria Lopez adds, "if that toad comes under threat, it's your duty to die for her."

TWO HOURS LATER, Cadets Wayne and Steinbeck have accomplished their mission: Betty is in the office. On the way over, the toad clearly took advantage of a moment when the terrarium opened slightly during some hard braking: she escaped and managed to take refuge in the most inaccessible place possible, way under the driver's seat. Anna Steinbeck, helpless with laughter, had to pull over into the emergency lane, and Wayne had to fold himself in four to retrieve the critter without crushing it between his fingers, and all this at the expense of an implausible number of F-words.

In a room at the FBI annex, cognitive science specialists have created a soft, comfortable, and colorful space in which the duplicated children can meet in a "play-based environment."

Sophia March and Sophia June are lying on the floor playing. At their age, the behaviorists reckoned, they're not afraid of new things: an Other isn't yet an enemy. Between the two of them, Betty's no longer an amphibian but a transitional object, croaking very appropriately. And the Eiffel Tower in her terrarium is now equipped with a state-of-the-art mic. The two shrinks are keeping a low profile at this little tea party: they're just two women sitting at a table, nibbling chocolate chip muffins and sipping orange juice, pretending not to pay any attention to the two little girls who are such identical twins. The children meanwhile are tackling everything—memories, what they like, things they know, Do you remember Norma's birthday? What's your favorite flavor ice cream? Do you know what an *Anaxyrus debilis* is?

At first, neither of them can trip the other up, but Sophia March very soon realizes that she's the only one who knows about the last few months. She's found the weak spot and is victorious. So, you don't remember what Liam said at my birthday! Or what Mommy gave me?

She gloats while Sophia June is crushed, until she suddenly thinks of a riposte, throwing down her challenge in a quieter voice, "Did Daddy make you swear too? Make you swear not to tell anyone, especially not Mommy?"

Sophia June whispers a few words in March's ear.

The two pediatric psychiatrists were waiting for this, they freeze, force themselves not to watch the girls. The barely audible whispering has been instantly transcoded into subtitles on their tablets. These may be a child's words, but their interpretation leaves no room for ambiguity.

Sophia March shakes her head and jumps to her feet.

"You're not allowed to talk about it!" she screams.

"But I can."

"It's not true, it's not true!"

"What's not true, Sophia?" asks one of the psychiatrists in a gentle, soothing, natural voice. Of course, hearing their name, both little girls turn around at the same time.

Sophia March knocks over all the cups, furious.

"Don't say! Don't say!" she shrieks at the other Sophia. "Daddy said not to say anything. It's a secret."

The other child clams up, terrified, her eyes lowered. The game is over. Betty has stopped croaking.

"Come on, let's go for a walk," says one of the psychiatrists, taking Sophia June's hand. "Let's see if your mommy would like to come with us."

THE SECRET is Paris. Sophia didn't enjoy it.

First, she was worried about Betty, who'd stayed home alone, with a few skinny little maggots slipped into her terrarium to keep her going for ten days. And then when Liam wanted to go on the tourist riverboats on the Seine, her father said she'd better stay at the hotel with him because she was bound to feel "seasick." And when her mother took Liam to the first level of the Eiffel Tower, he said she couldn't go with them because she was "tired," and anyway "that tower's shorter than any of our skyscrapers." Both times he took her into the bathroom and asked her to get into the steaming tub. And Sophia doesn't like being naked in the bathtub with Daddy, who gets naked too. He soaps her slowly, all over, I'm clean, Daddy, that's enough, That's good, sweetheart, now it's your turn to soap me, we won't tell Mommy, it's our secret. But Sophia's eyes try to avoid her father's body, her hands to forget what they have to learn to do. Her gaze clings to whatever it can find, the chrome towel rack, the soap dispenser bottle, the gilded taps.

And later, in May, when her father returned from Iraq, Sophia March didn't like the bathroom at home either. In Howard Beach too she came to know every crack in the paintwork, every flicker of the fluorescent ceiling light, every irregularity in the sky-blue tiles. She hates the smells—of soap, shampoo, all those things. But it's a secret.

SLIMBOYS

MONDAY, JUNE 28, 2021

STRATFORD ROAD, KENSINGTON, LONDON

"Have a maki, Mr. Kaduna," says the man from MI6, offering the tray of sushi to Slimboy March. "They're from the best Japanese kitchen in Kensington. Much better than Ishimi on Victoria Island."

But the musician's anger won't back down. In Lagos he agreed to board the private jet, and he took his twelve-string Taylor and his Gibson Hummingbird because they'd dangled the prospect of a duet with a living legend of pop. Once he landed on English soil, though, and throughout the journey to this Victorian house near Holland Park, the tall Black man with clipped Oxford vowels has assailed him with a long, abstruse monologue. There was now talk of a "rare moment," an "unprecedented phenomenon," but nothing about Elton John anymore.

All is not lost: in the middle of the living room is a spectacular red Steinway grand.

"You brought me all the way to London and I don't get to meet Elton? I rehearsed all through the flight."

It was true: Slimboy spent the five hours on the plane working on "Your Song," the hit that all singers—from Billy Paul to Lady Gaga—owe it to themselves to cover once in their careers. The score is for a keyboard, but Slimboy chose Rod Stewart's guitar version. On his Gibson, he started by playing it condescendingly, disdainfully, intoning its simple lyrics, *And you can tell everybody this is your song*... He very soon forgot that this white man's love song was fifty years old and all played out; he found himself captivated by the words, emotional as a teenager. He remembered that Bernie Taupin was just eighteen when he composed it, and he realized that every word of it was written for him, Slimboy, to speak about the loves he wasn't allowed to have and wasn't allowed to sing about. And as the Falcon began its descent toward Heathrow Airport, Slimboy was playing the song with misty eyes and couldn't do anything about it.

"This building is under protection, but don't worry. Sir Elton John is on his way, he'll be here shortly," the agent sighs. "And the proof's right in front of you—believe me, there are never pianos on Intelligence Service premises."

"So was that really his private jet?"

"Absolutely. I mean, the seats were in pink leather. But do you . . . do you understand what I've just told you? Are you ready for this meeting, Mr. Kaduna?"

"For the last time, I'm not Mr. Kaduna," Slimboy snaps. "What about you, are you really called John Gray?"

"You can call me John," the agent replies as he gives a nod to the officer guarding the door.

When the other Slimboy appears, the first one backs away and the new arrival freezes. The two men study each other, scrutinize each other at length. Freud talks about the uncanniness of the strangely familiar, about narcissistic doubles and internal mirrors. None of it really applies. Neither one of them is bothered by the strangeness or attracted to his double: too thin, too tall, too young even—they both realize they're not their type. Slimboy June finally comes into the room, walks toward the window through which he can see the old oak trees on Edwardes Square, then picks up a maki and puts it into his mouth, all with his eyes pinned on his double.

Slimboy March sits down, also takes a maki, and the dainty mouthfuls of rice gradually disappear. The MI6 agent wasn't expecting this. He thought they'd be unconvinced, would question each other, probing to find the flaw in the interloper, reassuring themselves there was no trickery, but no. The bizarre doesn't unsettle them, the unbelievable produces no terror. But it does work up an appetite.

Soon there's no sushi left. Without a word, Slimboy June points to a pale scar on his wrist. His expression is a question.

"Tom" the other replies simply, pulling up his sleeve to show the same gleaming line.

"Tom," he says again, "you know."

Yes, Slimboy June knows, and he is alone in that: after Tom was murdered he didn't want to carry on living and slit his wrist. His mother saved him.

"It was in Ibadan," he says, sealing their pact with this geographical detail.

The two men smile at each other sadly. It's an affectionate, knowing smile, a fraternal smile. At last there's no need to lie, no need to hide anything, or be ashamed of anything. The world hasn't changed, but both March and June feel stronger. Slimboy March stands up, goes to get the two guitars, and hands the twelve-string to June.

"The song 'Yaba Girls' . . ." June says. "I've listened to it. It's wonderful. And . . . did I really play with Drake? I mean did you . . ."

"With Drake, Eminem, Beyoncé. In May I played the Afrorepublik Festival here in London. And in two weeks' time I'm starring in a Nollywood rom-com, *Lagos Wedding*. I've also signed a new contract with Sony

Music, I'm sponsored by Coca-Cola, and I've set up their new label, RealSlim Entertainment. There, that's it."

Slimboy June smiles. He remembers the joke about when the Americans landed on Mars...they find two dudes from Lagos signing a contract.

"And look," Slimboy March adds.

He undoes the zipper on his hoodie and the words "100% human and valid" appear on his chest. It's a Rex Young T-shirt, a discreet rallying sign for the LGBT community and the few heterosexuals who dare to support it.

The two men laugh openly. All this thanks to "Yaba Girls"...Slimboy June isn't jealous of this success, he isn't even surprised not to be. He's happy, it's like a legacy landing in his lap. The man from MI6 was not expecting this.

"I've written a song too. In the hangar where they held us. 'Beautiful Men in Uniform.' That's the title."

"Beautiful Men? Don't tell me you're gay too?"

June strums a major chord and sings the melody, and March immediately finds a second part, improvising the harmonies. The two singers match each other, adding without trying to outdo. Together they improvise a musical punch line, and March suddenly sits up taller, his eyes shining.

"Wait!" he says. "We can just say we're twins. It would be easy. After all, we're Yoruba."

Yoruba, of course. It's obvious. The Tchaman are afraid of twins. The Mandingoes even more so. They have second sight, can read people's thoughts. The Ndembu, the Bantu, and the Lele think twins come from the world of animals. When twins are born in the Folon Region, they're abandoned far from the village for a day and a night so that they pose no threat to chiefs and witch doctors. The Luba kill one of the babies, because they bring bad luck. All over Africa people claim that only fetishes cause twin births, they're a sign from the sky, and always bring the evil eye. But more than a century ago the Yoruba stopped killing the children of the god of thunder, these babies that generate such fear. Over the years, the curse has mutated into a reverence, a cult. The fact is that among people of Yoruba ethnicity the rate of twin births is, uniquely, one in twenty; the village of Igbo-Ora has even proclaimed itself the twin capital of the world, and the names Taiwo (First) and Kehinde (Second) are common. So yes, why shouldn't Slimboy have a twin brother, a brother he lost and has found again? No one would be surprised.

"We'd need to fake the personal records," June suggests.

"It's just a question of money," March agrees.

The MI6 agent takes notes as if taking orders for pizzas.

"A new identity for which one of you?"

"For me, obviously," replies Slimboy June.

"We'll sort it out," says John Gray. "We'll come up with a story for you, and we'll create a digital ID for you. It's the sort of thing we know how to do."

"We could do gigs together, write songs together. Twins... we're going to be huge," says one of them, smiling. "Slimboys sounds good."

The other is about to reply, but a long candy-pink limousine stops outside the house. A short man steps out of it, wearing a duckling-yellow suit, a bottle-green felt hat, and enormous diamanté glasses.

THE GUARDIAN NIGERIA NEWS

FRIDAY, JULY 2, 2021

FROM SLIMBOY TO SLIMMEN

Slimboy has a twin brother. The famous writer of the global hit "Yaba Girls" discovered the fact in January, thanks to a posthumous letter from his mother. Too poor to raise both children, she had given up the second baby to an orphanage at birth and had subsequently been unable to trace him. Slimboy, who has three younger sisters, set out to find his missing brother, entrusting the research to Lagos detective Adawele Shehu, who specializes in missing persons cases.

"It wasn't easy," Shehu confided. "It took me nearly four months to identify this unknown brother. It has to be said that my client's fame, now that every Nigerian knows his face, made the job easier. I just had to find someone who looked very like him."

Femi Ahmed Kaduna has a brother, then. His name is Sam, and he too is a gifted musician, who performed at parties in Lagos when his job as a deliveryman allowed. Ironically, this long-lost brother lived not far from Lagos, in Ojodu. The very moving meeting between the brothers took place in total privacy. Since then the twins—who really are extraordinarily alike, as our photograph shows—have decided to tour together under the name SlimMen.

We wish this new group doubly good luck.

SAME PLAYER DIES AGAIN

MONDAY, JUNE 28, 2021

MOUNT SINAI HOSPITAL, NEW YORK

PHARMACOLOGY WOULD so like to be an exact science: every eight minutes the pump gives a soft beep and injects a two-milligram intravenous dose of morphine. This plasmatic concentration is minimal but effective; David Markle isn't in any pain. He's asleep, exhausted, in his room on the palliative care ward. His organism is all burned-out. If he were to wake, it would be to take one last breath.

Jody has gone home to rest. Grace and Benjamin will go to school tomorrow. But Paul Markle is here, complying with a summons: "an exceptional situation" were the FBI's words. When he arrived at Mount Sinai Hospital he was greeted by a woman from the bureau who explained everything. He shook his head and frowned; every inch of him refused to grasp the "situation." He was taken upstairs to a zone of the hospital that is now under military surveillance, and whose staff have all been evacuated, except for one nurse sworn to secrecy. Paul waits, he looks through the file that the Protocol 42 medical team gave him: the new scans and MRIs undergone by another David Markle.

Paul waits, but when he sees the man who comes into the room followed by two agents, the word "fuck" doesn't even come out of his mouth, his legs give way, and he has to sit down.

David looks at his brother Paul, then at the other David dying on a hospital bed. The pump's beep doesn't break the silence between them.

"We've told your wife," the FBI man tells David quietly. "Some agents have gone to fetch her. We're preparing her for this..."

"Let her sleep," says David. "It's better that way."

That voice. Just hearing it again, Paul is overwhelmed. He gets up, walks over to his big brother and takes him in his arms. It's his smell too, his smell from before he was sick, and his sturdy, solid, powerful body. He hugs him close, then steps back and studies him again.

"It's you," he says idiotically. "It's really you."

"Really me," the pilot replies. "Come, let's go out."

The psychologists are not sure whether to follow them, but a gesture from David implies that they should leave them alone. The brothers leave the dying David's room and sit on one of those gray leatherette hospital sofas that have more tragedies to relate than miracles. David closes his eyes; his head is spinning.

"What . . . What happened to me, Paul? I was told it's pancreatic cancer, which was diagnosed in . . . May?"

The doctor in Paul comes back to his senses.

"David," he says, squeezing his brother's arm. "Do you remember you had medical tests on Saturday? In the hangar. I was given the results just now."

David gets it. Dying is all the more intolerable if you know when. He can't sit still; he gets up, goes over to the half-open door, stares at the body in the bed: it's so thin, so weak. He looks away and comes back to sit down on the gravestone-gray sofa. When he speaks it's a whisper, as if he's afraid of being heard.

"Do you think that *I*'ll have so little time too?"

"It's as if we're starting the chemo and radio on March 12 or 13 instead of May 30," Paul says reassuringly, looking at the files. "And four months of treatment instead of one is huge, given how aggressive this cancer is."

Paul explains it all again: the problematic position of the tumor, the secondaries in his liver, the metastasizing in his small intestine: he can't operate any more than he could on David March a month ago. David June asks the same questions, puts forward the same arguments, and Paul gives him the same answers in the same words. Every now and then he can't help a "like I already said."

He can't come to terms with the fact that no, he hasn't told this David anything before.

"How long?" David asks again. "At least three months, it must be. More?"

"We'll try a different treatment. You were your own guinea pig; at least we know what won't work."

Paul smiles sadly. His faith in medicine and its protocols is stronger than him, that's why he chose this lunatic's profession, why he excels at it. In fact, he sometimes believes it's the job that chose him: he never loses hope, he can reassure his patients because he's very good at lying to himself too. But once again he's having trouble breathing. A man is dying in the next room, a man who is David. He feels like laughing and crying. He's lost.

"And Jody?" David asks.

"She's exhausted. You can't imagine what she's been through."

It's an unfortunate turn of phrase given what lies ahead for David, but never mind. Paul's phone vibrates. He glances at it and picks up.

"Jody?" he says quietly.

IT'S A TINY Japanese garden. A tall hedge of black bamboo cuts it off from the elms and birches of a small

English-style park; a stream flows from a modest waterfall, cutting between pale stones toward a tranquil koi pond; a gravel path leads to a short wooden bridge that gives access to an island only large enough for a couple of stone benches. The people who designed this garden intended it to be serene, to breathe life, but its calculated beatitude identifies it as a place where people walk for the last time. It stands in the middle of a luxury palliative care home, the privilege of those who have good health insurance and who want to believe that a Zen death won't be so final.

When Jody appears through the bamboo, escorted by Paul and a bureau agent, David sees her freeze, struck by a bolt with no thunder or lightning. Her whole body tenses, fights the urge to back away. Her face is thinner, it has dried out and hardened, her eyes are red with dark shadows under them, tiredness is written in her every feature. Eventually, with Paul's support, she comes over very slowly. She's walking toward a ghost. She crosses the bridge, sits on the other bench, stares at him for a long time, then looks away. Paul gives his brother a steadying wave and walks away.

They sit facing each other in silence for several long minutes. In the end, it's David who speaks.

"Believe me, I'd have preferred a city square with screaming kids. Anything but this dumb, kitschy place. The shrinks must have thought it was appropriate. I gotta say, I—"

"Don't talk," Jody says quietly.

David obeys her and listens to the soft rush of the waterfall, the cheeping of a house sparrow. All at once the green water is churned by the switchback action of a carp. Maybe this garden's not so dumb after all.

Jody suddenly starts talking, her voice shaky.

"I didn't want the children to come see you in the hospital, once you were intubated, knocked out by morphine. We can tell them you were getting better."

She says "you" indiscriminately to refer to him—so palpably alive—and to the other man who's about to die. It's her way of denying one reality and accepting a new one. Over the next few days, the psychologists will observe this reaction in everyone.

David nods. He wants to hug her, but can tell she's not ready; he can sense her fear, and some revulsion. Jody can't hear the waterfall or the bird. Her eyes are locked on the white gravel; she can't bring herself to look at him.

"I'm so sorry," she says. "I want to kiss you, but I can't."

Once the amazement had passed, once the questions that inevitably come to every mind had been asked, the first thing she asked Paul was, And the cancer? And when Paul eventually admitted the facts, when she realized that this David from before, this David who'd appeared out of nowhere might die all over again, she felt the blood drain from her. She's ashamed for thinking, Why did you come back, David, why? Was this all just a dress rehearsal, one month of pain to prepare for still more horror, more tears and powerless rage? She wants to believe heaven is giving her a second chance, but no, it will be a second agony, and all she feels is anger and disgust.

"As far as the children are concerned," she reiterates in a hard-edged voice, "you've been convalescing, yes. It'll be easier."

She doesn't add, I don't want the children to bury their father twice.

"I'll try to get better, Jody. For Grace, for Benjamin, and for you."

"Yes."

"And for me too. Let's be honest."

She looks up. He wants to make her smile, she doesn't have the strength for anything. She looks deep into his eyes to find the real him again, to banish the despair that she can't shake off anymore. He reaches out a hand, she accepts it, he squeezes hers, and she rediscovers his warmth, the way he strokes her palm with his thumb.

"And it's really you," she asks at last.

It's not a question. She was never in any doubt. David doesn't reply, eyeing her with an avid tenderness as if already wanting to keep hold of everything about her, as if the days were already numbered.

They don't notice Paul at the entrance to the garden, Paul who's just been handed a note by a nurse and whose eyes are now misted with sadness. Nor do they hear the order issued by the FBI officer.

Time trickles by, and it de-weaponizes pain.

A carp leaps out of the water then falls back down and the sound startles them both.

WOODS VS. WASSERMAN

MONDAY, JUNE 28, 2021

CARROLL STREET, BROOKLYN

HOW CAN A BODY contain so many tears? The two Joannas are crying, and the same idea comes to them at the same time. So many tears.

There are five people in total in among the sketches and gouaches in Aby Wasserman's big studio: the FBI psychiatrists awkwardly perched on high stools, the Joannas in an armchair and on an old sofa, with a dazed Aby lost for words. Without thinking, the cartoonist sat down next to "his" Joanna and can now read the distress in the other one's eyes. She too is the woman he hugged fiercely after her Paris–New York flight three months ago. He should kiss her, comfort her. But no. He's turned to stone.

They sit unmoving and silent for a long time.

"I need to get out," says one Joanna, and the two women stand up, open the French door, and hurry onto the large balcony that looks out over the street. Aby follows them.

Now they're out in the sunlight, with their bloodshot eyes, taking time out. Joanna has always believed in the benefits of being out of doors, she's never been in any doubt that the wind, sky, and clouds bring answers the way storks bring babies. When she was a child, if the world seemed to be against her, she'd go out to find peace in the park on the corner of West and Providence. She'd run along the asphalt path till she was out of breath, till her lungs were about to explode and she flopped to the ground with her back on the close-cropped grass, her arms splayed out in a cross and her heart pounding. The universe infiltrated her with every breath she took, and she gradually reappropriated it. But today the shimmering maple trees on Carroll Street have no simple answers to offer them. One Joanna blows her nose, takes a long slow breath, tries to steady herself. The other wipes her eyes.

"I don't want to steal your life," says one, sniffing.

"Neither do I."

"But I don't want to lose mine either."

"Aby?" says one of the women, turning to him. "Say something."

It makes him jump. His eyes were darting constantly from one Joanna to the other. Only a discreetly swelling stomach helps differentiate them.

"I'm really sorry. I'm out of my depth. I... I just have no idea what to say."

He looks down, contemplates the tattoo on his wrist: two palm trees on a dune. A tribute to his grandfather and the story of his life: as a child Aby saw "OASIS" on the old man's forearm, and asked what the tattooed word meant. The reply was, You see, Aby, my boy, an oasis means water in the middle of the desert, a place of peace and sharing, so I had this tattoo done when I was twenty, because it represented hope for a new life here after the war, it's a good-luck charm, do you understand that, Aby? *Ein Glücksbringer.* Little Aby repeated the word—*Glücksbringer*—and it fascinates him to this day that the German language has only one word, *Glück*, for happiness and luck: perhaps unhappiness is just being really down on your luck. On Aby's twelfth birthday his grandfather told him that, no, the tattoo wasn't the word he thought he'd read backward, it wasn't OASIS but 51540, his prisoner number at Auschwitz. The day after the old man died, Aby had a tattoo done on his own skin, in the same place: this oasis whose secret meaning only he knows and that has been a source of strength to him. But the two women are looking at him, and the tattoo he's staring at is no longer a refuge.

"So we got married, then? And we live here?" asks Joanna June. "What was our wedding like?"

Neither the "we" nor the "our" is premeditated. But they anchor into the language a sort of balance between

Joanna Woods and this Joanna Wasserman, who's carrying Aby's baby. She's not the perverse intruder, she's the poor insider who got left behind.

A summer breeze quivers through the silver leaves, and the noise of cars recedes. "The winds must come from somewhere when they blow." Why this poem comes to her, Joanna doesn't know.

"I don't know what we're going to do. Legally..." ventures the first Joanna.

There's no legal precedent, the other is about to say but immediately thinks, Fuck, that really is me all over, straight to the legal position. She remembers the Martin Guerre trial in France in the sixteenth century. An impostor called Arnaud du Tilh comes "home" to the village where Guerre was born, passes himself off as him, lives with his wife, and convinces anyone prepared to be convinced that he is who he claims to be. But in a spectacular twist, the real Martin Guerre returns, and the impostor ends up on the gallows. What's the point of mentioning it, thinks Joanna, guessing that the other Joanna has remembered the same story at the same time.

"It's completely different," she murmurs.

Silence settles over them. A discreet tap on the glass makes all three of them turn around to see the FBI agents who—either timid or intimidated—dare not come onto the balcony.

"Make yourselves a coffee," Aby says to get rid of them.

"What about Ellen?" asks Joanna June. "How's she doing?"

"She's okay, she's having her treatment today. And . . . I took a job with Denton and Lovell. I'm handling Valdeo, for the Hexachlorion trial."

"You didn't? With that piece of shit Prior? You . . . you did that?"

"He's not a piece of shit, that's a cliché because he's a billionaire."

Joanna June knows, it's so blatantly obvious: of course she would have done the same to pay for Ellen's treatment, but also because, well, it *is* Denton & Lovell . . . Without thinking, she reaches her hand to Aby, who takes it, also without thinking. Seeing this small gesture, the other Joanna finds there's no air to breathe, the pain crushes her chest. Her sister will always be her sister, but she has only one Aby. There are some loves that can be added together, and others that can never be divided.

"This is terrible," says Aby, taking her hand too. "I don't love both of you. I love just one woman, a woman whose name is Joanna."

He can't go on. The tears that were making his eyes shine start to flow, unchecked. So many tears.

ONE CHILD, TWO MOTHERS

TUESDAY, JUNE 29, 2021

RUE MURILLO, PARIS

TWO DAYS AGO the FBI PsyOps department contacted the special services in allied countries to communicate its protocol, broken down into five points: preparation, information, meeting, monitoring, and protection. But these formalities are no help inside this discreet Paris mansion that France's External Intelligence Agency has kept through its various incarnations; they're no help in this room with its net curtains drawn across the view over the Parc Monceau. The Lucie Bogaerts were confronted with each other fifteen minutes ago, and the aggression was instantaneous.

Total war. As soon as Lucie June was back in France she knew she couldn't avoid it, and Lucie March is equally determined. Her son, *their* son, the apartment, the films currently being edited, even down to clothes—a succession of elemental struggles and pointless battles.

The psychologists were prepared for this: Lucie and her son have been living together in a bubble of love and tenderness for ten years, and she's never contemplated shared custody with the child's father: the guy had been too young, he'd shirked fatherhood, never wanted to raise his son and had only consented to show any interest in him in recent years. And now Lucie must negotiate with this other "her," and meekly accept unbearable separations? Neither of them is prepared to sacrifice herself on the altar of the child's sacrosanct "emotional stability" that the child psychologists keep trumpeting, but what do they know? In a mother's love, the darkest selfishness battles furiously with the most dazzling generosity.

"Louis isn't ready for this," Lucie March says, not for the first time.

"He's just as much my son as yours," Lucie June retorts.

Lucie March stares obstinately at the floor and doesn't look up as she says "We need to think about his stability. It's a no."

It's a no? How does she mean "no"? By what right could anyone stop her seeing her son? Doesn't she understand that she's a mother too? That she's no less legitimate? Lucie June is consumed with anger and can't rationalize. Of course, the exact same anger is draining the other Lucie's cheeks of color and making her voice quaver.

"I won't stay another night at the hotel, not one," screams Lucie June. "I have an apartment. Can you imagine for just one minute what I'm going through?"

Lucie June takes a deep breath and reiterates, "You can't live in my apartment."

One of the psychiatrists represses a sigh. What they needed was a marriage counsellor, a divorce specialist. She is about to intervene when Lucie June adds reluctantly:

"Not all the time."

"The situation is . . . unprecedented, Ms. Bogaert," ventures the young man from Homeland Security, fresh out of his prestigious training school, in the 2020 "Hannah Arendt" year group, now catapulted into the crisis unit and bitterly regretting his appointment in Agriculture. He stammers on, ". . . We're working toward a solution."

"I'm no more 'surplus' than she is, this woman who's living in *my* apartment with *my* son. Do you know that I haven't been allowed to talk to Louis for five days?"

But Louis isn't alone in sparking all this fury. She also hates the way the other woman's chin wobbles when she's overwhelmed by anger, the tiny twisting at the corners of her mouth, the stubborn attempt to contain the fireworks behind a pretense of detachment, the way she pushes her glasses back up by screwing up her nose. So many readable signs on both their faces. And there was the shock of appreciating her prettiness, even though it's hers too, of seeing how slim her body is, how waiflike, so fragile that it can't help inspiring in men an avid urge to protect, a hunger for possession; and as Lucie June angrily studies Lucie March, she thinks of Raphaël.

She met him a year ago on a film shoot. A cameraman. Despite his stumpy frame and boxer's nose, Raphaël is attractive. She could tell he liked her. She calls him from time to time: if he's free, she goes over, goes in, hardly even kisses him. She undresses, lies down on the bed and wants him to take her, always from behind, pulling her hair and gripping her hips; she comes, then pushes him out of her, takes a quick shower, and leaves. She doesn't want anything more. It's not her secret garden, it's a wasteland. There were others before Raphaël. It's so much more straightforward when there's no love.

A few days before leaving for New York with André, she visited him.

As usual, she took off her coat, her watch, and the sapphire white-gold ring that André had given her, blurted out an I have thirty minutes, tops, and he sensed such urgency in her that he was thrown and couldn't satisfy her as quickly as she would have liked. He knelt between her thighs, wanting to lick her tenderly, but she pushed him away as she always did, No, stop it, not like that, and she brought him back to that canine position in which he could see only her hair, her back, and her ass. A few minutes later she was already showering, and Raphaël said, You know, Lucie, I'd like it if we didn't only see each other when there's a gap in your schedule, we could go out for a meal, to the theater. Lucie looked at him in silence, dried herself, and slipped on her panties and socks. Or we could take a few days in Bruges, he added, or Venice, wherever you like, just the two of us. She finished dressing then suddenly, coldly, she said, Just the two of us? The two of us? What, you think you love me because you get hard for me and that I love you because I yell Fuck me, take me, harder, is that it? Look, Raphaël, we're not together, this isn't what love is, this is nothing, it's nothing at all. It's chemistry, it's a scam. You don't get that it's a scam!

The young man was speechless for a while before losing his temper and barking, Get out, get out. Lucie shrugged, picked up her watch, put the sapphire back on her ring finger, and left. He shut the door behind her and went over to the window to watch her walk up the street, get onto her scooter, and disappear. He stayed standing there, shattered by the humiliation and pain caused by this woman he possessed when she was never actually his. He was sure that in a week, maybe a month, she'd call him again as if nothing—absolutely nothing—had happened. He would open the door and say, I thought you'd never come back. She'd stare at him in amazement. And take off her clothes.

Lucie June thought she'd never feel ashamed of a farce like this. What did it matter what Raphaël thought, or any of the others before him? But all at once, confronted by this other woman with her reptilian eyes, this woman who knows everything, right down to the sordid domination scenarios that she dreams up and that make her come, Lucie June is filled with chilling disgust. Suddenly she's stripped naked, ugly, pornographic. It's no longer a wasteland, it's a landfill site.

She shudders, wonders whether Lucie March is also thinking of Raphaël right now, whether she's still seeing him. And what does it matter?

"And another thing," Lucie March says. "I don't think Louis's ready to meet—I don't know how to say this, his two mothers..."

"He's a very intelligent boy, very mature," offers one of the psychologists. "All his reactions demonstrate that he'd be able to cope with the situation. And it's also for him to decide."

Because Louis now knows. The special services insisted that he come here with Lucie March, and he's been in a nearby room talking to a child psychologist for over an hour now. He gets it: he doesn't have two mommies, but two times his mommy. When the psychologist thought the time was right, she turned on the screen relaying the meeting between the two women, but on mute.

"That's so nuts" is all the child said, wide-eyed.

The therapist laughed and agreed. Yes, it's totally nuts. She tells him, again, that it's a secret, that he mustn't tell anyone, it would be dangerous. But that isn't what bothers Louis.

"Will I have to chose one of my two moms?" he asks. "Because when parents separate, their kids have to say who they want to live with, their mom or their dad. But, like, obviously this isn't the same."

Louis's right, it isn't the same, the psychologist agrees, but for the child's well-being some sort of pact needs to be agreed on; better than that—an alliance, an agreement that doesn't sacrifice any of them.

Louis wouldn't be able to put this into words or even acknowledge it, but his favorite mom is the one from three months ago, the one who called André every evening and took him to spend a few evenings a week with his grandma. Louis was such an essential element in his mother's life, but from the child's point of view the arrival of this white-haired, slightly mischievous beanpole of a man had come as a relief. It broke up the rut they were in, and Louis had enjoyed the calm, the laughter, and that thoughtful look his mother sometimes got. A less omnipresent mother had her advantages, and when Lucie broke up with André, and Louis was restored to his central position, the child took no pleasure in resuming their routines like an old married couple.

He's known André for three years, and in his timescale that's an eternity. The architect had taken to inviting them to his house in the South of France every summer. And it was there that André had brought an old box down from the attic one evening and taught him to play Dungeons & Dragons, to invent whole worlds, design castles, take on a character and fight off orcs and other monsters. He offered him a boxed set of multisided dice and showed him how to calculate the probabilities of every throw, how to choose the best weapon and the best tactics. Within a few games, Louis had become a level-three elf wizard, and his mother a dwarf archer. André taught him brainteasers too.

"I have a riddle for you," Louis says to the psychologist.

"Go ahead," she replies with a smile.

"The poor have it, the rich need it, and if you eat it you die."

The psychologist gives up.

"It's nothing."

"Nothing?"

"Nothing. The poor have nothing, the rich need nothing, and if you eat nothing you die."

"That's very good. I need to remember that one."

"To work out which mom I stay with, I could throw dice," Louis suggests.

The psychologist's first reaction is to smile. Mallarmé wasn't wrong when he said a throw of the dice will never abolish chance: it certainly won't abolish this unholy mess. And she so loved Luke Rhinehart's *The Dice Man,* a cult classic from the '70s in which a psychiatrist mired in boredom and dissatisfaction starts throwing dice to make his every decision in life. Mostly, she admires Louis's intelligence in adopting this strategy to avoid enormous tension, the spontaneous irony that proves his maturity. Then, in a flash, she realizes it's staggeringly obvious: Louis's right. That's what he needs to do to ensure he's still in control of his life but doesn't have to bear the weight of a decision.

"Yes, that's a great idea, Louis," she says and, wanting the child himself to work out the rules, she adds, "How do you think it would work?"

"At the start of each week, I'd throw the dice seven times, once for each day of the week. If it's an even number for Monday, that's one mom, if it's odd, it's the other, and so on."

"Why not?"

Rapid calculations tell her that the risk of either one of the Lucie's being deprived of seeing her son for a week is less than one in a hundred, less than one in a thousand for ten consecutive days. Neither Lucie would be sacrificed or would feel like contesting the result of a throw of the dice. They would work it out.

"Shall we go see them, then?" the psychologist asks.

Louis nods, and they head for the room where the two Lucies are waiting. When he's standing in the doorway he looks at one, then the other, and for a second time says, It's totally nuts. He comes into the room, and with out favoring one or the other, sits down facing them both and calmly explains his idea.

The two women try to contain the lava churning inside them; they smile at Louis, and each one tries to catch her son's smile. If Louis were a dog and one of them had a tasty tidbit, she'd hide it in her hand to lure him over. But they also watch him, both of them; they listen to him, and deep down, they admire this son of theirs who's just so wonderful.

When he's finished, there's quite a pause, to the point of being awkward.

"I thought of it 'cause of Dungeons and Dragons," Louis says, breaking the silence, and he smiles proudly, as if this explains everything. At this point both women nod their heads, resigned to his idea. Sometimes the worst solution is the best.

"I have a riddle for you," says Louis. "We were born to the same mother, in the same year, in the same month, on the same day, and at the same hour. But we're not twins. How come?"

Both Lucies shake their heads, mystified.

"We're triplets!" Louis announces, laughing.

PORTRAIT OF VICTOR MIESEL AS A REVENANT

TUESDAY, JUNE 29, 2021

YPORT CLIFF, NORMANDY

IT WAS HERE. The broom bends in the westerly wind and albatrosses glide in the English Channel's gray skies. The mist rising off the sea erodes the outlines of Yport's white houses far below. Victor is lying in the tall grass looking up at the clouds. A seagull alights near him, and he wishes it would come closer and even touch him with its wings, communicating some of its primordial life force to him now that he's reduced to nothing but doubt. He stands up, walks over to the cliff, sits on the edge of the precipice, and skims his fingers over the white chalk washed clean by the rain a hundred times.

Yes, it was here, right here, that the ashes of another Victor Miesel were scattered at the end of April. The hero of his first novel, *The Mountains Will Come to Find Us,* chooses to take his own life here, and Clémence Balmer remembered that, so she opted for this place. It was here that she read the words of Kohelet, son of David.

Vanity of vanities, says Kohelet.
Havel havalim
Havel, *says Kohelet, all is vanity.*
All streams run to the sea,
but the sea is not full;
to the place where the streams flow,
there they flow again.
What has been is what will be,
and what has been done is what will be done:
there is nothing new under the sun.

Then she gave a restrained, deeply felt speech about the importance of these rituals, these contrivances that the living come up with to make the unacceptable bearable. It started to rain, and she liked this good honest rain that came and disguised the tears she hadn't been expecting. "Death is never worthy of us, Victor, it's always solitary. But we can hope that this time for final farewells is at least useful for those who are left behind. If the Stoics are right, if there is nothing between people, no love or tenderness or friendship, but instead the body is everything, if it's true that all our feelings are rooted in ourselves, well then, Victor, these last words won't be pointless."

Clémence could very well repeat these same words to the ghost she's watching walk dangerously near the cliff edge. She calls out to him not to go too close to the edge, but can't make herself heard over the wind. Victor turns around, gives her a wave, and comes back over to her smiling.

"It's wonderful when a friend dies and you can think, still not me, then!"

Clémence is disconcerted: her Victor is definitely back. Very early this morning, an Airbus chartered by the army dropped him and the other French passengers from Flight 006 at the Évreux-Fauville military base. For hours on end they were given explanations. He is the first to have been released: there's no anticipated confrontation with another Victor Miesel. That makes half as much work for the psychologists, but the one allocated to him by the "services" won't let him out of her sight. As this situation isn't inventoried in any manual, all Joséphine Mikaleff can do is improvise.

"You were right to come here first to pay your respects," she says.

"I didn't pay my respects. I'm not in mourning for myself. For a moment I thought that coming to this cliff might somehow help me understand, but actually it didn't, at all. I just feel like I've been kept locked up for four days, like I left home in winter and arrived back in summer. Let's go have some lunch in town. I need an andouillette. And a glass of Médoc. Several even."

They climb into the black Peugeot and drive slowly to Étretat, with a man from the Protection Service for dignitaries and celebrities at the wheel. The young psychologist has taken the passenger seat, and Victor and Clémence are in the back. The car is silent, the only sound is the psychologist's constant typing on her keyboard. Victor loses himself in the landscape of grass and chalk, and his editor can't take her eyes off him. She had resigned herself to never seeing him again, and she doesn't know what to think of the turmoil that his reappearance has produced in her. Having reread all his books, she's closer to him than ever. His absence had opened the way for an infatuation in her.

Once in the restaurant, Victor chooses a round table and insists that they all eat together, including the police officer, even though this isn't regulation. He orders his andouillette and a bottle of 2016 Château La Paillette.

"Do you realize," he says, smiling at Clémence, "we had dinner together last week and it was the beginning of March. So, are you glad to see me?"

She looks at him thoughtfully, but her gaze drifts off far behind him. That walk through the rain and mud with the urn in her hands. The white swirl of ashes, the sound of the wind, the words from Ecclesiastes: "What has been is what will be, and what has been done is what will be done: there is nothing new under the sun."

"Clémence?" Victor asks, hauling her away from her thoughts. "Are you happy to see me again?"

"Yes, Victor, very happy. I'm so sorry. I've been through two terrible and very strange months. And now this. It's quite..."

She tries to find the words. There's a Jewish joke that says God often rereads the Torah to try to understand what's going on in this world he created.

"Why've you told me?" she asks. "Why me and only me?"

"I trust you more than anyone else, I know you're discreet. Did you tell anyone? No. You see?"

"It's only delaying the moment. Everyone will soon know it was your plane."

"Not necessarily," Mikaleff intervenes. "The list of passengers will be kept secret for all time, the services will guarantee that."

"I could disappear," Victor says, "start a new life with a different identity. The government has offered us that option."

"First of all, you don't want to, and it would be impossible for you," says Clémence, switching on her tablet and going to the publishing company's site. She clicks on "New books," *The anomaly,* and then the "media coverage" icon.

"More than one hundred articles and shows, and your face is everywhere. On the front page of this month's *Lire* magazine. Six translations already underway, and when they find out that you're...can you imagine the excitement...so for you to disappear...unless you have cosmetic surgery..."

Victor read *The anomaly* at Évreux base this morning. He recognized his style but couldn't find himself in it. He doesn't appreciate that formulaic sort of art and has no fascination for aphorisms. The enthusiasm generated by the book is beyond him.

"It's like Jankélévitch on LSD," he quips. "Another me. I hadn't written a line of it before I left for New York."

"I can see something of you in it, and I like it," says Clémence. "Otherwise I wouldn't have published it. You'll have to get used to it, it's sold more than two hundred thousand copies..."

"I should have tried LSD earlier..."

She closes up her tablet, and with considerable resolve, pours a glass of Médoc.

"We'll need to announce your 'resurrection.' Livio's going to be thrilled."

"What? Salerno?"

"He's the driving force behind your club of posthumous friends."

"He's not what I'd call a friend," says Victor. "We had mutual friends."

"It seems you saw a lot of each other before you . . . before the . . . Either way, he gave a wonderful eulogy at the crematorium, with that Italian accent of his and quoting from your books."

"Livio's always liked funerals. Eulogies are his absolute niche, he gets to be both modest and generous-hearted."

"I have to say," Clémence admits, "he looked like he was in his element. In any case, there's also Ilena. She's—"

"Ilena? She left me six months ago. Well, I mean nine . . ."

"You made up . . . in those last few months. She even says you were back together."

"I'd be very surprised."

The morning Ilena left him, last fall, they were at the Wepler and she was sipping her perennial "double decaf latte with extra hot water and not too much milk please," and was keen to inform him that she'd had a lover all along and "*his* crew mean well." Victor was so surprised that he made her repeat those words, and she did, angrily, breaking up all the syllables: "*he* screw me well." He shrugged his shoulders, laughed out loud and muttered, "Yeah, whatever, Ilena, whatever you say!" She got to her feet and added, "I pity you," making the word "pity" reverberate around the room for the edification of their paltry audience. Then she left without a backward glance, although not before casting her haughty eye over the room to check that no one present was in any doubt about how abjectly pathetic this man was. He watched her stride resolutely away, and acknowledging how absurd the situation was, gradually succumbed to laughter.

So, yes, he'd be very surprised if they'd had a reconciliation.

"Dying was a good idea," he sighs. "Basically, you're right, everyone's going to be very pleased to see me."

"Well, I am," says Clémence, laughing. "When the Homeland Security people came to the office and explained the situation and then brought me here, I was terrified. I thought I'd be meeting a . . . an alien. A man with empty eyes and an ice-cold voice, like in that film, you know, *Invasion of the Body Snatchers*."

"Sorry, Clémence, it's just the same old me. Actually, two questions. Practical ones. I need a working cellphone—the SIM in mine's been deactivated. I feel cut off from the world. I'd really like to call my 'widow' . . . and hear the happiness in her voice."

"You'll get all of that, Mr. Miesel," says the Protection Service officer. "You'll need to be careful whom you call."

"I also want to go home."

"A room has been reserved for you in Levallois, Mr. Miesel. In the counterespionage premises that belong to the General Directorate for Internal Security. We'll find you a hotel in Paris tomorrow."

"And then..." Clémence starts, but she doesn't know where to begin. His apartment being emptied by distant family members, who promptly divided up his furniture and put the apartment up for sale—"we can't ask top price because of the suicide, right?"—the tremendously proactive Friends' Society...Victor doesn't comment or seem outraged.

"As for your book collection," she continues, "there was a party at your place, and everyone helped themselves. There are lots left in cardboard boxes, stuff by Jarry, Dostoyevsky... No one reads them these days. Your cousins took the Pléiade collections: they're decorative shelf-fillers, and they sell well on eBay."

"The government is doing everything to ensure you recover your assets, Mr. Miesel," the officer tells him.

There's one question haunting Clémence, but the psychologist asks it before she does: "We already talked about this on the flight, Victor, but... what could have driven the 'other' Victor to take his own life?"

The writer looks amused.

"No one takes their own life, didn't they teach you that? There are just tortured souls who escape by killing their torturer."

"Couldn't it be because of... Ilena Leskov?" Mikaleff pursues her point. "I know *The anomaly* is being translated into a lot of languages, but your original French title, *L'anomalie*, is an anagram of *Amo Ilena L*—'I love Ilena L.'"

Miesel roars with laughter.

"Is it? Really? Who came up with an idea like that?"

"Ilena hinted at it in an interview."

"Thank goodness for Latin to make use of that *amo*. The only good language is a dead language, as General Sheridan might say. But joking aside, I have no idea why he did it. *I*'m not suicidal. Mind you, I'd gladly kill myself, especially as later will already be too late."

"Aha!" exclaims Clémence, opening her tablet again, scrolling through it feverishly and triumphantly showing Victor a phrase from *The anomaly*.

"You've just quoted from Victør Miesel."

She pronounces the name "Victerr," rolling the "r" and enjoying lingering on the "ø."

"Oops, it must be this Médocation I'm on, Clémence, that's all I can say."

His editor smiles at the terrible pun, opens her bag, and hands Victor a large envelope.

"Here. You had all this on you when you jumped."

Victor tears it open. Inside he finds his cellphone, his keys, and a red Lego brick. He delves into his own pocket, brings out the twin brick and sets it down next to the other one. He studies them, intrigued, straightening them. His memory fits perfectly with the recollection.

WEDNESDAY, JUNE 30, 2021

THE SALON, LUTETIA HOTEL, PARIS

Clémence Balmer has summoned the press for an event with the title THE DOUBLE LIFE OF VICTØR MIESEL, giving prominence on the invitation to this extract from *The anomaly*: "I'm afraid of putting too much faith in the incompetence of my future biographer."

The place is packed. Victor is waiting in a small connecting room with the team from Orange Tree Editions. The setup terrifies him: a raised stage, a table, and a chair each for Clémence and himself, facing hundreds of other chairs, all of them occupied. A good dozen television cameras are waiting for him at the back of the room.

"There are journalists from all over the world here," says Clémence. "Your book's coming out next week pretty much everywhere . . . Superfast translations . . . are sometimes less accurate."

"But still, I'm not George Clooney."

"You're much more. You're somewhere between Romain Gary and Jesus Christ. Suicide and resurrection."

Victor shrugs. Clémence dusts off his gray jacket affectionately, while he opens the door a crack to look at the room full of journalists.

"And my beloved Ilena isn't here? My widow must have stayed home enjoying this crew."

"Excuse me?" Clémence asks, frowning.

"No, nothing, *I* understand what I mean."

His editor checks her watch. It's six o'clock.

"We'd better go. We're running late because of security checks at the door. A lot of them want to open their eight o'clock newscasts with you."

"Does that whole circus still exist? Didn't twenty-four-hour news channels and the internet kill it off?"

"Ten million people watch those shows. Let's go. Thanks to that half a Lexomil, I can see you're super relaxed. Maybe too much. No clowning around, I beg you."

"Cross my heart and hope to die!" Victor jokes.

He comes out from the back room, steps onto the stage amid a burst of flashbulbs, sits on his chair, and stifles a yawn. He really is relaxed.

"Good evening, all of you," Clémence Balmer says, mic in hand. "I'll be brief because I'm guessing you have a lot of questions..."

Victor doesn't recognize any of the journalists here. There's little chance they'll be talking about literature—the papers have sent reporters, not book critics. If so much as one of them has read *The anomaly,* it will have been out of professional duty. When Clémence has finished her presentation, they all raise their hands. She calmly keeps control of the chaos and gives the first question to a tall man in the first row.

"Jean Rigal from *Le Monde*, Mr. Miesel. You feel like it's only a week since you left Paris in March. A lot has happened in the last four months, particularly for you, you've written a book and you've—well, the only way to put it is you've died. What's this incredible experience like for you?"

"I'm adapting as best I can. I've read 'my' book, along with my obituaries in various papers. Just reading those is enough to make you want to die."

"Do you think of *The anomaly* as a book you wrote?"

"Define 'you.'"

Victor suspects that Clémence is privately rolling her eyes, so he backtracks: "Forgive me that little flourish. I definitely recognize my voice in some of the book's wording. But that doesn't mean it's a book that I, the person speaking to you now, wrote. I'm getting the royalties, which is what matters."

"We said no clowning" is the clear message in the sigh from Clémence, who's regretting recommending that antianxiety pill.

"Would you say that your book contains the key to what happened in that plane?"

"Millions of people are looking for that. If there even is a key, they'll find it before I do. Especially as, and everyone knows this, when you have a hammer, everything ends up looking like a nail."

"Do you think we're all in a simulation?"

"I have no idea," Victor says simply. "To paraphrase Woody Allen, I'd say if we are, I hope the programmers have a good excuse. Because the world they created really is a hell of a mess. Except that, as far as I can see, *we*'re actually the ones making the mess."

"As you probably know, Mr. Miesel, almost all the passengers on the flight are refusing to reveal their identities. Why did you decide to live out in the open, so to speak?"

"I don't think I face any kind of threat. I have police protection, anyway. And psychological support. They've thought of everything."

"Do you think you felt the exact moment of what some people are calling 'divergence,' or more recently the 'anomaly'?"

"Of course, like everyone else on the plane. The turbulence stopped and the sun came streaming into the cabin. That last sentence is also the definition of Prozac."

A lot of people laugh, so does Victor; he's riding a bit of a wave, and Clémence is in despair about the coverage.

"Do you know why your 'double' committed suicide?"

"He probably wanted to die. That's the main reason for suicides."

"What exactly is your relationship with Ilena Leskov?"

"Currently nonexistent. At best, we could say it's antemortem."

Victor is now glowing, a living commercial for bromazepam.

"Anne Vasseur, *Times Literary Supplement*. Are you working on a new book, Mr. Miesel?"

Victor looks at the back row, where this delicately husky feminine voice came from. His face lights up. It's the young woman from the conference in Arles, the one who took an interest in Goncharov's humor.

"Yes. I'm writing at the moment."

Clémence turns to him in amazement.

"It's a classic theme," Miesel continues, "a woman reappears in a man's life when he thought he'd never see her again. It will be called *Ascot, or the Return of Whipped Cream*."

"What an extraordinary title," the young woman says with a smile.

"One last question," Clémence Balmer requests, guessing that her author now has better things on his mind than ensuring the smooth running of her press conference.

"Andrea Hilfinger, *Frankfurter Allgemeine Zeitung*. How would you define what happened in the United States yesterday evening?"

"Define it? I think the *United* States of America is just a name now. There have always been two Americas, and now they don't understand each other. Seeing as I tend to identify with one of them, I don't understand the other one either."

THE LATE SHOW

TUESDAY, JUNE 29, 2021

ED SULLIVAN THEATER, NEW YORK

THE HEAD MAKEUP artist for *The Late Show with Stephen Colbert* contemplates her work, enraptured.

"You're gorgeous, Adriana. I thought it was a good idea to style your hair a little differently."

"Stephen's finishing his introduction," the production assistant interrupts. "Come with me. When I touch your shoulder, you step out onto the set, okay?"

She doesn't wait for an answer and leaves the dressing room: the two young women walk along the corridor toward the lights on set and wait behind the black curtain while the group Stay Human finishes its number.

Facing the audience from behind his desk, Stephen Colbert checks his notes, and when the camera is back on him, the CBS star host draws his brows into a frown.

"This evening I have the privilege of welcoming a super-young actress whose fame is, well, totally in keeping with her age [*groans of disappointment*]. Please, remember your manners, I'm ashamed of you [*laughter*]. So, ladies and gentlemen, I'd like you to welcome . . . Adriana Becker."

Colbert opens one arm to the wings; the "Applause" panel lights up and is immediately obeyed.

A young woman steps forward: she is slight, almost a teenager, in jeans, sneakers, and a dark-blue angora sweater. Her hair falls to her shoulders in chestnut curls. The host goes over to her and gives her a kiss on the cheek to reassure her.

"Hi, Adriana. It's great to have you on the show."

"Hi, Stephen. I'm so happy to be here."

"And impressed too, I hope. First time on TV?"

"Yes."

"There's a first time for everything. I remember my first love, our first dinner in a restaurant, it was very romantic, in fact I even kept the check [*laughter*]. So, Adriana, you're twenty years old and you're an actor. You were in *Romeo and Juliet* back in May. And you played?"

"Juliet."

"Of course, you were Juliet. And where did you perform *Romeo and Juliet*?"

"At the Sandra Feinstein-Gamm Theatre."

She mutters the theater's name in a whisper, and there's some unkind sniggering in the auditorium. The super-young interviewee blushes. Stephen Colbert raises his eyebrows questioningly.

"It's... in Warwick, Rhode Island. It's a small theater..." she adds.

"Adriana, there's nothing to be embarrassed about. Matt Damon started out in a bit part, you know. He was a pizza-slinger who handed a Margherita to a customer and he just had one line: 'Five dollars, please.' He now claims it was a Four Seasons for seven dollars, but he's a terrible show-off [*laughter*]. I'm sorry, Adriana. So tell me, what's your next play going to be?"

"*Desire Under the Elms*, a three-act play by Eugene O'Neill. I'll be playing the part of the young girl."

"The young girl?... But there's going to be a problem, Adriana. I mean if there's only one young girl in this play. Wouldn't you say?"

Adriana Becker laughs. So does the audience, although no one understands. Stephen Colbert smiles and turns toward the wings.

"And now, ladies and gentlemen, I'd like thunderous applause for Adriana Becker! Yes, Adriana Becker!"

From behind the curtains a second Adriana emerges. Her clothes are identical, except that her sweater is red.

The entire audience is on its feet, stunned, whooping and clapping, while Colbert walks over to her, kisses her, and leads her over to the sofa where her twin is sitting. In the control room, the director takes a drag on her e-cigarette, flouting the company's regulations, along with legislation. This is fucking good television, and the channel's pulverizing ABC and NBC on the back of it. Behind her are about a dozen of CBS's social media team, busy tweeting, posting on Instagram, and creating Facebook Live streams. The number of likes and shares is going through the roof.

Here they are, side by side, a lock of red hair over one of their foreheads, a lock of blue over the other—a subtle touch from the makeup artist, subtle but suddenly blatant. The applause keeps on coming, then Colbert goes back behind his desk.

"Hi, Adriana."

"Hi, Stephen," replies the new guest.

"Aren't you twins?"

"No, absolutely not," both young women say at the same time, with the same smile and the same energy.

"Right, well, I think the audience gets that [*laughter*]. In the last few hours, you people are all anyone can talk about. I'm going to have to differentiate between you by saying Adriana June and Adriana March. June and March are the FBI code names, is that right?"

"Yes."

"June is in red and March is in blue, that's how I can tell you apart... Don't tell me that's wrong, the production invested a lot of money in those sweaters and dyeing your bangs!"

"Okay."

This same response comes simultaneously from the two interviewees, producing the same delight in the audience. Young Adriana, or rather both young Adrianas, are instant superstars.

"Adriana June, you didn't play Juliet, is that right?"

"That's right, I didn't."

"No, you didn't play Juliet, because *Romeo and Juliet* was in May. Tell me, when you landed at McGuire military base five days ago now, and were held there along with two hundred forty-two other people, were you convinced it was March?"

"Yes, Stephen. I can't tell you the exact date, the FBI has banned us from disclosing it. For everyone's safety."

"I understand. What I'd like to know, and I think the audience would like to know about this too, how did you find out... that you had a 'double'?"

He peers intently at the two young women before continuing: "Adriana March, very early last Sunday morning the FBI came to collect you and your parents, right?... in—" he unhurriedly consults his notes "—in Edison, New Jersey. Your parents must have been terrified... and you too..."

"Yes, the FBI agents told us that it was a question of national security. But they did try to be reassuring."

"Well, you're right, having two FBI agents show up at dawn is always reassuring [*laughter*]. Then what happened?"

"Then what happened was I was taken to the base by helicopter. And they—"

"First time in a helicopter?"

"Yes."

"It's noisy. A washing machine on the spin cycle. The blades, the updraft, and all that. I can't stand helicopters."

Colbert is toying with the audience's mounting impatience, but he knows where and when to stop.

"And once you arrived at the military base?"

"I was taken into a big administrative building guarded by soldiers, and I was shown to this ordinary room with a table and a few chairs. I sat down with a psychologist on one side of me and an FBI agent on the other."

"What did they say to you?" Colbert asks.

"That I shouldn't be scared, that I was going to experience something extraordinary."

"And that's when..."

"They brought me in," says Adriana June. "I also had a psychologist with me."

"It must have been a shock for you. And for the psychologists too..." [*laughter*]

"It took me a few seconds to realize that I was looking at... myself," continues the guest in the blue sweater. "My head started spinning, I wondered who I was, if I really existed."

"How about you, Adriana June, tell us what happened," Colbert says, turning his attention to her.

"Our flight had landed three days earlier..."

"In March, as far as you knew..."

"Yes. We hit terrible turbulence, the plane was damaged. I was detained with no contact with the outside world, no cellphone or anything..."

"You mean you couldn't even play Candy Crush? [*laughter*] So, on Monday morning, the third day..."

"These people came to fetch me, and they told me the same thing, I'd experience something extraordinary et cetera, et cetera, and I was going to meet someone that I couldn't possibly meet..."

"And who did you think they meant?"

"I know it's ridiculous, but I thought I was going to see my grandma again. She just died in January..." [*an emotional "Aw!"*]

"Oh, I'm so sorry to hear that, Adriana. My condolences."

"So, I walked into that room..."

Adriana June looks at Adriana March, who's smiling. The audience starts clapping again. Not wanting to lose the momentum, Colbert presses on immediately.

"Oh my God... In your shoes, I would have had a heart attack. In fact, I would have had two heart attacks. [*laughter*] Weren't you terrified? Adriana March?"

"Yes, of course I was. At first we didn't dare speak to each other, we just answered questions from the psychologists and the FBI woman. They showed us videos... explaining. It showed the exact time on the plane when... the moment of..."

"Of divergence or of the anomaly." Colbert finishes the sentence for her, looking at his notes.

"Yes. And then they suggested we ask each other whatever questions we felt like asking. The FBI wanted to prove to both of us that the other one wasn't... I don't know, some kind of clone. That we both had the same memories, the same life."

"The same life right up until March and that Paris–New York flight," Colbert clarifies. "So tell me, Adriana March, did you ask Adriana June something that only you knew?"

"Yes. Something that happened on New Year's Eve, but I'm the only person who knows about it," Adriana March replies shyly.

"Well, we're the only two people who know about it," adds Adriana June. [*laughter*]

Three people, in fact: the two of them and their younger brother, whose room Adriana should never have walked into without knocking and giving him time to close his laptop.

"Well, you're very lucky there," Colbert says with a suave smile, "I drank so much on New Year's Eve that my memories kick back in at about midday on January 4. [*laughter*] So are you now convinced that you're . . . both Adriana?"

"Absolutely convinced," they say at the same time, producing an ecstatic response from the captivated audience.

"You know, I sometimes think we came close to disaster, it could have happened to Air Force One. Can you imagine? Two presidents? [*shouting and clapping*] The pair of them would have brought Twitter to its knees within a day. I'm guessing you were given various scientific hypotheses, the ones we've seen all over the press recently . . ."

The two young women nod their heads.

"Is there an interpretation that you think is more plausible than the others?" he asks.

They shake their heads.

"Either way, you don't seem like simulations to me. There are some people who even think all two hundred forty-three of you are aliens. And you're going to invade the Earth. [*laughter*] And what are you going to do now?

Adriana June, you went home to your parents, of course you did, you live there..."

"They put me in my younger brother's old bedroom, he's a student at Duke. I saw him last night, when the FBI brought us home."

"His name's Oscar, right? How did he react? Adriana March?"

"He said 'that's nuts' at least ten times. And suggested we wear our hair differently."

The audience laughs, so do the Adrianas, and Colbert turns away from them to address the camera.

"Oscar is in the theater. We also invited your parents to join us, but they declined. How is this all working out with them?"

The two interviewees look at each other, and June is first to answer.

"My mom is scared. She didn't dare kiss me this morning."

"She's scared of both of us," adds Adriana March. "She can't tell which of us is which, and she thinks one of us..."

"Is 'fake,'" Adriana June fills in the blank.

"And your father?"

Both young women are silent. The production team regret not fully informing Colbert: an FBI agent and a psychologist arrived at the Becker home in Edison before the two Adrianas returned on Wednesday evening. They explained the inconceivable to the Adrianas' parents, at great length. Their mother kept saying, But how in God's name is it possible? And when the girls finally made their entry, their father, who'd been slumped listlessly on the sofa, sat up, terrified, backed away up the stairs without a word, and shut himself in his bedroom. It took a lot of negotiating through the door for him to agree to come out. His behavior since then has so alarmed the FBI that the bureau has insisted on having an agent on the premises at all times.

Colbert realizes he needs to avoid the subject. Before the silence gets awkward, he turns to the Adriana in the red sweater.

"Anybody would have trouble adapting to such a unique situation. Unique really isn't the word. [*laughter*] Your parents love you and they'll be happy that they now have *two* such wonderful daughters."

The audience applauds this fairy tale; on and on they clap, until Colbert has to interrupt them.

"And how are things between the two of you?"

"Good," says Adriana June, and Adriana March nods in agreement.

This is no white lie. The two young women aren't rivals. They have their life before them, a future to conquer, they don't yet have anything they need to share.

"Do you have a boyfriend, Adriana June? I'm not the Spanish Inquisition, no one would mind if you kept that information to yourself."

"No, I'm happy to answer. I'm single."

"Well, Adriana, admitting that here—and live—wasn't a good idea." [*laughter*]

Colbert turns toward the blue Adriana.

"How about you, Adriana March? Have you met someone since March?"

"Yes, three months ago."

"Thank you for sharing that with us, Adriana. What's his name?"

"Nolan."

The audience murmurs excitedly. Up in the control room, the production team is ecstatic: love is always a big draw.

"I think I'm right in saying," Colbert continues, "that Nolan was also in the cast of *Romeo and Juliet*. Don't tell me he was Romeo?"

"No, he was Mercutio."

"Ah, Mercutio! Romeo's best friend. Could we possibly have Nolan-Mercutio in the theater with us?"

A spotlight slowly scours the rows of onlookers, tilts down to the front row, and comes to rest on a young Black man. He's tall and slim, with a huge smile, and he gets to his feet amid enthusiastic applause.

"Ladies and gentlemen, please welcome Nolan Simmons."

Colbert gestures for him to step up onto the stage, and the clapping just keeps on coming, as anyone could have predicted. The Adrianas smile and wave, Adriana March simpers a little while Adriana June watches Nolan with an astonished smile that raises a laugh. She met Nolan in the wings, but she's acting surprised, it's her way of ensuring the attention comes back to her. Neither one of the Adrianas took much persuading to play this scene, and Nolan was barely more difficult to convince. *The Late Show with Stephen Colbert* is damn good entertainment, and these young actors didn't choose this profession in order to avoid the limelight and skulk in bashful modesty. They're all playing along, on with the show.

"You can kiss your girlfriend, Nolan. But don't get the wrong one!" [*laughter*]

The young man gives Adriana March a tender kiss on the cheek, then briefly shakes Adriana June's hand.

"Don't worry, son," says Colbert, shaking his head, "no one's ever been prepared for a situation like this. Tell me honestly, Nolan, if you'd met them in the dressing room would you have known who was who? And what if I told you that right from the start, we asked each of them to play the other part? What if we tried to trick you?"

A stunned muttering buzzes through the audience. Now genuinely unsure, Nolan loses his composure and instinctively backs away from Adriana March. It's not working. The audience is suddenly worried, there's an awkward tension, and Colbert immediately regrets his ruse.

"Don't worry, Nolan. She really is *your* Adriana. [*Oohs of relief*] That was a terrible trick to play, I couldn't resist it. Forgive me..."

Nolan takes Adriana's hand again, and Colbert grimaces. He's annoyed with himself for showing a cruel streak, and all because he let improvisation take over. He rereads his notes and comes back to his scripted suavity.

"So..." he says, "how are you going to share out the roles now?"

While the *The Late Show* reverts to its good-natured mood, uneasiness is settling over the control room, where some of the screens are relaying images from outside the Ed Sullivan Theater. The moment word was out on social media, dozens of Christian zealots started converging on the theater, and they've been laying siege to it for the last ten minutes.

"Who knew we had so many God fanatics in New York," the producer says with a forced smile.

The show's security has been doubled for the occasion. An inadequate cordon of policemen is trying to keep the crowd at a distance, but right in front of the surveillance cameras, demonstrators are yelling, spewing out their fear and loathing, and waving signs that read "*Vade retro*," "Daughters of Hell," "Spawn of Satan," "Blasphemy..."

"Blasphemy? Where's the blasphemy?" asks the producer.

"I read that they think the doubles are damned," ventures an assistant. "Among other things because of the tenth commandment."

"Which one's that?"

"You know perfectly well... 'Thou shalt not covet thy neighbor's wife; thou shalt not desire thy neighbor's house, et cetera.' Obviously, it's impossible for these people to respect that, because they own the same stuff. On the other hand, you could argue that they're not each other's 'neighbors...'"

"Yeah, right. I don't think these crazies are big on textual interpretation."

Out of nowhere, just as police reinforcements come to strengthen the line of defense, a Molotov cocktail flies in a parabola of flames and explodes in the entrance to the theater. The theater's security staff swiftly put out the fire, while the police take out their clubs, push back the demonstrators, and start making arrests. But their efforts are in vain; the small hyped-up crowd is swelling, pushing over barriers and trying to barge through to the theater's front entrance.

The show is nearly over, and Colbert, now tipped off about the incident, turns to address the audience.

"My friends, we're all going to have to stay in this theater a little longer than planned. There's a very aggressive demonstration going on outside, and there are clashes with the police. We'd be putting you at risk if we let you out now. And actually, that brings me to my last question for both of you, Adriana and Adriana: the FBI has already warned you about the dangers of religious fanaticism. There have been statements from the leaders of various congregations describing you—and I mean both of you—as 'the devil's creatures' and 'abominations.' Have you personally received death threats?"

"Yes, like hundreds, on my Facebook page, I mean, ours."

"I'm so sorry to hear that. So, what would you like to say to these people, who may simply be scared because they don't understand?"

Colbert allows a silence to develop. This is the show's moment of tension that everyone will remember. He and the two interviewees went over it at length, with the help of the specialists delegated by the crisis unit. It's a patiently rehearsed speech that needs to give the illusion of being off the cuff, and it's Adriana June who must deliver it—the psychologists were categorical about that—because she's the one whom most people will think of as the intruder.

"Well, obviously, I don't know how that plane came to land a second time," she says softly. "Nobody knows. *That's right, it's especially important to talk slowly, steadily, show that you're struggling to find the words, communicate your emotion.* What I'd like to say to all those people who are scared is me too, I'm scared too. If everyone could just try to imagine what we're going through. I wasn't, like, picked out for a reason, and I definitely wasn't 'chosen.' And neither was any one of the two hundred forty-three people on that plane. What's happening to me, what's happening to us, could have happened to anyone in this theater. I'm just anybody . . . *If possible, repeat that. Actually no, that's going too far.* There's nothing special about me, *leave a pause,* I'm just this twenty-year-old girl who lives in Edison and wants to be an elementary school teacher, *Don't say French teacher, a lot of people don't like the French, and don't say just 'teacher,' make sure you remember to say 'elementary school,' everybody likes a woman who teaches little kids,* I'm this girl who enjoys performing in amateur theater, *really emphasize the 'amateur,'* and she was on her way back from Europe in early March, *yes, and here it's better to say Europe than France,* only to find it's June, and she has no idea what's happening to her, but she just has to deal with it. *Another pause, stammer a bit, don't find the words right away.* And this other girl . . . who's here next to me and who's just as much me as I am . . . she has to deal with it too. This Adriana has lived through three more months than I have, but we have the same memories, we have the same faith in God, *shit, I almost forgot God, that was the most important part, they really made a thing about it, make sure everybody knows we're believers, I can't believe I nearly forgot,* we have the same friends, the same parents, we both love them as much as each other, we even have to share my clothes, because they're her clothes too."

"And plus," Adriana March interrupts, "we always feel like wearing the same thing at the same time." *That was one of Colbert's ideas, and a good one, actually. Wait for the laughter, there it is, then keep going.*

"That's right," says Adriana June. "So, from now on, obviously our two lives will go their separate ways. They've already started to. *Turn to look at Nolan, gauge the mood in the theater.* I mean, I don't know how this would work out if I'd met Nolan before traveling to Europe, if *I* was in love with him. *Don't make a big deal of it, just let the audience identify, get an idea of the turmoil.* That's one of the hundreds of things going around in circles in my head."

"I think," says Adriana March, *in a slightly different voice, emphasize the possibility of differences between you,* "I think all I want is for no one to be afraid of me, or the other Adriana, or of the two of us. For them to be kind. *Leave a really long pause here, then it's the conclusion.* We're lost, we need the love of all the people we love." *Look down, take Adriana June's hand, wait for the applause. If you can manage to cry, definitely go ahead and cry.*

A tear rolls down Adriana June's cheek, she didn't have to force it, she's overrun with emotion and could easily start sobbing. Adriana March moves closer to her and puts an arm around her shoulders while Colbert watches and smiles.

"Thank you so much, both of you. I know that a lot of people understand what you're saying. I have one last request: your brother told me that last Christmas you sang the famous bossa nova 'The Girl from Ipanema' for your family."

"Yes, the Amy Winehouse version, I did," says Adriana June.

"Well... the both of you, before you leave us, would you?"

The audience goes wild, and the two young guests smile.

"I should add that you haven't rehearsed this," Colbert says, lying shamelessly, given that they spent thirty minutes doing just that.

The drummer from Stay Human starts Jobim and Moraes's bossa nova gently on the hi-hat and the snare, the lights go down on stage, and two soft spotlights pick out the Adrianas, beaming red light on one of them and blue on the other, canceling out their differences. It was the production team's idea to play on the colors like this. Vinícius de Moraes once said that his song is just about time passing, the sad sort of beauty that belongs to everyone and no one, and the melancholy ebb and flow of waves. Ipanema Beach takes over the stage of *The Late Show* as one Adriana starts, joined in the second bar by her twin: "Tall and tan and young and lovely..."

The two Adrianas sing as a perfect duo about that graceful Ipanema siren walking over the fine sand toward the sea. One of them starts a phrase and the other completes it, they make a point of being a whole and yet apart, there's something almost magical about their harmonies, the effect is dizzying. And every frisson produced by this giddy-making loveliness comprises a homeopathic dose of terror.

"Fuck, this is good TV," says the director in the control room. "Fucking good TV."

THE VOICE INSIDE JACOB EVANS

TUESDAY, JUNE 29, 2021, 11:00 PM

ED SULLIVAN THEATER, NEW YORK

THE HAND OF GOD never weakens. And Jacob Evans's every move is guided by Him. Jacob was born to faith in Christ in Scottsville, Virginia, and he knows—because his father John told him so—that those who are not born of suffering are not God's creatures, for nothing is created except through Him, and the voice that won't stop inside his head keeps repeating the words he heard when he was just a boy working on the farm.

When the Abomination was revealed by the press and on social media, God guided Jacob Evans. On the first day, he and his brothers from the Army of the Seventh Day met in the Baptist church and listened while Reverend Roberts talked about the spawn of Satan, the faithless legions, and all those who have offended God because the Book of Revelation, the Apocalypse of John, says that there were lightning bolts and earthquakes and that terrible hail with hailstones weighing a hundred pounds fell from the sky onto mankind, and thanks to God, who is all knowing and who guides us, Reverend Roberts, and Jacob and all the other faithful along with them recognized the storm and the airplane caught in that sacred storm that the Lord put in its path. And all the people inside that plane blaspheme against God because of the scourge of hail for it was a very great scourge.

And ecstasy in the Lord flooded over Jacob Evans's body and His rage flowed through his arms, and He wanted Jacob to accomplish His glory in the world of men.

There are explanations presented and discussed over and over by newspapers, there are debates between experts and scholars, but *I will destroy the wisdom of the wise and I will set aside the intelligence of the intelligent*, because, yes, Jacob remembers Isaiah, he remembers that looking inside ourselves for our own salvation shows pride and contempt for the all-powerful God. This is also the message that Paul gives to the Corinthians, who want to be free of the word of God and seek wisdom in the vanity of mankind when men should be filled only with humility, with fearfulness of the Father, and with faith in our Lord Jesus Christ. *He is risen, he is truly risen.* And this message that God has sent with his Abomination offers salvation only in the glory of the Lord and the destruction of Evil. Jacob's eyes were closed, oh yes, but the Almighty has opened them wide to contemplate the darkness.

And at the very heart of this endless fire that has always consumed America, with this war waged by darkness over enlightenment, a war in which reason gradually backs down in the face of ignorance and the irrational, Jacob Evans puts on the dark breastplate of his own primitive and uncompromising hopes. Religion is a carnivorous fish in the abyssal depths. It emits the feeblest of light and needs a vast darkness around it to attract its prey.

For seven hours Evans and other members of the Army of the Seventh Day drove in a procession of cars bearing the cross of Christ the Savior. They screamed the Wrath of the Lord outside the military base, but the soldiers kept them at bay. But now, with the help of God and Instagram and Facebook, Jacob discovers that one of these Monstrosities will be parading itself before the world this evening. Jacob stares in disgust at an image of this girl and knows that she incarnates the Great Lie and the devious ways of the Fallen Angel.

Jacob is one of many who converge on the CBS theater, alighting at the Fiftieth Street subway station into the neon glow and multicolored lights of Broadway. They march through Babylon the Great, through the Great Prostitute incarnated in a city, but the police have blocked the southern entrance to the avenue and there are metal barriers preventing access to the theater. The fanatical crowd is growing, bolstered with each passing minute thanks to rallying cries on social media.

At midnight a first flaming bottle flies through the air and shatters against the brightly illuminated awning, the fire immediately causes a short circuit and shuts down thousands of bulbs, along with the glittering sign for *The Late Show with Stephen Colbert,* but Jacob marches on through the flames, He is *not afraid of Hell, and Jesus rejoices in his heart.* The police charge and arrest some of the rioters. And Jacob begs the Lord to let him approach the Impure, to let him accomplish His will. In the heat of the fire he prays to the Lord and knows that he will soon taste the sweetness of Paradise among the chosen.

From high up on His mountain, the Lord looks down on his lamb Jacob Evans and He guides him toward Fifty-Third Street. Jacob walks in His light, for *God alone knows the way.* And it is here, while his brothers in God are baying on Broadway, that Jacob sees a black limousine emerge from an underground parking lot only a few meters away from him. It turns left to avoid the faithful and their demonstration, but the road is full of traffic, and the car slows to a standstill outside a deli on Broadway. Its rear windows glide up as quickly as they can, but in the harsh light of a New York night Jacob glimpses the two young women with such identical faces. *Oh, the depth of the riches of the wisdom of God.* The Abominations are giggling, displaying their too-straight teeth in their repulsive mouths, and their angelic faces bear the perfidious face of the Angel of Darkness. *And the Lord shall guide my avenging sword.*

These Creatures must die, and *there shall be a sky to envelop all men,* and Jacob takes a Grendel P30 from his pocket, *and the light shall glimmer so soft and warm, sustain me, Lord,* and he fires through the window, which shatters *In the name of Jesus Christ I shall drive you out* and all around him there are screams of panic, he fires again and the shot destroys a face, *The Archangel Gabriel shall be upon me,* Jacob keeps firing and empties the magazine into another, blood-soaked Adriana before falling to his knees, *Jesus Christ is born,* then dropping onto the dirty asphalt, he's on the ground, Christ the Savior with his arms spread wide, *Speak one word, my Lord, and my soul shall be saved,* and while officers throw themselves at him and cuff his hands behind his back, while sirens wail around them in the glare of revolving blue lights and camera flashes, *The Lord is my shepherd, I shall not want,* a smiling Jacob Evans with half-closed eyes sees three spirits glide from the mouth of the dragon and the mouth of the Beast and the mouth of the false prophet, and these three spirits look not unlike frogs.

ERASINGS

WEDNESDAY, JUNE 30, 2021

CLYDE TOLSON RESORT, NEW YORK

00:43 in the FBI building. Every screen is now relaying twenty-four-hour news channels, and the Protocol 42 team watches as they air the double murder on loop. At 01:00, CBS broadcasts a special program: a devastated Stephen Colbert chairing a discussion with journalists who specialize in religious affairs. The plea for a cooling-off period devised by Pudlowski and her experts was pointless: on Hope Channel preachers are denouncing the worship of false prophets, and televangelists on Fox are condemning the crime, as is only fitting, while still railing and talking about the end of the world. In the morning, Gallup and other pollsters will scour the streets: forty-four percent of Americans think it's a sign of "the end of days," thirty-four percent of them think the end is "near," twenty-five percent even think "very near." One percent have come up with the idea that it has already happened. And places of worship all over the world will have unprecedented attendance throughout the day. When seven billion human beings find out that they may not really exist, it's not easy to comprehend.

A furious Jamy is striding up and down the conference room at Clyde Tolson Resort where the whole Protocol 42 team has now been convened.

"We need to guarantee anonymity for all the passengers," she says again. "Like with witness protection in Mafia trials. These people need to be able to disappear, to change identity."

Still, she did anticipate that God would be a problem... Given that nothing should contest His omnipotence, this Boeing appearing out of nowhere must be part of His design. Ironically, in the simulation hypothesis there's now one thing that's indisputable: Man really is the creation of a higher intelligence. But who would be prepared to adore the creator of a colossal role-playing game?

"Since the president's announcement," says Mitnick, "hospitals have reported a wave of suicides. A lot of people who were already vulnerable have taken that step. Conspiracy theories are proliferating: the whole thing is a setup, the suggestion of a simulation is intended to make any fight—against anything from capitalism to global warming—look pointless. The flat-earthers are saying it confirms their conviction. To name just a few."

"We should always be wary of the people who tell us to be wary," Pudlowski summarizes.

"Aliens are also making a hell of a comeback," Mitnick continues. "But, I mean, there was no avoiding that... There's this girl too. Tomi Jin, an influencer... She just posted this."

Mitnick puts up on one of the screens a selfie of a slim, dark-haired Asian American woman. It already has 1,512 likes. She has a lock of red hair over her forehead, and the caption reads "One, two, a thousand Adrianas." By two in the morning, it has been shared 12,816 times. It will be seven million times at eight o'clock. And by then thousands of people with Adriana June's red-dyed bangs will be marching in the streets, from Paris to Rio and Hong Kong to New York. Their message is obscure, but freedom of thought on the internet is all the more complete now that it's clear that people have stopped thinking.

Empathy, emotion, and the absurd sell well, so within a few hours stalls will be offering T-shirts with the slogans "Stimulate me, don't simulate me," "I'm a program, reset me," and "I am 1, U are 2, we are free." Comedians on the morning shows will venture into sketches about duplication.

"Do you know what a simulation is, Hillary?" the journalist asks the impersonator.

"Peter," Hillary Clinton's voice replies, "every woman in America knows what simulation is."

UP TO THIS POINT, about a hundred scholars have been speculating in a hangar. All of the sudden, there are ten million researchers on the planet feeling the need to shoot down in flames the scholars' theories by putting forward alternatives. The "photocopier" and the "wormhole" now have few supporters. And never mind if the most straightforward theory is also the most insane.

However, astrophysicists are not very big on the simulation idea. Space agencies even less so: Space exploration is already expensive, but if there isn't any space, the price is suddenly not worth paying. Particle physicists aren't keen on it either: What about all their beautiful particles, their quarks and gluons, and dark matter? Are they all virtual? And the massive particle colliders that they're so proud of, are they just a huge 3D joke? What about time? If time itself is contrived—just as it is in video games, where everything is calibrated and slowed to give humans a chance of playing—how do we measure real time in relation to our virtual time? Lastly, the biologists are up in arms: What about evolution, extinctions, and the loss of biodiversity? But they all know: whether or not it's virtual, the universe is entirely governed by laws that we understand increasingly clearly. Not one of these scientists hasn't been dabbling in simulations for years now, using a supercalculator that has increased its capacity a hundredfold in ten years. Not hard then for them to imagine the scope of machines billions and billions of times more powerful.

It would be better not to record productivity on Wednesday morning. In fact, the only people working are the men and women of Protocol 42. Because this Wednesday morning sees the launch of operation "Hermes." Meredith came up with the code name to represent the journey experienced by all the passengers on Flight 006 and the secrecy surrounding them—the time has come for them to disappear. At least Jacob Evans's crime will have helped convince the passengers that they are targets, and certainly in the United States, they all consent to anonymity. The NSA has erased all digital traces of the flight, and French and American agents have retrieved the flight logs. The general public knows that it was an Air France Paris–New York flight in March, but there were more than two hundred of those.

WEDNESDAY, JUNE 30, 2021

STUDIO 4, FRANCE 2, ESPLANADE

HENRI-DE-FRANCE, PARIS

THE TRUTH is that within a few hours, the world enters a vacuum of meaning. Religion is offering a false, doctrinal response, so philosophy steps forward to suggest an incorrect, abstract one. Talk shows proliferate all over the world, particularly in France, a country with a legendary concentration of media-savvy philosophers. One of them goes by the name of Philomedius. Got to hand it to him. And here he is on the set of a national channel with another guest—one Victor Miesel.

"I'd prefer not to give my opinion about this simulation idea," Philomedius says. "But I don't think it changes anything. I'm a materialist: there's no difference between thinking and believing we think, and therefore between existing and believing we exist."

"But surely, Philomedius," the presenter says, "really existing isn't exactly the same as being virtual."

"Forgive me, but it is, it's the same: I think, therefore, even if I'm simply a thinking program, I am. I feel love and pain in the same way, and I'll die just as surely, thank you. And the things I do have the same consequences, whether my world is virtual or real."

"Philomedius, next to you is the writer Victor Miesel, whose book *The anomaly* has become a cult hit, and obviously even more so now. Victor, you were on that flight, we know that your 'double' took his own life, and you held a press conference this afternoon. Thank you for being here with us. How do you see the future for these duplicated passengers?"

"There are more than two hundred of us who've had to look at the things our 'doubles' did between March and June, perhaps regretting they didn't take another route. Some may want to do things differently, or better, or do something else altogether. But I haven't been confronted with myself. But, actually..."

The author takes two red Lego bricks from his pocket.

"Ever since my father died, more than thirty years ago, I've always kept a Lego brick in my pocket. It wasn't a fetish or a lucky charm. Just a few grams of memories, almost a habit. I've been given the one that the other Victor had, and there are now two of them. I've forgotten which is which, and I've clicked them together. I couldn't tell you what they mean, but I feel as if I have more options, I'm freer than ever. But I still don't really like the word 'destiny.' It's just a target that people draw after the fact, in the place where the arrow landed."

In the studio audience, Anne Vasseur from the *Times Literary Supplement* is privately amused. She prefers the other joke that says that if an arrow is to hit the target, it needs to have missed everything else first. When she heard about Victor's death in April, she was shocked, upset even, and amazed by the intensity of her feeling. Of course, she'd noticed him in Arles, she'd thought his contributions intelligent and perceptive, and she'd been touched by his teenage-like attempt to strike up conversation with her over dessert. She'd been in another relationship at the time, and hadn't wanted to play. And then she'd loathed that facile moment of weakness and pride, she'd loathed the fact that he was attracted to her precisely because she was attracted to him. So she'd left Arles earlier than planned, ashamed of her selfish and inconsequential desire, refusing to be a woman who cheats, who takes her pleasure and causes pain and ends up not knowing where she belongs. She'd run away. She'd thought, briefly, that it would be better to live with remorse than regret, but she'd never looked for an excuse to track down Goncharov's translator. She saw this extraordinary 'resurrection' as a sign, an incomprehensible one but a sign nevertheless. And she, the literary journalist, had persuaded the editorial team at the *Times* to let her attend this conference, instead of a special correspondent. Now she sat watching a man who could in fact be, more than just briefly, a destiny.

"Tell me, Philomedius," the interviewer says, turning back to him, "if you were in their situation, how would you react?"

"First of all, I wouldn't have any feeling of unreality for very long. If I doubted my own existence, I'd only need to pinch myself. After that, granted, this other person would be an uncompromising mirror to contemplate, but more importantly, he'd be the only person to know everything about me and my secrets. If I were exposed like that, I might decide to change, or to run away from myself. The fact is, having two people in one life is one person too many. I'm sure I'd think it was all vanity—my apartment, work, all the material things... I'd concentrate on my inner core, on what needs preserving at all costs. I have a daughter, I love a woman, and when I say 'my wife' or 'my daughter' I understand everything I mean by that 'my'... If I had to share them, I might learn to relativize that craving for possession. To be honest, I don't know how I'd react."

"How do you explain Pope Francis's statement?"

"I'm sorry but I have no idea what the pope said."

"He said, and I quote, 'God is giving mankind a sign of His omnipotence and an opportunity to surrender to it and abide by His laws.'"

"He said that?" the philosopher asks, surprised.

"This morning."

"It has quite a whiff of 'Repent, ye miserable sinners' to it. I mean no disrespect, but I was expecting something a bit better from him. Mind you, all religious figures run on that software: 'Here are our beliefs, find the facts that prove them.' Like Voltaire's character Pangloss, they believe noses were made to carry glasses and that's why we have glasses. I haven't heard the voice of God in all this, nor seen Him appear in the clouds. To be perfectly frank, if He had something to say to us, it was now or never. Given the state we're in. No, the only true philosophical and scientific attitude is. 'Here are the facts, let's see what the possible conclusions are.'"

"And for the rest of us..." the interviewer says brightly, focusing on her other guest, "Victor Miesel, what would you say will happen now?"

"Nothing."

"Excuse me?"

"Nothing. Nothing will change. We'll wake up in the morning, we'll go to work because we still have to pay the rent, we'll eat and drink and make love just like before. We'll carry on behaving as if we're real. We're blind to anything that could prove that we're fooling ourselves. It's only human. We're not rational."

"What Victor Miesel is saying is rather like what you, Philomedius, mentioned in your article in this morning's *Le Figaro*. You described it as our need to reduce 'cognitive dissonance'?"

"Yes. We're prepared to warp reality if the stake is not losing altogether. We want answers for even our tiniest anxieties and a way of conceiving the world without reexamining our values, our emotions, and our actions. Take climate change. We never listen to the scientists. We spew out virtual carbon unchecked from fossil fuels that may or may not be virtual, heating up our atmosphere, that may or may not be virtual. And our species, which again may or may not be virtual, will be wiped out. Nothing's changed. The rich fly in the face of common sense and reckon they can save themselves, and themselves alone, and everyone else is reduced to living in hope."

"Would you agree with Philomedius, Victor Miesel?"

"Of course I do. Do you remember Pandora and her box?"

"Yes," the presenter replies, baffled. "I don't see the connection."

"There is one. If you remember, Prometheus stole fire from heaven and Zeus, wanting revenge on him and all blaspheming mortals, sent Pandora to Prometheus's brother Epimetheus. Zeus slipped a gift into her belongings, a mysterious box—except it was actually a jar—and he told her she must never open it. But she was too inquisitive and disobeyed him. All the evils of mankind that had been sealed inside it were then released: old age, disease, war, famine, madness, poverty . . . just one evil was too slow to escape, or perhaps it was obeying Zeus's wishes. Do you remember what that evil was?"

"No. Please explain, Victor."

"That evil was *Elpis*, the expectation of good—hope. It's the most destructive of all evils. It is hope that stops us being proactive and hope that prolongs people's suffering because, as they always say and in spite of all the evidence, 'it will all come right in the end.' What is not meant to be cannot be... The real question we should always ask is, 'How does it benefit me to accept a received idea?'"

"I see," the presenter says. "And, Philomedius, would you say that this is what's happening now, that each of us finds our own way of accommodating the reality we're being offered, is that it?"

"Yes. Absolutely. I'd like to remind you of something Nietzsche said: 'Truths are illusions which we have forgotten are illusions.' Right now, the whole planet has been confronted with a new reality, and it's challenging all our illusions. We're being sent a sign, that's beyond doubt. Sadly, thinking takes time. The irony is that the very fact of being virtual may give us even more of a duty toward our fellow human beings and our planet. And most significantly, it's a collective duty."

"Why's that?"

"Because—and a mathematician has already made this point—this test hasn't been set for us as individuals. This simulation is thinking on the level of an ocean, it couldn't care less about what each water molecule does. The simulation is waiting for a reaction from the entire human race. There won't be a supreme savior. We need to save ourselves."

LETTERS—THREE, EMAILS—TWO, SONGS—ONE, ABSOLUTE ZERO

SATURDAY, JULY 10, 2021

CARROLL STREET, BROOKLYN

THE ENVELOPE is addressed to "Aby and Joanna Wasserman," and Joanna recognizes her own fine, cramped writing. When Aby opens it they find one sheet of paper folded in four and two other sealed letters.

Dear Aby and Joanna,

In this envelope there's a letter for you, Joanna, and I know that you'll read it to Aby because that's what I would do. And one for you, Aby, and you alone.

Like both of you and like so many of the people who were on board that plane, I've tried to find answers, even just clues, in The anomaly, *the strange book written by that French author who was on the flight. I didn't find anything except this: "We must kill the past to ensure it is still possible."*

We wanted to resuscitate the past too, and we took ourselves off into the sympathetic arms of nature in that log cabin in Vermont. Aby had taken me there, taken you there, Joanna, for those long, freezing, snowy days when we decided to have a baby. Aby, what we had together then was so powerful that we wanted the memory of it to keep us going and to dictate the route that all three of us should choose.

But when we walked along that stony little path between the spruce trees and the firs, the path that—so symbolically—was too narrow for us to walk side by side, you trailed miserably between the two of us, my poor Aby, like a spaniel between two masters. Your sad smile was a constant apology for spending time with the other Joanna and for having to get back to her soon. You were never there, plainly and simply there, with her or with me. Instead you were just torn in two. You did a lot of painting, you couldn't stop, it was your way of avoiding questions that have no answers, and I'm leaving with the watercolors that will always remind me of you.

That's right, I've gone, I've left you alone in that log cabin full of sadness, before we destroyed one another. Joanna, because you're carrying Aby's baby you guessed I'd be the first to back down, to cave. The first to run away. And of course I knew that you knew.

I ran away.

I went back to New York and, after contacting Jamy Pudlowski, presented myself at the FBI's Manhattan headquarters. In just a day they'd created a new identity for me, with six years of digital life, and—just as a precaution—my name is now Joanna Ashbury. Ashbury, it sounds like a little English town that has nothing special except for its Norman church. And then there's the connection with Woods: Ashbury—buried ash. It would be kind of funny if they'd done it on purpose.

So, Joanna Ashbury's going to be working in senior management for the FBI's legal department, and, thanks to the NSA, she now has a Stanford degree to her name. The bureau also offered to cover the costs of Ellen's treatment. It's a generous offer, and I didn't refuse. But still, don't give up your job at Denton & Lovell, Joanna, not that I need to tell you that, I know what you decided.

Obviously we'll see each other again. We'll run into each other someday visiting Ellen.

I wish you all the happiness in the world.

Joanna Ashbury

Dear Joanna,

It's so weird calling you that.

You're name's now Wasserman and mine's Ashbury. Wasser like water and Ash like ashes—there's so much irony in this whole thing. Joanna Ashbury sounds a little like John Ashbery, and that reminds me of his long poem Self-Portrait in a Convex Mirror, *that I promised myself I'd read, if you remember. He talks about a painting by Parmigianino from the cinquecento. I liked the poem and wanted to find out about the painting.*

One day, when the painter was very young, only twenty-one, he saw himself in one of those convex mirrors and decided to do a self-portrait. He had a curved panel of wood made the same size as the mirror, so that he could create the image in the exact same shape. In the foreground at the bottom he paints his hand, it's huge and so beautiful it looks real. His face, in the center, is hardly distorted at all, and it's endearing, angelic, he's almost a child. The world revolves around this face and everything is distorted, the ceiling, the light, the perspective—it's a chaos of curves.

That painting isn't an image for the two of us, or for you, the mirror of my mirror, but it really should be an allegory for something, because I stayed there looking at it and suddenly started to cry—I've done so much crying recently. Right then I realized that that oversized hand was grabbing me, threatening me, stealing everything that belonged to me.

I had a dream while we were in the log cabin in Vermont. You suddenly died and I went back to my old life, I was so happy that you were dead. I comforted Aby and it was so easy to win him back, to make him forget you. I woke at dawn and couldn't get back to sleep so I went out onto the terrace with a coffee. You were already out there, you couldn't sleep either. Just like me, you'd made yourself a coffee, and just like me, you were barefoot, your hair was held back with a silver barrette like mine and you were holding your cup in both hands in the exact same way. Opposite us the mist clung to the mountain and the sun still wasn't quite ready to break through, and we exchanged an icy look. I got it, you'd just killed me in your dream too. That was when I decided to leave. Not because I was scared but because jealousy and pain were making me so hideous and I could see that ugliness all over you, plain as plain can be.

I don't know where I'm going. But I know that if I'm a long way away from you, from both of you, I still have a chance of remembering who I am and who I want to be.

Joanna

Aby walks away along the balcony and opens the letter that's meant for him alone; and every word he reads adds slightly to the crushing weight in his chest.

Dear Aby,

You're the only person I love and I'm leaving.

A year ago we didn't even know each other. And you, this guy who doesn't believe in anything, you called it a miracle, and I smiled, me, this girl who's always talking about how people meet.

I know the other Joanna will show you my letter to her. I won't add much to it.

The day I came to the apartment from the military base, you suggested the two of us go out to the park opposite your studio, to the bench where we've had so many conversations. Sitting there, you put your arms around me, my head dropped onto your shoulder and you put your hand on my stomach. I knew instantly that you did it without thinking, it was a tender ritual established between the two of you: your hand protecting your child—yours and hers. But there was nothing to protect in my belly, Aby, nothing, just my longing for you. You were embarrassed, you took your hand away and talked about I don't remember what, and everything about your expression said that you hoped I hadn't noticed. Then we went back to the apartment and I felt empty too, emptied of all strength, just like my belly was empty of life.

And remember that night when we were at your cabin in Vermont, that hot clammy night when I led you out into the forest and I so wanted you to make love to me under the trees, but you no longer dared to make the slightest move toward me or the other Joanna, you didn't want to ignite the tiniest spark of longing. I wanted you to take me, that's right, I wanted to feel your powerful desire thrusting inside me. And when I suddenly ran away it was because I was filled with disgust at myself. Aby, what I wanted more than anything was for you to make me pregnant too, for fate to go ahead and give me some way of competing.

Just look at the person I've been turned into by this pain. I have to go. Don't worry, my darling Aby: you've read War and Peace *more than once so you know what General Kutuzov knows—the two most powerful warriors are patience and time.*

Another man will come along, another meeting of minds, another miracle. I'm sure of it. I'll love again. At least love stops us constantly looking for some meaning to life.

I'm looking at that incredibly gentle portrait you painted of me in the sunset, with my head resting on the wooden beam and my eyes closed.

I love you, I'll always love you, and you'll know I do because, in the weirdest way, I'll be right beside you.

Joanna

THE PREVIOUS DAY

CLYDE TOLSON RESORT, NEW YORK

"ARE YOU OKAY, Joanna?" Jamy Pudlowski asks through the door in the FBI's all-gender restrooms.

No, Joanna June is not okay. Too much Scotch and too much pain. Her head and heart are spinning, she wishes she could collapse but she would just dirty her clothes.

Joanna wrote those letters a few hours ago, thinking she would never succeed in mailing them. She slipped them into her purse, and those letters are now like a revolver that someone's made the mistake of buying: It's hidden in the nightstand but the fact that it's there gradually fills the whole room, becoming an obsession, and because that revolver wants to be used, it ends up making a murderer of them, or a suicide. Joanna June can't bring herself to burn the three letters, and they insist on being slipped into a mailbox.

In order to leave the man she loves a woman must dismantle the world. Joanna June had to rewrite their story, had to dig up doubts that she'd buried and exhaust the attraction she felt for Aby in the same way that she could rob a word of all meaning if she repeated it dozens of times. She'd learned to unlove his too-blond curls, his bootlicking goody-two-shoes act, his skinny-boy awkwardness, his slightly snobby clothes, the way he wanted to joke about pretty much anything, even the way he burst out laughing like a kid. She remembered being uncomfortable about his elation, his urgent hurry to get married, to lock them both into a contract, as if it might all disappear overnight, as if he didn't entirely trust her, or himself or them. Over the course of one painful night she forced herself to relive every moment she'd spent with him, and discovered a chilliness in herself as she contemplated this disgustingly tender display. And, very gradually, she unraveled the emotion until she felt a growing aversion. The lawyer had become the prosecutor; she mercilessly put all her intelligence into serving the crime, and the prosecutor took this Aby with his thousand perfections, this simple branch on which Joanna's love had crystalized endless glittering, shifting diamonds of salt and poured the rain of indifference over it. And then the crystals dissolved and the charmless, leafless branch reappeared, dull enough and ordinary enough to make her weep.

So, when she actually mailed those three letters and for an hour afterward, Joanna no longer loved Aby. Then all her love came flooding back, and she opened the bottle of Talisker.

FROM: ANDRE.VANNIER@VANNIER&EDELMAN.COM

TO: ANDRE.J.VANNIER@GMAIL.COM

DATE: JULY 1, 2021, 09:43

SUBJECT: SEPARATION

Dear André (what else can I call you?),

I'm writing to you from the Drôme. I'm going to stay here for a while, and you can stay in my apartment, your apartment, in Paris for as long as it takes. I'm attaching the complete email exchange with Lucie from when we returned from New York. If you read them, you'll understand. I wrote a lot, she didn't reply much. You see plenty of "I don't want to hound you/pester you in vain," which were all lies because I wrote again and again, pointlessly. And that last email, which goes on forever—Jesus, be brief—the one that ends with the pretentious thing about walking "the longest of possible paths, together." I was by turns bombastic, insistent, tearful and plaintive, and even after she'd evicted me from her life, I still tried to get her to backtrack.

I'm not your enemy or your rival, or even an ally. But I have my past in my mailbox, and if you don't want it to be your future, do something.

See you soon,

André

FROM: ANDRE.J.VANNIER@GMAIL.COM

TO: LUCIE.J.BOGAERT@GMAIL.COM

DATE: JULY 1, 2021, 17:08

SUBJECT: YOU AND ME AND ME AND YOU

Dear Lucie,

I'm writing from my new email address to yours because the old ones belong to other people, and, like you, I've added a J for June. Why are we the ones who have to adapt? I suppose those four months that you and I haven't lived give the other André and Lucie the advantage.

We now both know what happened to "us." "You" left me, tired of my eagerness and impatience. I've read the emails that "we" sent each other, another Lucie's words describing how she drifted apart from another André. I've read sentences that I recognized as my own, in all my vulnerability, and my stupidity too.

I'll make this short. Being with me was never a rational choice on your part. And yet you approached me. Being with you was a miracle, but I also managed to lose you.

People rarely have the opportunity to save a relationship before it's even in danger. I want to have a second chance before I ruin the first one.

I love you. Hugging you close... but not too tight.

GHOST SONG

Music & Lyrics:

Femi Taiwo Kaduna & Sam Kehinde Chukwueze

Here I dance with a holy ghost
On a sandy Calabar Beach.
Because now love's so out of reach.
Oh we didn't see them comin'.
I loved your skin, that was our sin,
That's why they burned you in a tire
And threw our rainbows on their fire.

The Anomaly

I still remember every kiss,
So much about you that I miss.
Oh fallen hearts in the abyss.

I sing about a long-lost ghost
On a sunny Calabar Beach.
Even love's now out of reach.
Hear the dogs barking around us,
The wind blowing over the dust
Of my sweet love gone in the dark.
Let's go, let's swim with one last shark

I still remember every kiss,
So much about you that I miss.
Oh fallen hearts in the abyss.

As I walk with you, lover Tom,
On a weeping Calabar Beach,
Look, even hate is out of reach.
I want a mist of forgiveness,
But then I'll beg for nothing less
To cover up the blood and tears,
I just want love, I'm asking please.

I still remember every kiss,
Everything about you I miss.
Oh fallen hearts in the abyss.

To cover up the blood and tears
I just want love
I'm asking please
I'm asking please.

THURSDAY, JULY 1, 2021

CLYDE TOLSON RESORT, NEW YORK

"WOULD YOU LIKE to hear the recordings again, Mrs. Kleffman?"

April June shakes her head. Jamy Pudlowski watches as she sways in her seat, her expression blank. A game, a mouth, some soap, the whole world is swirling around her, and each word resonates without achieving any meaning. The SOC officer hands her a glass of water, but April has to put it down because her hands are shaking so badly. The business with the plane, and now this.

"The child psychiatrist let your daughter talk, she didn't steer her in any way. She established trust, and Sophia explained each of her drawings, she talked about the secret. Do you understand?"

April is paralyzed with shock. Clark, her own daughter, the bathtub, every ounce of her refuses to conjure the suggestion of an image. *April tender, April shady,* said the poem that Clark didn't write. The officer leaves long pauses in her explanations, but she keeps going, her voice gentle.

"Mrs. Kleffman, my name's Jamy. May I call you April?"

"Yes, that's me," April says in a toneless voice.

"Have some water, April."

April does as she's told, like an automaton. *April soft, so sleepy warm . . .*

"Yes, thank you, ma'am."

"April . . ." Jamy says. "Can you hear me? Your daughter can get through this. She was able to talk. And that's important, talking is very important. The cognitive therapists were with her for a long time, they discussed her fear of water and of the dark and her relationship with her body. They've given a reassuring prognosis about the short-term effects of the trauma that Sophia has experienced. But of course we can't be sure about her future development, Mrs. Kleffman. We hope everything will be okay."

". . . everything will be okay."

"Here's what's going to happen: your husband will be tried, and given Sophia's testimony, both Sophias' testimony, I wouldn't be jumping the gun to say he'll be found guilty. Because, since you were in Paris, in the last three months... that you haven't had... your daughter, well... the other Sophia has been abused in your home. Do you understand? In the state of New York, the sentence for this crime is ten to twenty-five years."

"Twenty-five years. Yes."

"It could be less if he agreed to attend therapy, to be monitored, to move away. You'll need to explain this to your children, especially Liam, who'll be angry... with you, with his sister, even with himself..."

"Has... Liam...?"

"No. You can be sure of that. The interviews leave no room for doubt."

April runs her fingers over her lips, her eyes staring vacantly, then she slides a hand through her hair. Jamy watches her compassionately.

"You could change your name, move to another state," she says. "Your double's doing just that. She already accepted our suggestion. I've negotiated with the army and you will keep your husband's pension as if he'd been killed in combat."

"Killed in combat," April repeats feebly.

She's thinking about foals, like the ones she used to draw for her mother. Foals. They're blood-colored, hovering in a steel-blue sky. It's cold, it's so cold. Everything's stopped moving. Absolute zero. *April caught in the icy storm.*

"You will have medical and psychological support for your children and yourself."

April doesn't have time to do anything, her eyes widen in horror and nausea rises inside her, an uncontrollable bilious black wave of it, she wants to throw up, but she can't manage even that.

THE LAST WORD

OCTOBER 21, 2021, 13:42

THREE TIMES the pilot of the Super Hornet asked for the order to be repeated. But he's just the last link in a chain, and what's the point of a hand if it refuses to obey the brain?

The decision has just been made in "The Tank," the Pentagon's inner sanctum. It's a windowless, fortified space, officially room 2E924, that looks like an ordinary company conference room with its table in golden oak, its revolving leather chairs, and timeless décor. In a painting on one of the walls, President Abraham Lincoln is holding a strategic meeting during the Civil War. He is surrounded by Commanding General Ulysses S. Grant, Major General William Tecumseh Sherman, and Rear

Admiral David Dixon Porter. All these officers on canvas have witnessed the most secret decision ever made by the chiefs of staff of the various armed forces, a decision that has been debated at length and on which the president wanted to have the last word.

The missile detaches from the wing of the fighter jet, which is heading northwest. The AIM-120 immediately activates its rocket propulsion and in moments has achieved cruising speed, leaving behind it a straight gray trail. The sun bounces off its steel casing, it is death gleaming bright. At Mach 4, the target is only fifteen seconds away.

In Paris, Victor and Anne are looking out over the Luxembourg Gardens, having a last coffee on a café terrace before heading off for dinner. It's late October, but the summer is still holding on, an Indian summer, as they say. Anne looks up at Victor and smiles at him. He has never felt so alive, he sometimes thinks that the other Victor's death has made his own existence both fragile and precious. He has put the two Lego bricks on the table, like two bright-red sugar lumps. He's snapping them together and breaking them apart again without thinking about it.

Vanity of vanities, says Kohelet.
Havel havalim
Havel, *says Kohelet, all is vanity.*

Victor has just written the last word of the slim volume that describes the plane, the anomaly, the divergence. For the title, he considered *If on a Winter's Night Two Hundred Forty-Three Travelers,* but Anne shook her head, then he wanted to make those the opening words, and Anne sighed. In the end it will have a short title, only one word. Sadly, *The anomaly* is already taken. He doesn't try to explain, but to bear witness, in simple terms. He has narrowed it down to just eleven characters and senses that, unfortunately, even this is too many. His editor begged him, Please, Victor, it's too complicated, you'll lose readers, simplify it, do some pruning, cut to the chase. But Victor did as he pleased. He opens the novel vigorously, with a Mickey Spillane–type pastiche about a character who remains a mystery to virtually everyone. No, no, it's not literary enough for a first chapter, Clémence criticized, When are you going to stop playing games? But Victor's more playful than ever.

Thousands of kilometers away, in Mount Sinai Hospital, Jody Markle has no tears left to shed and closes her eyes. She's losing David for the second time. He's been deeply sedated for four days, because even the French nanomedication can't control his pain now. Paul is standing by his brother's bedside, thinner, drawn and silent. A noise of breaking glass outside distracts him. He opens the slats of the blind, leans forward and looks down: in the parking lot two men are throwing insults at each other over a shattered headlight, while on the monitor in the room the electrocardiogram's undulating profile flattens to a smooth line, and its soft beep becomes a continuous note.

In Lagos, the SlimMen concert is finishing as the tropical night closes in. At the end of the concert a surprise guest comes onto the stage for the last song, amid cheering and clapping: a short fair-haired man in a sequined pink suit and huge lit-up gold glasses. More than three thousand young Nigerians join the performers in the song's refrain, all of them aware of its hidden meaning:

I want a mist of forgiveness,
But then I'll beg for nothing less
To cover up the blood and tears,
I just want love, I'm asking please.

Joanna March's belly has swelled, and the baby may come earlier than anticipated. It's a girl and she will be called Chana: it was the name of a forgotten Japanese princess and it means "year" in Hebrew. Joanna has some free time, because the Valdeo trial won't be going ahead. A deal was struck with the plaintiffs, and Hexachlorion has been withdrawn from the market. She never went to that meeting at the Dolder club where the theme was to be immortality, nor the ensuing dinner, when the conversation turned to places on the planet to escape the effects of climate change and influxes of migrants. Prior has bought a hundred hectares in New Zealand.

Aby would have liked to keep writing to Joanna June, in a murky cocktail of distress and guilt, but she refused to keep in touch. Later, maybe. She's met someone at the bureau, an expert in art trafficking. He thinks it's serious, she's not sure but wants to believe in it.

It's the beginning of spring on West Antarctica's ice sheet, and the Thwaites Glacier—a great raft of ice two kilometers deep and the size of Florida—may well break away in three months' time, raising seawater levels by more than a meter, but Sophia, Liam, and their mother have left the flood-risk house in Howard Beach. The Junes have move to Akron, near Cleveland, and the Marches to Louisville. The army and the FBI kept their promises, and in return the two women have agreed never to contact each other. They could have common ground in Clark, but the terms of his sentence preclude any further contact with his family. And the levels of anger in both Liams have gradually subsided.

Blake is wrong to be worried. No one at the FBI is still looking for him. Using two blurry images taken in customs at Kennedy Airport of a man who might be the passenger from seat 30 E, the NSA has used facial recognition software to identify 1,049,278 individuals. Of that million, 1,553 are people photographed in East Coast airports the following week, but that proves nothing; 4,482 other faces don't match any profiles, and appear only in photographs, sometimes in the background. Granted, the man was duplicated, but he's obviously trying to go unnoticed. And anyway, what is he guilty of, apart from breaking a door in a hangar and stealing a car?

André March puts a blue ceramic jug on the sideboard in the kitchen of his brand-new house in Montjoux. In early August he went to a concert in Montjoux's temple, and met a woman who lives in the neighboring village and plays double bass: he was ready. This tall, very dark-haired woman with bottomless blue eyes makes him laugh and never stops giving up smoking. She sometimes wears baggy overalls whose yawning gaps are a delight for André's hands, and he's discovering the pleasures of electric bicycles. After they made love this morning, she went back to sleep in the bedroom, and while he sets the table for breakfast, Lucie March calls him just for the pleasure of talking to him. She's working "way, way too much," she says, but she's calming down, coping with the routine that's fallen into place between her and Lucie June for spending time with Louis. Who's doing well. "Amazingly well."

The boy doesn't mind that his "other" mother, Lucie June, is pregnant. The center of gravity of that Lucie's life has shifted so far in the space of a few months that the unimaginable has become possible. Are you sure?

asked André June, feeling happy and anxious in equal measure. Yes, she really is sure. It's a new pivotal point, and a sort of revenge on this fate. She never called Raphaël again, and no other casual lover has taken his place.

Adrian and Meredith are in Venice, Italy, Europe. They're trapped in their hotel by the *acqua alta*, but this transient confinement isn't so tragic: their sun-filled room overlooks the Fondamenta del Passamonte, the room service is above reproach—the hotel director thought he recognized Adrian as an American actor, but who exactly?—and his less and less white, less and less spotless shirt, a souvenir from the White House, is sprawled across the floor with a black dress on top of it. They're talking quietly, hidden under a pyramid of sheets, and Meredith's clear laughter rings out

The Department of Defense shut down Protocol 42 in September to concentrate on Operation Hermes. The task force's speculations went on all through the summer, but still no one came up with a way to disprove or confirm any of the theories. Nor have Americans found out about the other plane, the one in China. There's no news about its passengers.

Jamy Pudlowski is drinking a dry martini in one of Quantico's bars after a final training session. Two days ago she gave the green light to the latest protection plan for the passengers of Flight 006, and she herself is being transferred to the West Coast, to San Francisco, where she'll be starting next week as director of the regional office and its seven satellite offices. If anyone asked her what she's thinking right now, she'd just order another dry martini.

The side camera under the Super Hornet's left wing follows the AIM-120's trajectory, and in the underground command center at the White House the president of the United States is watching a huge screen with his eyebrows knitted together and his fists balled. Yes, it was a difficult decision, and I made it alone, because it's my job to make decisions alone. When he was told that a third Air France Flight 006 had loomed into the Atlantic skies with the same Captain Markle at the controls, assisted by the same Favereaux and with the same passengers on board, the president gave the order for the aircraft to be destroyed. We really can't keep letting this same plane land.

Let's have one last coffee, says Victor, would you mind? He draws Anne to him, strokes her cool fingers and kisses her gently on her lips, which she opens slightly. His breath smells of tobacco and menthol. And that is when it happens. At first it's just a breath of wind, a fleeting whirl of dead leaves on the ground. A soft, soft note hums in the air, a very low F. The air quivers, and the sky becomes clearer, but almost imperceptibly. A well-dressed woman pulling a shopping trolley stops outside a bookshop, a man in a raincoat is out for a walk with a big black dog, a young woman on a bicycle pedals past them, stops, checks her phone, and smiles. It's a peaceful moment, serene.

The missile is only a second away from Air France Flight 006, and time stretches and expands before the explosion.

It's difficult to describe what happens, there's no word in the language to define accurately the slow vibration through the planet, the infinitesimal pulsing that is felt at the same time all over the world, just as much by the cat that was sleeping by the fire in a log cabin in Arkansas as the greylag goose flying across the skies over Bordeaux, and the Zambezi falls and the pristine snow on Annapurna, the Rialto over the Grand Canal in Venice, and the congested main road in the huge Dharavi slum, in the dirty sponge left on the edge of the sink in Montjoux and the punctured old tire on a garage forecourt in Mumbai and the red cup f c ffe wi h its I y bra d g i tor
Mı el' h d a d ı th b l

on An ' t gue No e c d a c ly sa h w ti e gr

ua ly sp d un l t re w a u

re l, b r l y pe c pt

le w h i t e n

o i s e

d st

e

n

d

ACKNOWLEDGMENTS

Ali Amir-Moezzi, Paul Benkimoun, Eduardo Berti, Élise Bétremieux, Hadrien Bichet, Nick Bostrom, Hélène Bourguignon, Olivier Broche, Sarah Chiche, Christophe Clerc, Claire Doubliez, Paul Fournel, Jacques Gaillard, Thomas Gunzig, Jacques Jouet, Philippe Lacroute, Jean-Christophe Laminette, Daniel Levin Becker, Clémentine Mélois, Anaëlle Meunier, Victor Pouchet, Anne-Laure Reboul, Virginie Sallé, Sarah Stern, Jean Védrines, Pierre Vivares, Charlotte von Essen, Ida Zilio-Grandi.